KISS KISS FANG FANG

A SUCKY ROMANTIC COMEDY

PENELOPE BLOOM

Want a free book exclusive to my subscribers? Sign up to my no-spam VIP club and get FREE copy of Miss Matchmaker instantly. Click Here>>

1
CARA

In the movie version of my life, the director would probably start with a brief tease. It'd be one dramatic snapshot to show you just how abnormal my mostly normal existence was about to get.

They'd probably open with a black screen that slowly brightened until a fuzzy image became clear.

There I'd be, looking like I just got thrown from an exploding building to land on the wet pavement. Face up, of course—for cinematic reasons.

The camera would rotate and rise upwards so you had plenty of time to study my face and the "what the hell am I doing here" look written all over it.

The average viewer might not notice the smoking gun in the scene right away. But that was okay. It would add to the drama.

If they were a person of taste, they might go straight to the awesome Chuck Taylor's I snagged on clearance.

If they were a nitpicker, they might get stuck on my black-haired pixie cut that was in desperate need of a trim.

And if they were an asshole, they'd probably laugh to see a gym membership card on my keychain—the same keychain that was dramatically strewn a few feet from my outstretched hand.

And *yes*, I'd been on a little fitness hiatus since New Year's. Okay? And no, I wasn't talking about this past New Year's or even the one before it.

But even the assholes in the audience would feel bad when they noticed the most important detail in the scene.

Cue the slowly growing pool of blood spreading from behind me.

A good director would change the camera angle at this point. Maybe something low that gave a shot of my impressive A-cup cleavage and let you see *him*.

There he'd be, approaching me from the shadows with concern all over his offensively hot face.

Somewhere between admiring his impeccable jawline and to-die-for eyebrows they'd see the teeth. *That* is when the real question would start to form.

They'd ask themselves, "Are his canines extra-long, or is it just my imagination?"

If I wasn't passed out, I would've happily cracked my eyes open to say that, "Nope. You've pretty much got it on the nose. Good job, detective."

As with any proper tease, the scene would cut away abruptly and bring you straight to the soul-crushingly ordinary existence of my Monday morning.

Temporarily ordinary, at least.

I LOOKED FOR SOMETHING TO SPREAD ON MY BAGEL BEFORE I rushed out the door. Birds were chirping outside, the air was pleasantly cool, and some asshole had left the cream cheese out on the counter until it fossilized. I gave the tub a dejected jab with a fork, then stuffed the bagel between my teeth and shouldered my bag.

I had class to get to, then my internship, then my late-night gig. Just another day of chasing the dream.

"Hey." Zack appeared in the cramped, deteriorating kitchen. He played on the basketball team for our college, along with all the other guys I lived with. And *no*, there was absolutely no shenanigans going on, if you were wondering. The situation was a combination of coincidence, guys who weren't pervs, and me not having enough disposable income to be picky.

Besides, I was thirty years old, and if dating was a menu at a fancy restaurant, college guys were the section in another language. It probably would've been more accurate to say the entire menu on dating had gone up in flames when I decided to sacrifice my personal life to keep up with my academic goals.

Zack was wearing a tank-top and his wild, curly brown hair was even messier than usual. "Have you seen the cream cheese?"

I had a bagel in my mouth, arms full of books, and a bag on my shoulder that weighed as much as a tank. All I could manage for him was to make an indistinct noise and point my eyes toward the cream cheese container I'd knocked into the sink.

"Ah, right on." Zack pulled out a piece of bread from a bag that I had reason to believe was doubling as a mold and fungus culture. He ran *tap water* into the hardened cream cheese, then jammed a knife around in the container a few times until it softened and started spreading it on his bread.

I knew I'd been living with a pack of mannerless, barbaric college guys too long when I didn't even vomit all over myself at the sight of his antics.

I was using my butt cheek and a tip-toe technique to push the door handle down when Zack lifted his knife and pointed it toward me. "Hey, wait a sec."

I bulged my eyes. This was worse than the hygienist trying to ask me about my day while she had four power tools jammed down to my tonsils.

"You going to be coming home super late again?"

I nodded my head.

Zack made a face to show his disapproval. "You coming from that place you do the tours? Just text one of us. We'll come walk you back."

I spit out my bagel and tried to call on some of my experience as a high school soccer player to knee it up and into my half-open bag. All I managed to do was knock it away, where it landed on edge and rolled under the couch. "I don't need a personal escort," I said. "But thanks."

"No," Niles said. He was coming down the stairs as he spoke. Niles was the kind of tall that meant he had to duck his head to get through doorways. He was also so rail-thin that he could've probably walked through a fence by turning sideways, too. He had big, expressive eyes and a shaved head. "You shouldn't be walking home that late by yourself. You at least need something. Do you still have that pepper spray Mooney gave you?"

I felt like my shoulder and arms were going to disintegrate if I had to stand there holding my stuff any longer than necessary. "I know you guys mean well, but seriously. I don't need a squad of over-protective, freakishly tall little brothers. I'll be fine. I promise."

Zack and Niles shared a disapproving look on my behalf.

I let myself out before they had time to argue more. As much as I appreciated their concern, it all only felt like a reminder of where I was. Thirty, still living in college-style housing, still trying to make a name for myself in my field, and *still* a student.

There was also the ever-present, ever-depressing thought that I was spending the twilight of my most datable years with my eyes glued to microscopes and my nose buried in books. I worried I'd wind up achieving all my goals only to find there was nobody who was still waiting around to share my life with.

But I did what I always did and shoved those concerns down to my core where they could fester away in the background.

I sat through my advanced hematology lecture while furiously scribbling notes. I crammed for a biomedical theory test in the brief break between classes, inhaled my lunch while watching an online class lecture on my phone, and finished the day off by falling down a small flight of stairs in front of an army of sorority sisters practicing some kind of cultish chant.

I rode the bus to what I liked to think of as an internship, but my graduate professors not-so-kindly called a "borderline illegal enterprise where I was more likely to catch a deadly pathogen than contribute to my thesis." If my translation was correct, they didn't approve. But most of them saw my particular field of interest with blood as an insult to the field. I wasn't supposed to want to modify blood. It didn't matter if it could help people, what mattered is that it simply wasn't done.

At least some people didn't share their belief, even if it did mean I had to resort to unpaid work with a woman nobody took seriously.

I let myself in the rickety fence in front of Anya Yuvinko's house. It was nestled in a residential section of downtown on a pretty street. The black paint, crumbling stucco, and long-dead plants made it function more like a wart on an attractive girl's nose.

I found Anya in her basement, like usual. She had several centrifuges spinning down vials of blood and she was hunched over a microscope.

Anya used to be a leading researcher relating to all things blood and hematology in Russia. Some sort of falling out had occurred, and she'd more or less fled to the states. Now her sole focus in life was finding out how to splice human blood with cat blood. She… really wanted cat ears. I wished that was a joke. Regardless of whether Anya had lost her mind, she had all the equipment I needed and none of the pretentiousness to stop me from doing my own work.

She was in her late forties with short blonde hair she cut choppily herself. She usually worked in bath robes, moo-moo's, or whatever else she could find.

I set down a few cans of ravioli and instant noodles on the desk by the stairs when I came down. She never acknowledged the food I brought, but I also never got the impression she really left her house. Sometimes I wondered if she'd just starve to death if I didn't bring her something to eat.

"You will extract plasma now," Anya said in perfectly annunciated English. She had no hint of an accent, but she frequently struggled with grammar in ways that made her either difficult to understand or accidentally hilarious.

I got some of the menial tasks she needed help with while my mind picked over my own plans for the day.

If I had to describe my academic interests in layman's terms, I'd say I was basically obsessed with blood. Not in a creepy, *I take baths in the stuff* kind of way, either. My interest was because I felt like the healing potential of blood still hadn't been unlocked. My dream was to find a way to make a sort of synthetic super-blood we could inject into ourselves to fight off infections and disease before they started. Anya was just one unconventional step I'd had to take in my pursuit of that goal. The other was the fact that I hadn't so much as been on a date in at least five years.

But there'd be time for men later. Maybe when I was in my forties. I heard great things about the dating prospects for sexually inexperienced women in their forties, after all.

2

CARA

I stifled a yawn as the last of my tour group headed back home. I'd changed clothes after my internship into something that was more *me*. I liked wearing outfits that were a little out-there. Sneakers were usually a must. I might wear an old torn t-shirt from a show I'd been to years ago with a black plaid skirt one night and heels with a flirty dress the next. The point was having fun with it. My outfit was basically my version of those mood boards my elementary school teachers used to put up.

Tonight, I'd opted for black Converse, an "I came for the turkey" t-shirt with suggestive drops of white splattered around the letters. I was also wearing a neon blue and black plaid mini-skirt. The intended message? *It has been a long ass day and I have no interest in making small talk, thanks but no thanks.*

But I also tended to dress a little drearier for my late-night gig giving haunted tours of downtown Savannah, Georgia. I typically ended the tour at the old Mercer-Williams house.

I was just walking around making sure all the doors were locked when I decided I couldn't wait until I got home to pee. I wasn't supposed to use the bathrooms in the tour locations, but I'd been holding my pee so long I was either going to squat in an alley somewhere or desecrate the haunted mansion.

I stealthily pushed open the creaky front door and tripped on the loose floorboard. I wound up crashing face-first into an antique table, which knocked several picture frames over.

Whoops.

Thankfully, I was alone, unless the ghosts I told my tours about were real, at least.

I tried the bathroom on the first floor even though I knew the water hadn't been turned on for decades. Sure enough, it hadn't magically been activated so I could relieve myself.

I knew I usually heard pipes rattling from the basement, so I headed through the darkened manor down the stairs.

Distantly, I thought how most sane people would probably be scared out of their minds right about now. I'd just spent the last two hours explaining to wide-eyed tourists how dastardly and haunted this house was. In truth, the place *did* creep me out. I always had the sense that I wasn't alone here, but I hadn't had any of the ghostly encounters other tour guides claimed to experience.

There were stories of former tour guides killing themselves here. People getting pushed down stairs. Phantom hands grabbing ankles and leaving marks.

But my personal stance on the paranormal was "maybe, but probably not." I thought it was fun to talk about. Unless a ghost decided to formally introduce itself, I was going to remain a skeptic. So the only fear I really had going into the darkened basement was of giant rats.

I had to cross the large basement area to a door I'd never bothered to open. I was crossing my fingers there was a toilet behind it. I tried the handle and found it locked.

"Shit!" I hissed. That was it. If I didn't find a way to a toilet in the next five minutes, I was going to pee myself. It was that simple.

I went to a precarious, tall standing shelf lined with endless buckets of paint and heavy tools, hoping to find some kind of key. I stood on my tiptoes and saw something metallic hanging just over the edge of one of the top shelves.

"Don't do it, Cara. You're not coordinated. You will die."

I ignored my own advice and planted one foot on the first shelf and tried to reach for the key. It wasn't enough, so my full bladder compelled me to climb up one more shelf like it was a giant ladder.

I barely got the key between my fingertips by stretching as far as my short frame would allow. I was on one tip-toe with my fingers fully extended like Harry Potter about to grab the snitch.

That was the moment I felt the shelf lurch.

I was falling forward toward a brick wall.

Oh hell no.

I closed my eyes and held on for dear life.

There was a huge collision and clatter of thousands of things falling from the shelf—thankfully not including the stupid thirty-year-old thing clinging to it. My forehead banged against a paint bucket and something bounced up then pounded painfully against my back.

"Ugh," I murmured. I slid my hand between my legs to make sure I hadn't peed myself. "Hah," I said, finding I was dry. "I still got it."

With some premature old woman grunts, I pulled myself out of the spilled carnage of tools, cans, and now-broken shelves. When I got a few steps back, I saw the shelf and its contents had broken a door-sized hole in the brick wall.

Shit. I was going to get fired.

I wasn't sure what I expected on the other side, but I did *not* expect to see a perfectly preserved room.

I stood there staring at the opening as dust filtered down from the disturbed rafters overhead.

Why was there a room in the haunted mansion behind a bricked-up wall?

I took a half-step backwards, then looked at my hand. *I was holding the key.*

Some things in life were more important than the loss of your job, damaging historic locations, or potentially disturbed ghosts. One of those things was a full bladder, so I quickly rushed to what I prayed was a bathroom.

Sure enough, it wasn't.

I closed the door anyway and found a bucket I could use. If I had to choose between discreetly finding a way to dispose of a bucket of my own urine and peeing my pants, I'd take the bucket.

I was in the middle of hiking up my skirt when I heard footsteps. Multiple pairs of footsteps.

3

CARA

I clapped a hand over my mouth and tried not to make a sound.

I wasn't imagining it. Footsteps. Shifting rocks. *Voices.*

I was in a haunted mansion at one in the morning and I wasn't alone. I distantly wondered if pepper spray worked on ghosts.

"Quiet," a woman's voice said. There was a strange, formal stiffness to her voice. Almost like an accent but not quite.

"I've been quiet long enough," a man replied in a deep, resonating voice.

"Look at this," another voice said. There was a pause, then the rattling sound of paint cans being moved. It sounded like they were rummaging through the pile of things from the shelf. "How long have we slept?"

"Too long," replied the man with the deep voice. "Look."

Another pause, then a slow, amazed laugh from the woman. From the direction of their voices, I thought they might be reading one of the informational plaques the tour agency had put up explaining the history of the house.

The woman spoke. "Looks like poor old Mercer is long dead."

"This door wasn't here before," one of the men said.

"Do you smell that?" The woman asked.

"Smells like a human."

I really wished I didn't still have to pee. When the door opened, it took everything I had not to lose control of my bladder.

Two men and a woman were waiting in the darkened room. They were all dressed like something out of an old movie with layers of well-made, formal clothing. They were pale, lithe, beautiful people. The woman had black hair, eyes a startling shade of blue, and curved, full lips that somehow hinted at both innocence and an edge of something more dangerous.

The man on the left had dirty blond hair slicked back over a smooth forehead, eyes that twinkled with danger, and beautifully sculpted, sharp features.

The other man was broader with a square kind of perfection to him. He fixed dark eyes on me, then took a step closer. "Hello."

He was the one with the resonating voice. "Hi," I croaked.

"I'm Lucian Undergrove. This is my brother, Alaric, and my sister, Seraphine."

"You were trapped behind that wall?" I asked. I could feel myself trying to slam together puzzle pieces that didn't fit. The biggest, most confusing piece was how three very much alive people had just come out of a wall I knew had existed ever since I'd been working here. "Was there a... tunnel in there?"

The three siblings exchanged a quiet look, then Lucian nodded. "Something along those lines."

The two in the back were looking at me in a way that made me uncomfortable. The woman, in particular, had an intensity in her eyes that I hadn't seen since I accidentally showed up to prom in the same dress as one of the cheerleaders.

"I'm just going to take this bucket and go," I said, lifting up the bucket and showing all of them, as if it explained everything.

Lucian put a hand on my arm. It was cold. It looked even whiter than I'd realized against my skin, too. "I'll need you to forget you met us."

A loud swallow clicked in my throat. "You got it. I was never here."

"No," he said, eyes taking on a heavy, oddly magnetic quality. "I need you to really forget." He reached out and brushed a slender finger down my nose, then half-smiled at me, revealing a handsome little vertical dimple on one side. "It's a shame, though. I think I would have enjoyed getting to know you."

I tried to say something, but it felt like I had suddenly become full-blown, can't-even-talk-properly drunk. Some kind of slurred sound came out of my mouth, and then the inside of my head was spinning.

4
CARA

I had a cup of coffee in my hands as I sat at the breakfast table back home. Four tall basketball players surrounded me with varying levels of consternation on their faces.

Zack folded his arms. "So, you're really not going to tell us who he was?"

"I already told you I don't remember anything." It was mostly true, at least. I remembered trying to find a key for a bathroom. And I remembered falling from the shelves. I assumed I must've hit my head somehow, but that admittedly didn't explain why my head didn't hurt. It also didn't explain how or why some mysterious trio of strangers had apparently dropped me off last night.

"The girl was *thick*, dude. Like," he grinned stupidly. "*So thick*." Mooney said.

It had taken me a while to learn to keep track of my four oversized roommates when I moved in last year. But I had it down now. Zack was the walking science experiment who existed primarily on expired food. Also, the shoulder length-curly brown hair was his thing.

Niles was the tallest of the group with the shaved head and an unhealthy obsession with cleanliness. Unfortunately, instead of using his powers to keep our place neat, he just avoided the kitchen entirely and kept his own room clean.

Mooney was the muscular one who had a new girlfriend every week. He had the whole short on the sides long on top style and a toothy smile full of white, orderly teeth. He could charm the pants off women, but only if he did it before they got to really know him.

Last but not least was Parker, who had a scraggly, patchy beard and had never met a conspiracy theory he didn't love.

Together, they were like my mostly incapable team of personal super heroes.

Zack was nodding his head as he ate something out of a Tupperware with a fork. Judging by the smell, it was long gone. "The vibe was really off, though. Did you see the look in their eyes? Creepy, if you ask me."

"But you'd still smash the girl, right?" Mooney said, tilting his head and raising his eyebrows.

Zack made a *pfft* sound and laughed. "I mean, obviously. Just saying it was weird."

Parker ran his fingers down his face, seeking out a little patch of his beard thick enough to tug at. "I don't know. From the way you guys described them? I'm thinking something's up."

Niles eyed what Zack was eating, then shuffled to the other side of the room, shaking his head. "You always think something is 'up,' Parker."

"Yeah, maybe," Parker said. "But did you hear about the Mercer house last night? A tour guide showed up this morning and they found a demolished wall. And they aren't saying what they found inside, but the girl they interviewed looked completely sketched out. Super suspicious."

"Wait," Zack said. Without looking, he tossed his Tupperware toward the sink. It bounced off the countertop and clattered to the tiles out of view.

"Kobe!" Mooney said, laughing.

"No," Zack said, waving his finger around as he tried to grasp at some mental straw. "The Mercer House? That's where you work, right, Cara?"

I thought about the ladder. *Oh, shit.* Did I break a wall?

"I work a lot of places. But yes, that's one spot the ghost tour hits."

The guys all exchanged a look, except Mooney, who was cleaning something from under his fingernails.

"Oh, come on," I said. "What are you trying to say?"

Zack just shrugged. "I don't know. But I do think you should let one of us tag along with you tonight if you're doing another ghost tour."

"I don't need an oversized babysitter."

"The fact that you came home with three strangers and can't remember anything from last night suggests otherwise," Niles noted.

I finished my coffee, then went to gather my things for the day. "You know," I said, shouldering my bag. "Try getting four hours of sleep a night. You'll probably forget a thing or two."

Niles narrowed his eyes. "Wait. Is that supposed to convince us you *don't* need someone keeping an eye on you? Because it's having the opposite effect on me."

Zack nodded. "I'll go with her tonight."

I stared at him. "Seriously?"

Zack bent down, picked something up from the floor, then popped it in his mouth with a cocky smile. "Seriously. I'm going to keep an eye on you tonight, like it or not, Care Bear."

I grinned. "Great. I'll let the alley cats and rats know there will be less food to go around, then."

5
CARA

I found myself checking my phone all day through my classes. The demolished wall and the curiosities on the other side had ignited a bit of a local firestorm of interest. I figured it was only a matter of time before the media got a hold of the names of the tour guides who had access to the Mercer house last night. I considered coming clean when they reached out.

I could just tell the truth. It had been an accident. I must've hit my head, and I don't remember anything else.

Except I did *know* three mysterious strangers had escorted me home afterwards, according to my roommates.

Anya lobbed the crust of her peanut butter and jelly sandwich at my head. "Focus, Cara Skies. Samples will not look at themselves."

Startled, I looked up and realized I'd been in the middle of moving a sample of blood to a slide, but it had sat on the little clear rectangle of glass too long and coagulated in the open air. I swore to myself, then went to clean up my mess. "Sorry," I said. "I had a crazy night last night."

Anya was absorbed in what she was doing at the computer and waved her hand in dismissal—either of my apology or that she could possibly care about how my night had been.

A short while later, there was a loud knock at her door. We both looked up, then Anya made a "don't just stare at me, go get it" gesture with her hand.

I set down what I was doing and hurried upstairs toward the sound of more insistent knocking. I hadn't realized how late it was until I saw there wasn't even a hint of sun coming through the windows upstairs anymore. That meant I needed to leave soon for my tour-guide gig, assuming I wasn't going to get fired the moment I arrived.

I opened the door.

I was expecting a delivery guy or maybe even a resourceful news anchor who had thought to contact the tour company and ask who had been working yesterday.

Instead, I saw a mountain of a man flanked by two women. The man was huge with nearly black eyes, hair, and pale skin. The man was dressed like some kind of biker king with a thick leather jacket despite the heat and pants that hugged long, powerful legs.

The two women at his side wore disinterested, annoyed looks. One had short cropped hair and high bangs that managed to put an exclamation mark on her perfectly sculpted features. The other woman wasn't blessed with the same genetics. She had a too-wide mouth, eyes that were a little too feral, and a cruelty to her face that I couldn't quite put my finger on.

"Um," I said. "If you guys are selling Girl Scout cookies, we already got some last week. So..." I started to close the door, but the man planted a huge hand in the center of the door and shoved it open.

"Where are they?" he asked. His voice was deep and growly.

"We ate them all?"

"Where are the Undergroves?"

I let out a sigh of relief. "You guys are lost? Is that what this is? I've never heard of 'the Undergroves' but it's probably a lot easier to just plug it into your phone."

The man took a step forward. I was struck by the fact that he didn't appear to be sweating even in the slightest. If I wore that getup for two minutes I would've been dripping. "I'm not playing games with you, Cara Skies. Tell me where they are. Give me the Undergroves, and I'll consider letting you live."

I raised an eyebrow. "*Okay*. Clearly you have the right name, but the wrong person. I have no idea what you're talking about."

The man let out a low growling sound. He stared into my eyes —*into my soul, actually*. He seemed to come to some kind of conclusion that pissed him off, because he broke eye contact and turned toward the women.

"I think he wiped her," he said.

"I wipe myself, thank you very much," I added.

The look he gave me over my shoulder was a healthy reminder to keep my mouth shut. I wondered if I could close the door and they'd forget about me but decided staying perfectly still was probably the safest bet. Maybe creepy people in the night were like dinosaurs. If you don't move, they can't see you.

Wait, had I heard that was just a myth they made up for a movie? I couldn't remember but did my best statue impression to be safe.

"We could use her as bait," the woman with the cruel eyes suggested.

Nope. Not liking the sound of that. Maybe I could run. But something about the force I'd sensed when he pushed the door back open made me wonder if a simple locked door would do anything more than piss this guy off.

"If he planned to keep her as a pet, he wouldn't have wiped her," the man said, as if he was explaining something very simple to somebody stupid.

Why is this guy so obsessed with wiping? Maybe it was some kind of disgusting kink of his.

"Can we have her?" the pretty one asked. She had a tinkling, high-pitched voice with a lilting edge of a southern accent.

The man eyed me. "No. Jezabel will keep an eye on her for the time being. There's still a chance the Undergroves might decide to come back for her."

The pretty one rolled her eyes. "Can't Leah watch her? I'm hungry."

I took a slow, shuffling step backwards. *Maybe if I move slowly enough, they won't realize I'm moving.* I tried to *be* molasses. I *was* the line at the DMV. I *was*—

"Where do you think you're going, human?" The cruel woman asked. Leah—I thought it was.

The man faced me. "Come." he said, curling a finger in my direction.

I was about to make a smart assed comment about how it was just like a man to think the female orgasm was voice activated when I realized I was walking toward him. *No.* I definitely hadn't decided to do that.

He fixed me with those black, empty eyes and stared. "You don't remember us. You never met us."

I frowned. I was in the middle of trying to piece together how that might possibly make sense when the trio turned and left.

I hesitated, then closed the door. Did he seriously think I was going to forget *that*? And why had the woman called me "human?" Was that some hip thing the kids these days were doing? Maybe they thought it was a fancier way to say "man." "What's up, hu-man!"

I tried to shrug it off as three weirdos. Except those three weirdos knew where I'd been last night. They also were asking about some mysterious group of people who appeared to be tied to the demolished wall at the Mercer House.

I couldn't help wondering if there was a connection to the three equally strange people my roommates described dropping me off. From their descriptions, it was three *different* weird people.

What the hell was going on?

6

CARA

Zack was about as good at stealthily tailing me as a t-rex would've been in a backstroke competition. He towered over the group of tourists I was leading around the spooky sights of Savannah. He also had his eyes narrowed and kept jerking his head in random directions, as if expecting to see people peeking out from around building corners and parked cars.

Either this Leah woman decided she had better things to do than tail me, or she was much, much more discreet than Zack, because I hadn't seen even a glimpse of her.

I was surprised to find the media frenzy around the Mercer House had apparently already fizzled out since morning. There was some police caution tape around the building, which had restricted my tour to an outdoor slow-walk where I explained some of the mysteries of the house and its past. But as far as I could tell, nobody was inside.

When the last of my tourists finally headed off, it was just me and Zack

"Well," I said, spreading my hands. "It looks like you scared off any bad guys. Good job."

He was really playing up the powerful male guardian thing, because his only response was to narrow his eyes and look around suspiciously. "For now."

I grinned. "Alright, Batman. Are you ready to walk me home?"

Me and Zack had made it about halfway home when he sniffed at the air like a dog catching a whiff of bacon.

"What is it?" I asked. "Do you smell some expired eggs? Maybe a mushy banana?"

"No," he said. He scrunched up his face, nose still twitching. "But *fuck* it smells good. You don't smell that?"

I shook my head.

"Hold on." Zack looked around, then seemed to zero in on something in the direction of a creepy, dark alleyway. He walked toward it.

"Uh," I said. "Aren't you supposed to be guiding me home safely? I don't think leaving me to go explore a dark alley is a great idea."

"No," he said. "I just want to see what that smell is. I'll be like ten seconds."

I folded my arms, waiting as I watched him creep-walk toward the alley and move into the deeper shadows between the buildings. All I could make out was his tall, broad-shouldered silhouette as he ducked and looked behind a dumpster.

I had done a pretty good job of feeling like Miss Tough Guy until that moment. But the weirdness of the last two days came rushing up on me in a gut-clenching burst of paranoia.

I looked over my shoulder, then checked the other direction, sure I was about to see a beautifully terrifying, pale-skinned woman coming toward me.

All I saw was the empty streets except for a couple walking together in the far distance. The guy was laughing about something and the girl was rolling her eyes so hard I could read it in her body language.

When I looked back toward Zack, all I saw was the alleyway. No tall shadow sniffing out what was probably a bag of garbage. "Zack?"

Oh, come on.

"Zack!" I yelled, a little more insistently this time.

I spun to look behind me, which only managed to create a new "behind," which I had to spin and look at. I thought my heart was going to explode if it beat much faster. "Zack! Get your ass out here right now! I am not going in there after you." I was practically whispering, and not sure how I expected him to hear me.

I was also crouching and holding my hands up like I knew how to throw a punch to save my life—*Let the record show, I certainly did not.*

I hadn't heard a single sound, but when I spun around to look in a new direction for the hundredth time, I saw the woman with the high bangs. I thought her name was Leah, if my adrenaline-filled memory was working properly.

"Oh," I said. I felt my eyes go wide and my body turn completely still.

She let out a tinkling laugh as she walked toward me with a confident sway to her steps. She tilted her head sideways, as if she was watching a somewhat interesting new animal for a few seconds before deciding if she wanted to smash it under her boot or jab it with a stick. "You know we can still see you when you don't move, darling." She stopped just in front of me, then made me jump when she lurched forward and said, "Boo!"

I blinked a few times, inching backwards. "What do you want?" I asked. "If it's money, I swear I'm dirt poor. But I have some gift cards back at the apartment. I could absolutely hook you up. Maybe a free ghost tour?"

The woman kept walking toward me, forcing me in an endless backward, shuffling retreat. "Maybe I just like the way you smell when you're scared."

I resisted the urge to give my pits a discreet sniff. Clearly, this woman was deranged. "Okay," I said shakily. "Well, hope you enjoyed your sniffs. I've got to go find my friend, though."

"I'll take care of him. Don't you worry about that."

Icy tendrils of fear slid under my skin, making it rise up in goosebumps. "That guy from earlier today," I said quickly, still backing up. "He was your boss, right? I thought he only wanted you to follow me. So you should reconsider whatever it is you're considering. You might piss him off."

"Boss," she said, showing a flash of rage at the idea. Then she hesitated as a thought seemed to occur to her. "Wait. You shouldn't remember that."

I nodded quickly. "I know. I'll do like he said and not tell anyone who wasn't there. I just thought—"

She glanced over her shoulder, then took another step closer, eating up the distance between us. There was danger in her eyes, and I was one more *boo* away from blasting her with pepper spray and taking my chances.

The deadly playfulness seemed to creep back into her as she tapped her full lower lip in thought. "I wonder..."

She widened her eyes, then fixed them on me and kept advancing. I felt a kind of magnetic pull, then the briefest hint of... *arousal?*

There was a mental sensation of sliding down toward something, like a black pit I knew there'd be no climbing out of. But before the sensation took me, a vision of a startlingly handsome man I'd never seen flashed in my mind. He was wearing half a grin and showing off the vertical line of a dimple on one cheek.

Then the sensation was gone. Leah ran her tongue across her teeth, laughing in slow confirmation of something. "One of the Undergroves bonded you, didn't they? It's a powerful one, too. I've never seen a human resist our call so easily."

She might as well have been talking a different language. None of it made sense to me, and the only thing I was worried about was Zack. I was the reason he was mixed up in this mess, and I wished I could at least know he was okay. "Where's my friend?"

"The tall, pretty one?"

"The last part is debatable, but yes. The tall one."

"I'm saving him for later, I think."

"What does that even mean?" I forgot my fear for a moment and let out the frustration in my voice. "Why are you people harassing me? What did I do?"

She ran a pink tongue over her teeth, then flicked her eyebrows up once. "You let them out."

"Let *who* out?"

"The Undergroves."

I threw my hands up in frustration. "Okay? Assuming that's true, it doesn't mean they care the slightest about me. So—"

I gasped. All I felt was a sort of forceful thud in my stomach. I stumbled backwards, then looked down in complete confusion at the red stain on my shirt.

Blood. Was that blood?

My blood?

I looked at Leah, then saw her fingertips were wet and red. I looked at my stomach again and fell to my knees. "Why?"

She shrugged. "Because even Bennigan isn't always right." She gave me a girly wave, then back stepped and disappeared into the shadows.

I flopped on my back and looked up at the sky. So this was it. Dead by... what was that? A fingertip punch? *Stupid.* I was surprised that it didn't hurt more. All I felt was a sort of cold spreading from my stomach that carried numbness where it went. I wondered if that's how it would happen. Gradual spreading cold that reached my brain and ended everything.

I found myself wishing I hadn't let Zack tag along. What had I thought he'd accomplish against those three? I'd known there was something wrong about them, and I'd still let him come.

I heard footsteps coming toward me.

"I'm dying, okay?" I said, feeling annoyed. "You got me, so just fuck off and let me die in peace."

"No," a man's voice said. A deep, resonant man's voice that I was sure I'd never heard but immediately felt like I knew. "I don't think I will."

I blinked, realized how blurry my vision had gone, and rolled my head to the side. "Oh, hi," I said weakly.

How long had I been laying here bleeding? I patted the ground by my side a few times and determined the puddle of blood was large. My expertise in hematology told me it was approximately more blood traveling out of my body than was ideal.

"Are you Bennigan?" I asked.

The blurry figure tensed, then I saw him looking around us. "No," he said. "Bennigan is a bastard."

"And you're not?"

There was a pause. "Whether either of us like it or not, it appears you're about to be bonded to me. Even if I am a bastard as well."

"Is that like when a baby lizard thinks the first thing it sees is its mommy?" I felt like I was getting delirious. I grinned, though, finding the idea funnier than it should've been. "Are you saying you're gonna be my mommy?"

I thought the man was smiling a little, but everything was getting too blurry to be sure. He pulled something shiny from his pocket and cut his palm. "Drink," he said.

I shook my head, hearing the soft patter of his blood hitting the pavement beside me. "That woman said someone bonded me already. Sorry to break it to you, but I'm already taken." My voice sounded distant and floaty to my own ears.

Everything was spinning now, like the world was trying to fling me off into the abyss.

I was dying.

The man hesitated. "That's not possible. Now drink."

Before I could react, I felt hot liquid dripping across my mouth and running down my cheeks. A little bit of it slid down my throat before I could decide to be disgusted and close my mouth. "Is that *blood*," I sputtered.

"*Drink*," he said more insistently. He pushed his palm to my lips and forced more of the blood into my mouth.

The little bit that had made it into me was doing strange things I could already feel. My stomach rumbled and moved like I'd just tried Zack's diet plan for a few days. But the coldness was fading, and I was feeling less foggy.

And it tasted good. Strangely good. Like fancy red wine or some kind of sauce that was so good you'd find yourself licking up the last drops from the plate when the meal was through.

When he pulled his hand away, I found myself hungry for more of it, as insane as it was. I lifted my head and reached for his hand, but he shook his head. "No. You shouldn't have more than you need. It wouldn't be safe."

I wasn't sure why, but I thought he was implying it wouldn't be safe for *his sake*, not mine.

The man looked up, and I realized two dark figures had appeared at his side.

"She's being followed. Make sure that changes."

"Yes, master," one of them said sarcastically, and then both figures were gone as quickly as they'd come.

"What's going on? Are you guys superheroes? Are you Blood Man?" I still felt woozy, like I was halfway between drunk and dead tired.

"You'll sleep soon. When you wake, you'll feel better. Your wounds will be healed. And…"

"And what?" I asked. I could already feel the most powerful urge to sleep I'd ever felt rising up.

"And I'll explain the rest when you find me."

"Wait. Zack... Where is he."

"We took care of him. Stop worrying and sleep."

"You *killed* him? You bastard!" I reached up to grab his suit—what kind of person wore a suit at this time of the morning?

"No," he said, gently pushing my hands back. "We sent him home and made sure he won't remember a thing."

My vision was finally getting clearer, and I saw how breathtaking the man was. "Wow," I said dreamily. "You are pretty."

His face had been a mask of serious manliness, but my comment drew out a smile. It also showed me that his canines were unusually sharp and long. He also had a cute little vampire dimple I thought I could've tucked a penny into.

Wait. *Vampire.* I'd seen enough movies to connect the dots forming rapidly in front of me. I was about to ask him point blank, but he put a hand on my cheek. There was something in the way he looked at me. Like he'd known me for years. It was the way teenage girls dreamed about being looked at and never quite found. It was a lost, hopeless look. A *I will walk through fire for you* look. A *I will pick up my clothes and never leave a mess in the kitchen if you'd just be mine* look.

I had a brief image of him waiting in the kitchen for me with an apron that said, "I Fanged The Chef". Then I saw a little sharp toothed baby crawling on the ceiling and hissing at the cat.

Okay. Maybe I was already dead. At the very least, I was certainly delirious. That explained the vampire thing. It was just my mind playing tricks on me. Sexy, mouth-watering tricks that looked amazing in outdated, strange clothes.

He looked very serious. "Sleep, Cara. We'll speak again soon."

And then my world blinked out.

7

CARA

I blearily made myself a cup of coffee in the kitchen, navigating my way through the utter mess of dirty plates and half-eaten food.

I was still waking up, and I found myself picking over the fuzzy remnants of a dream I had last night. Except about two sips into my coffee I nearly dropped the cup on the ground when I remembered it wasn't a dream.

I yanked my shirt up and touched my stomach where I could still feel an echoing memory of icy cold and the impact of a creepy girl's fingertips.

"Nice belly button," Zack said. "But it's not ladylike to show it off like that."

Parker was sitting at the breakfast table with his laptop open. He didn't even look up before he spoke. "The belly button is the most disgusting part of the human anatomy. End of discussion. Please put that away."

I yanked my shirt down and glared at Parker. Then I set down my cup and rushed over to hug Zack when I remembered where we'd left off last night. "Oh my God, you're okay."

"Uh, yeah. Those tacos *were* highly questionable, but it wasn't anything a good night's sleep couldn't sort out."

I pulled back, searching his face for any sign that he was messing with me. "The tacos?"

"Yeah," he said slowly. "The tacos."

"The tacos," I repeated, nodding. "Right."

I finished my breakfast while the rest of the guys straggled down to eat.

Mooney was dating some girl from the track team now and it led to a grossly immature bout of innuendo jokes from the rest of the guys. Parker hijacked the conversation when he decided to explain how likely it was that entire civilizations of mole people could actually live beneath us and we'd have no way to know. But nobody asked about last night.

I kept waiting for the interrogations to begin. My roommates were as overprotective as it got, and none of them even hinted that last night had been unusual. They didn't even seem to remember the broken wall at the Mercer house or any of the fear they'd had for me just last night. In fact, the whole city seemed to have forgotten about the tantalizing Mercer House Mystery as the news had called it overnight.

Maybe I was losing my mind. In fact, I was starting to think that might be preferable to the alternative. Because either I was losing my mind, or the world was turning itself upside down right in front of me.

My suspicion of going crazy only got stronger a few hours later when I was finishing up my classes. All morning, I'd felt a growing sense of unease. It started out on the level of being cramped in an airplane seat for too long. Just a case of restless legs and the need to stretch them.

But hour by hour, the feeling of unease intensified. It turned into something almost like hunger, but for some flavor I couldn't identify. By the time my classes were done for the day, I was done fighting it. Something almost physical was *pulling* me in a certain direction. I turned my body toward it and started walking. The momentary relief I felt was enough to compel me to run.

Every step closer I got felt like an immense weight off my shoulder, so I ran and ran with no idea where I was going. All I knew was that each step was like the relief of emptying my bladder after drinking a jumbo-sized coffee and trying not to leave class to pee through a two-hour lecture.

I was out of breath and sweaty when I finally stopped outside a manor house in one of the historic districts of Savannah. I found myself walking up the steps to the front door and knocking. *You are absolutely losing your mind, Cara.*

Except something kept replaying in my mind. I could still see the blurry impression of the man who had saved me. I could remember sensing that he *knew* I would come find him again.

When the door opened, I got my first full-resolution look at the man from last night. And *wow*, it was quite the look.

He was dressed in a severely outdated set of formal clothes. His dark hair was thick and kind of begging to have my hands run through it. He had a fascinating combination of squared off, rugged handsomeness but with such perfect skin that I couldn't decide if he was pretty, gorgeous, beautiful, or sexy. All I knew was my breath caught because I'd never seen anyone quite like him and I'd never seen eyes like those. They were surprisingly dark, but oddly captivating and expressive.

He also had the most immaculate, thick black eyebrows that formed a perfectly roguish little swoop above his eyes. They were brows made for suggestive glances and playful, lopsided arches.

"Um," I said. Hearing my own voice felt like getting hit with an ice-cold bucket of *what the hell am I doing*. "Believe it or not, I have no idea how or why I'm here."

"You're here," he said breathlessly. He was watching me like a dog might watch a strip of bacon.

"For some reason." I laughed a little, more out of discomfort than finding any real humor in the situation. *Why was a man as bone-breakingly hot as this guy looking at me like he wanted to strip me naked and give me the best sex of my life?* "I don't even know your name, let alone why I came."

"I'm Lucian Undergrove. Come in," he said, gesturing.

But he didn't move from the door, so when I stepped forward, I was forced to brush against his body. The simple contact of my shoulder against his firm stomach was enough to make my blood feel like it was about to boil. The man was built out of lean muscle and sharp lines.

I pressed the backs of my hands to my cheeks, feeling how incredibly flushed I was.

What the hell?

But when I looked at the man, I saw he wasn't doing much better. He looked like he was barely holding something in.

"Don't try anything funny," I said, summoning some courage I didn't quite feel. Worse, I was pretty sure I actually wanted him to try several funny things that started with the removal of clothing. "I bite," I warned.

"Me too," he said, the corner of his mouth twisting up sexily. His eyes were absolutely smoldering, and I thought I was probably burning about fifty calories a minute with how much heat my body was generating around him.

"What's happening?" I asked. I didn't ask the real question on my mind. *Why do I feel an overwhelming urge to jump your sexy bones even though I don't know you?*

His nostrils flared out with each breath he took in. "It's the bond," he explained. "It will be strongest at first and fade with time. Sit. It will be better if we're not quite so close." He took a merciful step away from me and motioned to a chair in his old-fashioned living room that was lined with deep red wallpaper, stained brown wainscoting, and plush rugs.

I felt like I needed to get farther from the man, because I was worried I was going to do something absolutely insane if I didn't. I rushed over to the chair and sat, breathing out a brief sigh of relief once I was seated.

He moved to the other side of the room, clearly making an effort to keep his distance as he planted his hands on the back of a couch across from me.

"The less you know, the safer you will be."

I suppressed the vivid, erotic images that were already playing like a flipbook in my mind. Sweaty, exposed skin. Moving bodies. Lips pressed together.

The fantasy version of this guy had the most impeccably firm buns I'd ever laid mental eyes on, too. My mouth was practically watering.

I blinked, then shook my head. "What did you do to me?"

"I saved your life."

"And made me violently horny in the process?"

His smile was strained. "It will pass."

"I need to know more than that."

Lucian sighed. "When a human drinks the blood of... one of my kind, a bond is formed. It's the first step of a—" he cut himself off, clearly struggling with how much he wanted to conceal from me. "The first step of a process," he finished, choosing his words carefully. "All we need to do is control our impulses and the temptation will pass."

I stared blankly. "I feel like you're talking in code. Can you please just tell me in plain English?"

Lucian's nostrils flared again, and he still hadn't stopped looking at me like he was on the verge of tossing the couch and rushing toward me to devour me. *The scary part was that I wanted him to.*

"Put simply, we must not have intercourse. You would become like me if we did. I must also not feed on your blood. And there are a few other more ritualistic things we should avoid that we don't need to concern ourselves with."

A surprised laugh slipped out of me. "I'm sorry, but have you considered that maybe you're just crazy? Obviously, you're really attractive. Maybe you've built up this fantasy world where women can't resist you because you're... what, a vampire? Maybe you're just really hot and really tragically confused."

There was that smile again. It was disarming, like there was a more playful side to his personality he was keeping on a leash for now. It wasn't a crazy person's smile, I thought. Then again, Ted

Bundy was dashingly handsome, too. It didn't make him any less of a horrible person.

"You can fill in whatever details you want about our situation, Cara. As long as we don't sleep together, this will all pass, and your life will eventually return to normal."

I ran my palm down my mouth and searched the ceiling. "You mentioned danger. What would possibly be dangerous about knowing these things?"

"There are others like me. Others who place very high value on not being known."

"Like that Bennigan guy and the two women?"

Lucian nodded. "Others, too. But Bennigan has a talent for holding grudges. He's the greatest danger. *For now.*"

"Were you trapped in that wall? The one at Mercer House?" It felt like my brain was zig-zagging between a thousand unknowns and didn't know quite where to start.

"Yes. But that's enough questions for now."

I folded my hands together, frowning at the man. "Let's say I actually believe all of this. What am I supposed to do?"

"Unfortunately, that part isn't really up to you or me. The bond will force us to stay close. *Very* close. We'll need to find a way to blend into each other's lives."

"What do you mean?"

"Being away from each other will be like experiencing withdrawal from an addictive substance. You'll need to stay here, and we'll have to think of a way to make you blend in."

"No," I said, laughing. "I have classes. Roommates. People don't just disappear. I have no idea how long you were trapped in that wall, but there would be search parties and news stories if I vanished."

Lucian ran his thumb across his chin. "Then I will need to blend into your life as well."

I looked at his clothes and his ridiculously model-like features. "I don't think you're going to blend in to my life."

"Nor you to mine, but we'll have to try."

There was a loud thump, then muffled curses as something heavy tumbled down the stairs in the other room.

I got to my feet, looking toward the sound. "What was that?" I asked.

Lucian looked like he was about to sigh. "That is my roommate. Vlad."

I looked at him through narrowed eyes. "You seriously have a roommate named 'Vlad?' Let me guess. He's a vampire?"

Lucian gestured in the direction of the noise. "See for yourself. But don't get too close. Vlad has a fondness for torturing virgins."

"Did you just imply I'm a virgin?"

Lucian's lip twitched in amusement. "You smell like one."

I glared at him, unsure how I was even supposed to respond to that. But I decided I was in a weird enough situation that I should at least *consider* some of this could be true. So I cautiously approached the stairs.

I saw a man with long ringlets of dark, curly hair and a five-o-clock shadow. He was currently face first on the ground, groaning.

"Are you okay?" I asked.

Vlad rolled to the side, resting his hands on his impressively round belly as he gasped for air. "Yes. I don't feel pain." He had a thick, stereotypically vampirey accent. He winked at me. With another grunt that I was starting to suspect was more for effect than out of need, he got to his feet and brushed off his clothes. He was dressed a little bit like a cross between a medieval duke and a swashbuckling pirate, with embroidered vests, leather pants, and boots with curled up toes.

"I'm Cara," I said.

"Vunderful," he said, rolling his eyes. Despite Vlad's out of date style and lack of self-care, he still managed to appear strikingly handsome. Not my type, but handsome.

"Lucian!" he called out, walking past me toward where me and Lucian had been sitting earlier. "You can't bring your food home to toy with it. Not unless you want old Vlad to take a nibble first." He barked out a laugh, then broke into a coughing fit.

I frowned after the man. *What the hell?*

"How do you two know each other?" I asked. Vlad was pouring himself a glass of liquor. He took a mouthful, swished it around, and then spit it violently into the trash can, wincing.

"Vlad is exceptionally old," Lucian said. "Ancient, actually."

Vlad gave a theatrical bow with a little circling wave of his arm and a flourish of his other hand. "They used to tell stories of me. Then they told stories about the stories. Now it's all but forgotten."

I was still trying to come to terms with all of this, but only having one foot in the door of belief helped me to take the roommate situation in stride. "Is there any chance you used to impale people on sticks, Vlad?" I asked, moving to lean in the doorway.

I'd been joking, but there was a sudden feverish excitement on Vlad's face and a look of dismay on Lucian's.

"Please don't ask him about torture," Lucian said. "He will talk your ear off."

Vlad swooped closer to me so quickly I wasn't sure I'd actually seen his feet move—*or touch the ground*. He was inches from my face, smiling wide and sinister. "You're a fan of my work? I could show you a live and in person demonstration, if you wish it? I promise, nobody will ever poke you like I will poke you, dearie." He sniffed deeply, then his grin widened. "A virgin, as well?"

"Why is everybody here so intent on calling me a virgin? *And smelling me?*"

"Vlad," Lucian said, tone laced with warning. "You will keep your hands off the virgin. She's mine."

Vlad made a pouty face but wiggled his eyebrows as he slid backwards from me. "Another time, perhaps."

"For the record, I've never confirmed or denied this virgin thing you two keep assuming," I said, though it sounded like neither of them cared to listen.

"No. You will not be impaling Cara at any point," Lucian said. "She's not my food, either. The two of us are temporarily bonded, and I'm going to see to it that she gets to return to her normal life when it has passed."

"Perhaps I could torture her just for a little while and clear it from her memory afterwards? Surely you wouldn't deny old Vlad *that* small favor?"

"Surely I would," Lucian said. He was standing now, and the way he was squared up with Vlad made me worried the men were about to start throwing punches.

Except Vlad belched loudly, then went back to take another swig of liquor, which he spit out in the trash can a moment later. "Suit yourself, Lucy Boy. I won't poke your pet. For now." he turned toward us both with a maniacally raised eyebrow. "But I bet you will let *him* poke you before long, eh?" Vlad wandered off, cackling at his own joke.

"I apologize for him."

"Neither of you ever actually said how you know each other."

"Vlad may not look like it, but he's very powerful and feared. Well, he's feared by those who haven't met him recently. So long as I put up with his personality faults, Bennigan will not be likely to move against me and my family."

"Right," I said, not really sure I believed any of what he was saying. Then again, it was hard to deny what I'd seen with my own eyes, assuming that wasn't all some fever dream.

I also couldn't deny the fact that separating from Lucian didn't feel possible right now. There was a physical need to be close. Even considering splitting up made me feel sick to my stomach, and *that* was something I needed to deal with, even if he was a delusional, hot lunatic who thought he was a vampire.

8

CARA

Lucian drew the attention of just about anybody we passed with a functioning pair of eyes. I assumed a man who looked like he did was impossible to miss on a good day, but the way he was dressed wasn't helping, either.

I led him into a store where I hoped we'd find some updated clothes for him, even though he insisted on formal wear. At least it would be a modern suit, instead of whatever it was he was currently wearing.

"Aren't vampires supposed to burn up in the sun or something?" I asked as I held up a suit to his tall frame and tried to decide if it was a good fit.

"No. The sun makes us mortal. It saps our energy, too, but it's not fatal for an older vampire like myself."

I studied him. "Is that why you look kind of high right now?"

His eyebrows furrowed together. "No. That would be because you are very short, and I am quite tall."

"No, doofus. High is like—"

He flashed that disarming smile again. "It was a joke. Yes. I don't feel myself in the sunlight, but the risk should be minimal. Bennigan won't put himself in danger to face me in the open. He'll want to find where we sleep and strike like a coward would, assuming that's his plan."

I worked my lips to the side, setting down the latest suit. "We need to work on the way you talk if you want to blend in. *'The risk should be minimal'*" I mocked in a deep voice.

"You'd prefer I talk like the locals?"

"Can you?"

Lucian's eyes were half-lidded, and it was almost enough to make me laugh seeing him like that. He looked like he was about to start spouting off about how aliens were the ones who really built the pyramids. "I will increase my—" He paused. "I'll try."

"See? Maybe you're not completely hopeless."

It was taking everything I had to ignore the pulsing need I felt toward him. I was still allowing for the possibility that he was just a deranged hot guy who didn't understand the effect he had on women. But I was also beginning to believe this was no ordinary attraction I felt. Even when I walked a few steps from him to go look for a tie, I felt pulled back to his side.

The more dangerous part was how I felt like my normal barriers had been knocked down ahead of time. Things that should've seemed like too much and too fast didn't instinctively feel wrong. I could imagine wrapping my arms around his arm and leaning into him. I could easily drape a tie around his neck and run my hands down his chest before stepping back to see how it looked.

It all felt too easy, and I was currently engaged in a mental battle to stop myself from listening to my tainted instincts.

He also had a way of looking at me like he'd been dreaming about me for years. It was an addictive amount of attention he seemed to shower onto me, but I needed to make sure I didn't let myself get too comfortable with it.

I'd decided to refer to Lucian's current state as sun drunk. He really did appear out of it, and he was either crazy *and* a great actor, or what he'd said was true.

I eventually collected five or six suits, ties, belts, and shoes I liked best for him to choose from. Lucian surprised me by buying all of them, apparently unconcerned about the price.

Add rich to the growing list of descriptors for this guy, I thought.

"What do you do for a living, exactly?" I asked while he pulled out conspicuous wads of cash to pay for his clothes. The money looked old, which made the cashier have to call her manager to verify it still would work at the bank.

"That's complicated."

"Then try your best to help me understand."

Lucian paused in the shade outside, clearly still feeling somewhat off from the sunlight and not looking forward to going into it again. "I was an artist. *Before*," he added.

"Really? What medium?"

"I painted. I also did some work with sculptures. But I don't do that anymore. It reminds me of what I've lost."

Lucian was doing that hot guy thing where he kept clenching his jaw again and again, which made a bundle of muscles on his smooth jaw bunch and unbunch.

Sensitive topic, it seemed.

"Well, what do you do now? Or what were you doing before you got bricked up in a room for a hundred years."

"I was what you might have considered a law enforcement officer. But within the vampire world."

I raised an eyebrow. "Vampire cop? That sounds like some low budget sitcom."

"Vampires are still held to standards, even if they would all prefer to live outside any sense of order."

"Hmm," I said. "Does this have anything to do with the Bennigan guy and why he seems to hate you so much?"

"Do you always ask so many questions?"

"Yes," I said. "What do you do for fun?"

Lucian looked down at me incredulously. "I like to brood in isolated castles on hilltops, especially if a thunderstorm is coming."

"Seriously. What do you like to do?"

"I used to enjoy traveling. Seeing architecture and new things. Okay? Can we go on with your daily tasks yet?"

"We still have plenty of time. I missed my morning classes for this, and I don't need to be at my internship yet. You said *used to*. Why? You can't travel anymore?"

"Because reasons I don't need to share with a human," he said through clenched teeth.

"But you kind of like this human, don't you?" I teased.

"I'm bonded to this human, which doesn't give me much of a choice."

"Right," I said. "You like me."

I stepped out into the sunlight and left him no choice but to follow behind me. He shielded his eyes and looked even more pale than usual but was keeping up with me all the same.

"Okay," I said. "First test is you need to come with me to my internship at Anya's. If she asks who you are, we can just say you're my boyfriend, okay?"

Lucian was looking loopier the longer we walked around outside. I'd given him a pair of sunglasses to help disguise exactly how out of it he appeared. But he wasn't even walking completely steady anymore.

"Hey, are you in there?" I asked, nudging him.

Lucian gave me a thumbs up.

I grinned. I thought I liked him better when he wasn't so in control. The big, hot, stumbling mess at my side was at least less intimidating. "Are you sure the sun isn't going to kill you? You're not looking so good."

"I may have neglected to mention my kind usually limits our time in the sun to very brief, necessary exposure. This is more than I'm accustomed to."

"What does that mean?"

Lucian shrugged. "I suppose you may end up needing to drag me to our location."

I shook my head. "Not happening, shades. Come on, let's pick up the pace and get to Anya's."

Lucian managed to keep up until we got to Anya's.

Anya was wearing a thick, pink, fluffy bathrobe. Her hair was leaning to one side in an act of defiance towards gravity, and something was stuck in her eye. She grunted at me, then gave Lucian a curious look.

"This big man is?" she asked as we headed down the stairs.

"Drunk. And high, I think. But he's, um,"

"Her boyfriend," Lucian interjected. "We've developed very strong feelings for one another. It's quite serious."

As if to demonstrate his claim, Lucian put his arm around me and pulled me into the side of his chest. I felt myself blush both with embarrassment and with the explosion of mostly irrational horniness that blasted through me at the simplest touch from him.

"He's making it sound more serious than it is," I said, trying to pry myself from his grasp.

"No," Lucian said with a calm, reassuring little chuckle. "I'm afraid, if anything, I've underplayed the intensity of our feelings." We reached the basement, which gave Lucian the unfortunate chance to stop and tilt my chin up so I had to look into his obnoxiously amused eyes. "Every time I look at my darling Cara, I think my heart might burst."

"Your balls are going to burst if you don't stop," I warned through tight lips, hoping Anya wouldn't hear me.

He raised one of those thick, perfect eyebrows of his and grinned. "In fact, the thing I love most about her is how willful she is. *How passionate.*"

I was going to kick his undead ass if I got the chance for this.

Anya, who normally paid almost no interest to anything except her hopeless quest, was hanging on Lucian's every word. "Star crossed love," she whispered.

"No, no," I said quickly, stepping back from Lucian, which only let him smoothly take my hand and accidentally spin me in a kind of dance move I wasn't supposed to be capable of. Next thing I knew, he had a hand on the small of my back and our bodies were pressed close together.

"Yes, yes," he said.

Anya clapped her hands, then wiped at her eye. "Is beautiful. So beautiful."

I discreetly lifted my knees between Lucian's leg in a ball-kicking equivalent of a warning shot. He flashed that dimple at me, then let me go. "She is, isn't she?"

"Why don't you make yourself comfortable on Anya's lovely couch?" I suggested. "I don't know where you got all this sudden energy to profess your undying love for me, but just a few minutes ago you looked like you could really use a nap, right?" I added, giving him the eyes that said *you had better play along, asshole.*

Lucian hesitated just long enough to let me know he was not just hot, ancient, and most likely a supernatural creature. He was also a devious flirt who enjoyed seeing me squirm. But after a few heartbeats, he dutifully yawned and nodded. "A nap would be rejuvenating."

"Yes. Now go lay your big ass on that couch. I need to get to work."

Lucian shot me one last blood-heating look, then went to stretch himself out on the cat-ravaged couch.

I grinned to myself, then sat down and tried—but mostly failed— to ignore the huge man lying just a few feet behind me and the pulsing thrum of my heartbeat. It was strange, like each beat of my heart sent out a little probe in his direction, checking that we were still close enough.

I started going through the motions of work. Removing samples from the fridge and spreading them on slides. Checking them under the microscope and running their numbers to gather data on various treatments I needed to test.

I'd been working for about an hour when a thought occurred to me. I glanced at Lucian, who was sleeping on the couch. I wasn't sure if he was messing with me, but he was lying on his back with his arms crossed over his chest and his legs sticking straight out like the picture of a vampire in a coffin.

I rolled my eyes but couldn't help smiling.

When Anya wasn't watching, I pricked my finger and put some of my own blood on a slide, then looked under the microscope.

At first glance, it was completely normal. Just the endless sea of red blood cells bobbing around like abandoned floaties in a huge pool. But there was something wrong.

Little black, spikey things were moving around the sample with purpose. They'd occasionally swarm a damaged cell, vibrate against it, and then it would look completely repaired when they moved away. But more oddly, I noticed they were all drifting in a certain direction. Each of them was moving to the right of the slide and beginning to gather at the edge of the sample.

I frowned down at it, trying to puzzle out what it meant for a while before I lifted my eyes from the microscope and looked to my right.

To where Lucian was lying on the couch.

I studied the sample again and confirmed the little black specks were now all crammed up against the edge of the sample on the right side like they were trying to get to him.

I sat back in the chair, staring at the wall, heart thumping away like I'd just run a marathon.

All day, I'd been letting the impossible facts Lucian presented me with to slowly sink in my brain. It had honestly been easier to turn it all into a difficult to believe joke. Just something to play along with while I tried to make sense of whatever was going on with my body and the weird craving I had to be near him. But seeing the sample of my blood made it all feel concrete in a way nothing else had yet. The proof was right there in my blood.

I'd drank the blood of a vampire, and now I was pretending he was my boyfriend. *Oh*, and some sort of magnetic magic black dots were now flooding my blood and drawing me toward him like he was a drug.

Wonderful.

9

LUCIAN

I knew I needed to get back to Alaric and Seraphina soon. They'd be worried.

Yet I found myself trailing after Cara as she gave a group of people some sort of "haunted tour" through the city of Savannah, which had grown considerably since I'd last seen it. In fact, I'd come to the city when it was little more than a town and I'd known many of the vampires who were prominent in the area at the time. I'd also been present for many of the events she described, like the mass burials when the yellow fever came or the hanging of Alice Riley in the town square.

I watched Cara as she went through the motions of the tour. She was a peculiar human, even by the standards I was coming to understand of these modern women. Cara dressed somewhat randomly. The night I'd seen her she had been clad in black and aggressive clothes that were at odds with her slender, feminine frame. Today she had worn a simple, pastel pink skirt and a white blouse that completely changed her look. She'd seemed like a woman who would speak her mind and never dream of apologizing the night before, and today she looked more delicate—as if the sharper edges were subtle things that would only be discovered upon closer inspection.

She was fascinating.

She wore her black hair just down to her jawline, where it swooped forward into two little points. A solid line of bangs hung just above her eyebrows, making her hair like a frame for the simple, clean features on her face. But the most arresting thing about her might have been her mouth, which seemed to telegraph her feelings as openly as a book, whether she wanted it to or not.

She pressed her full lips together when I was irritating her. When she was aroused, she breathed through her mouth, showing just the hint of two flat, slightly oversized front teeth. When she was amused, she always bit her lip before she smiled, as if she was trying to stop the expression from coming by force and failing all the same. My favorite might have been when she was angry, which seemed to set her lips into a silent, shifting state where she was half forming the words she was about to hurl my way.

The woman was a constant surprise and yet somehow comfortably predictable. She was full of life and energy in a way that made me feel more alive than I had in decades, too.

She was currently making up some nonsense about how the bumpy sidewalk outside one of Savannah's many graveyards was actually caused by unmarked graves buried beneath our feet. I grinned, watching the members of her tour look down at their feet in horror.

I added a new expression of her wicked mouth to my list. When she was lying for fun, she held part of her lower lip between her teeth on one side.

The tour ended at the Mercer House, which woke a strange kind of bitterness in me. I didn't enjoy thinking about the wasted years we had spent sealed in there or the oddness of knowing people like this were touring the house all these years.

It was hard to think of much beyond the blinding throbs of need I felt toward Cara. I'd been bonded before, but it had never felt *this* difficult to resist. Maybe it was my long slumber or maybe it was how Cara had been on the brink of death when I'd brought her back. All the blood she'd lost meant there was more room for mine, perhaps.

It could also have had something to do with the fact that I pushed my will on her that first night we escaped from the room at the Mercer House. I'd heard stories of extremely powerful vampires bonding humans with nothing more than a suggestion. I supposed being dormant didn't stop me from becoming more powerful while I was trapped, and maybe I'd jumpstarted the bond before I even realized as much.

Whatever the cause, it was taking every ounce of my control to stop from kissing her. Touching her. *Taking her.*

Cara felt like a precious thing. Watching her walk around unclaimed was as hard as passing by a diamond ring lying on a busy sidewalk. Surely at any moment, another hand would snatch out to grab her if I didn't first.

But I knew what would happen if I gave in to my impulses. I'd be damning her to the existence I lived. To an eternity of watching the world grow to dust around her, where her only companions would be others like me. The deadly, the deranged, and the ones who hadn't quite lost their minds yet.

That was all there was in this world.

"You're looking better," Cara said when the last of our tour group was gone.

I pointed to the moon and stars above us.

She nodded. "So how do we do this last part? If I'm not home, my roommates are going to send out a search party. But I've never... taken a guy home with me. I'm not sure how that will go over with them."

"Your roommates? Who are they?"

"Zack, Niles, Mooney, and Parker. They're guys who go to the same school I do."

"Men?" I asked, feeling my temper flare. "You live with four men?"

She smiled. "It's nothing like that. I am dirt poor. They had an extra room and put an ad out. I met all of them before I agreed to stay there, and they all seemed super nice. None of them have ever tried to make a move or anything like that. They're basically like little brothers to me."

"I see," I said. "And you're worried these little brothers will not approve of me?"

"They're protective. They might interrogate you. So it's going to seem weird if you don't know the first thing about me."

"Okay," I said. We began walking in a direction I assumed was toward her house. I knew I'd need to drag her back to my world tomorrow and make sure Alaric and Seraphina didn't end up going on some sort of suicide mission assuming Bennigan had taken me captive.

"You've got to try really hard to talk normal, okay?"

I nodded. "What do I need to know about Cara Skies, the abnormally short human?"

She gave me a wry smile. "I didn't know vampires were teases."

"I was a person before this was done to me."

She looked curious but appeared to decide the most pressing issue was getting me to pass this pending interview with her roommates and didn't push for details.

"Then I should ask questions about my new girlfriend," I said, watching the little tick of frustration and amusement on the corner of her mouth.

"You should."

"Do you have family?" I asked. "I imagine someone with close family ties might not resort to living with four men."

"You imagine correctly. My family is dysfunctional, at best. I have a dad who cheated on my mom and now lives in Wyoming with a woman he calls his sugar momma. Then I've got a mom who never stopped feeling sorry for herself and gambled away everything she got out of the divorce. She lives in Florida and her only passion in life is going on sunset casino cruises when she gets her social security checks."

"Should I pretend I understand what most of those things are?"

Cara smiled a little sadly. "Probably better if you don't. The short version is my parents are in no position to be involved or really care about what I'm doing."

"Brothers or sisters?"

"Nope," she said. "It's pretty much just me. At least that's how it feels."

I didn't plan on it, but I put my arm around her and pulled her into me as we walked. I felt her stiffen at my touch, but she relaxed a few steps later, surprising me by allowing the contact. "For the duration of our bond, that won't be true," I said.

"Maybe that'll be nice for a change. A temporary one," she added.

I had enjoyed teasing Cara and testing her to see how she'd react to provocations, but I felt myself in danger now. I liked how it felt to walk with my arm around her. I liked listening to her speak and studying the many different ways that tempting mouth of hers spelled out her thoughts. Most dangerously, hearing that she was alone in the world made me want to protect her some way. To give her the bond she was missing.

I wanted to fill that space for her, except I knew I couldn't. I was poison and she was a fertile plant in need of water and sunlight. It didn't matter how much I might've wanted to be that nourishment she needed. All I would bring her was decay. More pain. More heartache.

"And what about your interests?" I asked, hoping to draw myself from my spiraling thoughts. "What does Cara Skies do for fun?"

"Well, I had this friend in high school named Lana. She ended up getting diagnosed with a rare blood disease. I remember when I first found out, I figured they'd say they knew all about it and they had a cure. Or at least there would be some experimental treatment they were going to try. Except they just had no idea. Like there was absolutely nothing they could do, and she ended up wasting away.

"I didn't exactly have the grades to make it into any kind of medical program at a college. I also didn't have the money. But watching that made me realize I wanted to do something worthwhile with my life. Even if it was just figuring out how to help people who were diagnosed with what she had. So I took all the part time jobs I could find, saved money, and eventually got into the cheapest community college I could. Then I knocked out the pre-req courses and applied to basically every hematology program in the US until I got in here.

"So as far as 'fun' goes, I've been too focused on making this happen to stop and smell the roses, I guess. My life has just been school and chasing after this goal, no matter the cost. Well, until some asshole decided to bleed in my mouth."

I still had my arm around her, and I gave her arm a little squeeze, grinning at that. "You are quite the impressive human, Cara Skies."

"That's highly debatable," she said. "Goals and accomplishments are two dramatically different things. So far all I've accomplished is absolutely nuking my social life and focusing on nothing but school for most of my adult existence."

"I've lived a very long time, and I've never seen someone truly determined fail to accomplish something impressive. It may not always be the goal they set out to reach, but energy tends to create outcomes. Put enough in, and something comes out."

She smiled a little wryly, then pulled herself from my grasp and backpedaled to look at me as we walked. "And what is it you've put your energy in for your long, geezerly existence, Lucian? I imagine somebody doesn't go on living for a million years without some sort of grand purpose?"

"I imagine we are close to your apartment," I said abruptly. "I should make sure I know as much about you as I can before we arrive."

She gave me a knowing look but let me continue asking any questions I could think of without turning the subject back to me.

"You know," she said. "I looked at my blood under the microscope today. It's fascinating. Have you ever seen what your blood does to a person? On a microscopic level, I mean?"

"No."

Cara started trying to explain her findings to me, but I found I only understood about every third word of what she was saying. I instead lost myself in the fullness of her lips and the glimpses of her pink tongue pressing against neatly arranged, white teeth.

She was clearly passionate about blood, because she spoke about it for nearly ten minutes before I interrupted. "Will your roommates ask about anything else?"

"Oh," she said. "What else... Okay, well, this is embarrassing, but I kinda told all of my roommates that I wasn't going to date at all until I was done with school. So they are probably going to wonder why the sudden change."

"And what do I tell them?"

"I don't know," she said with a sigh. "Tell them you made me suck your blood and now we can barely stand twenty feet apart and the urge to let you fang me dirty is kind of all-consuming."

She clapped a hand over her mouth, cheeks going red.

"Fang you... dirty? Is that some sort of slang?"

"Does your blood normally make people say things they only planned to think?"

"No," I said, grinning. "But if it makes you feel any more at ease, I am also finding it very hard not to dirtily fang you."

Cara snorted. "I really didn't expect a vampire to exist. But if someone had told me they were real, I wouldn't have imagined it would be so much fun to hang out with one—even against my will."

"You're not so bad for a human, either."

10

CARA

I let Lucian into the apartment and silently prayed the guys would be asleep or out. Instead, I found all four of them standing around the kitchen. They stared at us wordlessly, clearly in a state of pure shock.

"Guys," I said. "This is Lucian. My... *boyfriend*."

"We have very strong feelings for one another," Lucian added. "And she's deeply interested in the study of blood. Her parents—"

I elbowed him. So much for the whole smooth vampire charm. He was about as subtle as a baby bull.

"Boyfriend?" Mooney choked. "When did you even have time to *meet* somebody?"

"He was in my class. He's really into blood, too," I said, spit balling.

Lucian nodded. "It's true. I love blood."

"Talk less," I hissed out of the side of my mouth.

"Do you play ball?" Zack asked. He moved a little closer, confirming Lucian was almost as tall as all of my oversized roommates. "You're pretty tall."

Lucian hesitated. "Ball... Yes. Quite often."

The guys exchanged a look. I could see the idea forming in their heads and knew he would've been better off saying he didn't play. "We'll have to get you out on the court soon," Zack said.

"The court. Yes. I have a great deal of experience in the court," Lucian said.

I blinked, trying to get his attention so I could urge him to shut his stupidly hot mouth.

"Is that right?" Niles asked. "Did you play in Europe or something? You've got a kind of funny accent."

"Yes. I was present at several courts across Europe. But it has been some time."

They were all frowning. I could see they were on the verge of getting too suspicious and asking the wrong questions.

Lucian appeared to sense it too. "Gentleman," he said in a deep, more confident voice. "Look into my eyes, please."

What is he doing?

"You will forget you met me tonight."

"Hey!" I said, whacking his arm. "What are you doing?"

Lucian looked down at me, ignoring the glazed-over faces of my roommates, who were still watching him. "I'm wiping their memories. We can try again tomorrow. And again, if needed."

"You can't just wipe people's memories when you make a bad first impression."

He gestured to my zombified roommates. "It's quite easy. I can do this every night until we get it right, actually."

"No," I said. "Jesus. We need to teach you some etiquette or something. I don't care if you *can*. You shouldn't."

Lucian frowned. "Why?"

"I don't know? What if you're scrambling up their brains every time or giving them cancer? No more memory wiping. Okay? That's a rule from now on."

He appeared to chew over my command, then shrugged. "Unless it's to prevent direct danger to you, I won't wipe any more memories."

"Good enough, I guess. Now come on. I'm going to show you where you're sleeping on the floor in my room."

"Wonderful." Lucian said. He paused, then stepped back in front of my roommates. "You will also clean up this kitchen in two minutes. It's filthy. Have some self-respect."

I was about to tell him to stop mind controlling my roommates but decided that I could let some abuses of his power slide. At least for now.

I NORMALLY TOOK CLOTHES OFF TO SLEEP, BUT CONSIDERING THE circumstances, I went into my closet and threw on an extra thick hoodie and some pajama bottoms. I considered an extra pair of underwear too, but decided I was fooling myself. If Lucian started waving his vampire cock around, it was going to take more than a couple layers of panties to stop it.

I climbed under my blankets and eyed him suspiciously. "You're not going to try anything, are you?" *Cue my stupid, "bond brain" hoping he would.*

"I'm going to try to rest. Though I usually sleep during the day. This will be an adjustment."

I yawned. "Just stay on your side of the room and I'll stay on mine, okay?"

Lucian looked unconcerned and sat down in the corner.

I was trying my best not to do anything that might tip the scales in the battle waging within my mind. Even a subtle act of kindness might be too much, but he looked pathetic sitting there with his long, sculpted legs on the hard floor.

I sighed, then lobbed a pillow at him. I picked up an extra blanket and threw it as well. "I don't know if vampires use pillows and blankets, but there you go."

Lucian gave a slight nod of appreciation, but it still didn't look like he planned to lie down.

I sat in silence with my eyes closed for a while, occasionally sneaking a look in his direction. Half of the times I looked were to make sure he was still staying on his side of the room and the other half were because the man was a work of art. Pale blue light was filtering through my window, and it was hitting his smooth skin just right, making him look like some kind of god of the night.

I let out a frustrated sigh, then sat up a little, looking in his direction. "How does it work, anyway? The whole vampire thing, I mean."

"What do you mean?"

"Like in some movies vampires have to kill people to feed. Sometimes they turn anyone they bite into a vampire too. Sometimes they sparkle in the sunlight. What are the rules?"

Lucian tilted his head. I'd already noticed a pattern with him when he wasn't sure if he should answer my questions. He'd hesitate, then spoke slowly when he finally answered, as if he was reading from a script he'd just mentally scribbled down. "Feeding is not fatal for humans."

I waited. When he didn't say more, I decided to press him. "That's it?"

"We use our power of suggestion to make them forget they ever saw us, and they are somewhat weak from blood loss the following day. That's it."

"Then why do you look like there's something you're not telling me?"

"Because it's as I told you before. The less you know, the safer you are. Your goal should be to wait out the worst of the bond, then pretend you never met me and forget my kind exist. The more you know, the harder that will be."

"Why can't you just wipe my memory? It doesn't seem to faze you at all to do it to other people."

"The bond lends some of my power to you. Especially now, it would take a great deal of effort to wipe your memory."

"Wait. When Bennigan came to Anya's, he tried to make me forget I'd seen him. It didn't work, and that was *before* you made me drink your blood. What does that mean?"

Lucian nodded, as if he'd already thought about that exact point. Then I saw the same unwillingness to divulge more.

I folded my arms. "I'm in danger. You said it yourself. I think it should be my choice to decide how informed I want to be about that danger. Don't you?"

Lucian watched me for several long moments until I thought his eyes might actually be seeing straight into my thoughts. Finally, he looked down, nodding. "There have been cases where a human bonds with one of my kind without the transfer of blood. It's extremely rare, and in every case I know of, the bond that developed from those instances was unusually strong." He raised his eyes to meet mine again, and I felt a surge of heat flow through me from his smoldering gaze. "And every one of those cases resulted in a pairing."

I didn't need to be an expert in geezer slang or vampire vernacular to figure out what he meant by "a pairing." I swallowed. "So far," I added.

"So far," he agreed.

"Do vampires get married?"

"Yes."

I laid back down and rolled to the side, trying to sleep again. A few minutes later, I opened my eyes and turned toward him. "You're not going to drink my blood while I'm sleeping, are you?"

"No," he said. "Drinking your blood would consummate the bond and turn you into a vampire."

"Oh, yeah. I remember you saying that. But what if—"

"Sleep, Cara Skies."

I saw Lucian was lying on his back again with his arms crossed over his chest and his legs straight out. I grinned to myself, then tried to get comfortable. It was going to be a long night. *And a long day after.*

11

LUCIAN

Cara had let me borrow some clothes from her roommates. I was outfitted with a hooded garment, gloves, sunglasses, and an ample application of a substance she called "sunscreen." Armored as I was, the sun seemed to take its toll all the same, if maybe a little more slowly.

I followed her to her academic studies and watched the changed world as we traveled. I had already lived longer than I thought the mind was truly capable of coping with. But I had always watched progress crawl by. It was only when I looked back that the technological and societal changes seemed startling.

Ever since Cara released us from what I'd begun to think might become an eternal slumber, I was struck by the way the world had moved on. It was like a dose of mortality. A small taste of death, almost.

I looked around and saw time would happily pass without me. It would keep plowing forward, relentless and unforgiving, whether or not I was still creeping in its shadow.

Today, Cara was wearing a torn t-shirt with lightning bolts and electrified puppies on it with equally shredded jeans and black boots. I frowned. "Do you need money for new clothing? Yours appear damaged."

She laughed. "It's a style. Kind of. I mean, I guess it depends who you ask. And if you asked most people, they'd probably say I was too old to even make an attempt to express myself with clothes."

"I enjoy seeing the different things you wear. It's interesting."

She smiled wide and open, then chewed her lip. That was a new expression, I noted. Genuine happiness, maybe? Whatever it was, I decided I liked it. "Thank you, Lucian. That's really sweet."

"Yes, well, women in my time wore gigantic dresses and about ten layers. I am thinking I prefer the direction fashion has gone since I was detained."

Cara looked suddenly thoughtful. "Do you... *Did* you date humans? Or are humans just like food to you guys?"

I had a vision of Marabella. The images of her as a girl of seventeen waving to me from the fence that separated our family's land was faint. The more vivid image was of her hunched over, old, and wrinkled in a rocking chair. I'd been watching her from a distance, separate from the stream of time everybody and everything I'd ever known was chained to.

It had been the first time I sensed the real cost of what was done to me. The price I paid was knowing I'd outlive everything I ever cared about. I'd watch it all fade and die. Eventually, I'd feel like I did now. I would look at something pure, sweet, and full of life and feel only pain. Because I knew I couldn't stay part of Cara's life a moment longer than I had to. She'd grow old and live a life. She'd die and I'd carry on.

But she couldn't be mine.

Cara smiled playfully, then bumped my nose with her knuckle, making me flinch. "You went all misty eyed there, Lucian. Were you thinking of some girl you had the hots for like a million years ago?"

I shook my head. "No. My kind do not make a habit of dating humans. Relationships where only one half of the equation gets old and dies tend to create complications."

She pursed her lips. "Yeah. I guess that makes sense." She bumped her shoulder into me, eyes twinkling with mischief. "You're saying you wouldn't date me because you'll be too pretty for wrinkly old me in ten years?"

"It would be a cruelty to both of us if we pursued a relationship. Just a promise of loss that would hang over both our heads."

She nodded, studying her lap. "Yeah. I was just kidding, obviously. Besides, I've said since I was a little girl that I would never, ever date a vampire. So…"

I chuckled. "I'm sure you did."

"Well, um, we're not technically supposed to bring friends to our classes," Cara said. "So if my professor asks, you're a foreign exchange student, okay?"

We didn't talk as much for the rest of our walk, partly because the sun was draining me more quickly this time. I suspected the more I exposed myself in a short period of time, the more it would tap my reserves of strength. If the bond didn't fade soon, I thought we might need to find another arrangement to keep me from day walking as much as I had been.

I was grateful when we reached the shade of a tall, sleek building that was swarming with young students wearing bags on their backs or carrying books at their sides. "What is a foreign exchange student?"

"It's like when someone from another country comes to live with you. They sort of have to follow you around like a puppy since they're out of their element. So maybe they'll let it slide. We can say you're from Transylvania."

"Now it's you who is the tease."

The hint of red that crept into Cara's cheeks made me want to pull her close. The bond thrummed inside me, pounding with a physical force in my chest and head, practically demanding I reach out to her. Demanding I have *more*.

I closed my eyes, calming myself and controlling the urges.

"By the way," she said once we started walking again. "Were you able to sleep last night?"

"Yes," I said. It was a lie. I'd been awake the entire night while I did my best to suppress the urge to go to her. In fact, I hadn't truly slept since my brief nap on the smelly couch in Anya's basement. I could feel the heaviness of sleep calling me, even now.

"And you?"

"Yes," she said, biting the inside of her bottom lip. *A lie.*

We sat in a large auditorium where a small, bent over woman proceeded to drone on about some scientific jargon I couldn't begin to follow. I blinked heavy eyes, then stifled a yawn.

I was not going to fall asleep in a room full of humans. If I forgot the obvious danger, I could at least think of the indignity of it. My kind had always gone to great lengths to protect ourselves when we slumbered. Resting now would be unconscionable.

It was a complete and total embarrassment I would not allow.

12

CARA

Lucian's head was heavy on my shoulder and I could see his eyes were closed behind his sunglasses. The weirdo had slumped over, then crossed his arms over his chest and forced his huge body into a sitting version of the stiff "vampire in a coffin" look.

I tried not to notice the looks he was generating, especially when he started snoring softly.

Seriously? What kind of vampire snored?

I hardly heard a word my professor said because I was too distracted by the man who had his head against my arm. He had great hair, I noticed for about the hundredth time.

I looked down at the silky, thick black hair that was against my arm, then chewed my pencil, feeling my hand twitching upwards.

No. You are not going to sneakily feel his hair. You are not—

I took a small lock of loose hair between my fingers and gently stroked it. *Soft.*

I pulled my hand away, shaking my head. *Get a hold of yourself, Cara.*

I lasted about two more minutes before I had my entire hand on his head, drinking in the cool, soft smoothness of his thick hair. *God,* he was so gorgeous it wasn't even fair. I wondered if that was a vampire thing, or just a Lucian thing. Did those little black specks in his blood go through his system and find ways to make him more irresistible? Straighten out a nose here, thicken an eyelash there. Sculpt a ridiculous jawline here, fill up some ridiculously kissable lips there.

But then I remembered the Jezabel woman. She hadn't been unattractive, but she wasn't the picture of beauty like the other vampires I'd seen. Maybe the pretty ones just lived longer? Except that made Vlad an anomaly. Though he would've been strikingly handsome if he made an ounce of effort, I suspected.

The more time I had, the more I found myself wanting to ask Lucian a million questions. How old was he, anyway? How did he become a vampire in the first place? Had he ever been married? Had kids?

I was thinking about everything but my class when I realized people were getting up and leaving. Lucian stirred, and his eyes were on me before I realized my hand was still buried in his hair.

I snatched it back, then flashed an unsteady smile. "Sorry," I said.

He straightened, then cleared his throat. "It appears I drifted off. Briefly."

"Actually, you fell asleep hard. And it was pretty much right away." I glanced at the clock. "And it wasn't that brief. This was a two-hour class."

"Nonsense," Lucian said, standing up and stretching out his legs and arms. "Where do we travel next?"

I grinned. "We 'travel' to advanced biochem. And if this class put you to sleep, I'm going to need a bucket of cold water to wake you after that one."

"Cold water is fatal to my kind," Lucian said.

I paused as I was getting up. "What? Really? *God*, Lucian. You need to tell me this stuff. What if I'd spilled my drink on your or something?"

He showed a slow forming smile. "That was a joke."

I punched his shoulder softly. "It wasn't a funny one."

My mind wandered as we headed to biochem.

I was dragging a vampire around with me from class to class. A vampire dressed in a hoodie and sunglasses, even though it was a relatively warm day.

I thought it was still going to take time before I could completely grasp the entirety of the situation. There was only so much my brain could absorb in such a short period of time, after all. But one thing seemed to be forming into crystal clarity.

Lucian wasn't like any guy I'd ever met. And it was more than the whole supernatural angle. He paid a different sort of attention to me whether I was speaking or just looking out the window. He made it seem like I was the most important thing in his world, even if he kept talking like he'd vanish from my life the moment the bond was gone.

Temporary or not, it felt good. Dangerously good.

He was giving me a taste of the kind of fast and furious relationship I'd resigned myself to never have. After all, devoting myself to academia and the long hours that were probably ahead of me bent over microscopes was probably a death sentence for my dating life. By the time I emerged from a sterile lab at age fifty, my dating prospects would have depressingly dwindled.

So maybe I should've felt like I'd suffered some injustice by being nearly killed because of Lucian and now "bonded" to him. Instead, I felt gratitude. He was giving me a little taste of the fun I knew I was leaving behind, and I may not be immortal like he claimed to be, but I had a feeling I'd remember these days for the rest of my life.

Lucian leaned in a doorway, clad in his shades. He let out a long groan.

"You okay?" I asked.

He nodded. "All this sunlight tires me."

I gave his broad back a sympathetic rub. "I know. I'm sorry. Maybe if the bond loosens up some you can crawl around in the tunnels beneath campus or something. I bet you love creeping around tunnels, right?"

Lucian side-eyed me. "I will not creep through tunnels. Though I do admit I find the damp darkness rather pleasant. There's also something comforting in the close-quarters."

I grinned. "Are all the other vampires as cliché as you?"

"I am a unique individual."

I rolled my eyes. "I'm sure you are. Are you ready to start walking, unique individual, or do you need more time?"

"I'm fine."

We headed outside toward the biochem building, gathering a constant barrage of blatant stares from anyone who noticed us.

"Garlic?" I asked. "Does that hurt you?"

"No. I quite enjoy the flavor."

"Crosses?"

"Nope."

"So how *do* people hurt vampires?"

"That question is a dangerous one."

"For you."

"And you," he said, looking very serious.

"Fine. How old are you?"

"That's not a polite question to ask a vampire."

I grinned, pushing the doors open and heading through a breezeway toward the science building. "Seriously?"

"I was born in 1712 in a village not far from here."

I'd gathered that he was old, but I hadn't quite been prepared for just *how* old. "Wow. And you don't age?"

Lucian shook his head. "Physically, no. We grow stronger with time."

"So... You have like, super powers?"

"Enhanced senses. Strength. Healing capabilities. But most of my kind develop far more in one direction than any other."

"So what's your thing? A super strong nose? Because that would probably be the lamest, right? Watch out! Here comes Vlad! He's going to sniff out what you had for breakfast and then shame you for eating leftover pizza at five in the morning!"

Lucian eyed me, amusement twinkling in his dark eyes. "No. I've always healed more quickly than average. It's the only reason I can walk this much in the daylight. Even an elder vampire would only be able to manage a few minutes of direct sunlight. But I'm hard to kill."

I frowned. "People have tried to kill you?"

Lucian nodded. "Many times. I don't recommend it."

I thought about seeing my own blood dripping from Leah's fingers. I put my hand to my side, remembering the cold that I'd felt there. I had mostly succeeded in suppressing the memory, but it still bubbled up from time to time, unbidden. "No. I don't blame you."

Lucian put his arm around my shoulders, and I leaned into him.

It was that easy.

I wasn't sure if I was supposed to blame the bond for how natural it felt to be close to him, or if that was just *him*. But I did know it felt good. It felt right.

I would've thought my brush with near-death would've made the danger of his world feel real enough. But knowing others had tried to kill Lucian helped it click into place. People had tried to kill him. And three hundred years was a long time to make enemies. It also made me think about what was out there. If Lucian had lived that long, how old and powerful were the vampires who wanted him dead? The ones who wanted *me* dead because I was bonded to him?

"How long does the bond take to fade, anyway?" I asked as we took our seats at the back of advanced biochem.

"A few weeks."

"A few *weeks*?" I asked. "You didn't think that was important enough information to lead with the other day?"

"It will take as long as it takes. We just need to make sure we don't sleep with each other while my blood is still inside you."

The girl in front of us turned her head slowly to look at us with a horrified but curious glance.

I smiled. "He's a foreign exchange student. English is tricky."

Lucian smiled from behind his sunglasses and silly hood. "I'm from Transylvania."

"Right," The girl said, turning back around. She shoved her things in her backpack and moved several rows forward.

I didn't really have a successful social life before Lucian Undergrove entered my world, but I had a feeling he was going to set fire to any slim hope I ever had of being normal.

13

LUCIAN

Cara began walking back toward her apartment after her final task of giving tours finished. The night air was crisp and refreshing, even more so after an entire day of subjecting myself to the sunlight. But I was growing hungry.

Intolerably hungry.

Cara gave me a few silent looks before she finally stopped, putting her hand on my arm. "Are you okay, Lucian? I thought you'd be feeling better with all the moonlight. *Or something*," she added, sounding less sure of herself.

"I need to feed."

Her eyes narrowed. "You mean like in a vampirey kind of way?"

"Yes. I need blood."

Her gaze darted across my face, and I realized she wasn't sure if I was implying I wanted *her* blood.

"No," I said. "Remember? It needs to be someone else."

"Who?"

"Anyone."

"And you promise they'll be okay?"

"Would it matter if they wouldn't?" I asked, irritated by her question and admiring of her courage to care at the same time. "Would you stop me if I said they'd die?"

She looked down. "I just want to know whether I need to hate myself for not trying to stake you through the heart or something."

"They will be fine. I swear it."

Cara followed me as I searched. It wasn't long before I saw a pair of young women traveling together.

"Stay here," I said, motioning for Cara to wait back slightly.

She looked unsure, but obeyed, even as I felt the bond urging us to stay close.

"Excuse me," I said, getting the attention of the two women. "I'm not from here. Could you help me with something?"

The women shared a look, then smiled conspiratorially to each other and nodded, coming closer to me. I had no true preference for feeding on men versus women, but over the years I'd learned the way I looked made it much easier to lure women close enough to feed. Men were more likely to simply run.

I waited until I had both of their gazes. I cleared my mind, then reached into theirs and calmed them. The sight of pulsing veins in their necks was enough to enlarge my canines, and moments later, I was feeding.

I knew it was ridiculous to care that Cara was watching me with a horrified expression. It shouldn't have mattered, especially since I wanted to remove myself from her life as soon as the bond allowed. I was also still hoping she'd agree to let me wipe her memory of this entire adventure when it was all through.

But as I drank my fill from the first woman and moved to the next, I knew I was only trying to fool myself.

I didn't *want* anything that involved losing Cara. I already wanted to keep her for as long as I could. Selfishly, I wanted her to be with me for my cold eternity because I knew it wouldn't feel as cold if she was there, too.

I took only as much blood as I needed, then discreetly wiped the encounter from the women's memories. They'd find the twin puncture wounds on their necks tomorrow but would come up with some way to explain it.

I walked back to Cara, wiping my mouth with a cloth from my pocket. "I feel better now."

Cara's lips were pressed together, and she wasn't meeting my eyes. "Good. I'm happy to hear it."

She started walking quickly, and in no particular direction as far as I could tell. I watched her back, thinking of the things I wanted to say. There were many. And I didn't know if I would've been saying them for her benefit, or my own.

I never asked to be this way.

I'd take it all back if I had the choice.

Many times, I've wished I was human. I've wished I could live and die a normal life with a normal person like you.

But I said nothing. I didn't deserve to make excuses for myself. I knew what I was.

I chose to continue my existence. I could've found a place in the sun and waited for it to end me if I wanted. I could've let Bennigan tear me to pieces. There were a thousand opportunities to let this end, and yet I kept fighting to survive.

Feedings like she'd just seen were the cost of my existence, and I wasn't going to apologize for them.

14

CARA

I swallowed uneasily. The place Lucian had taken us to looked exactly like the kind of place you went into if you wanted someone to drug your drink or steal your money. *Or both.*

"You're sure about this?" I asked.

Lucian had seemed off ever since he fed on those women, and to be honest, I'd felt off, too. It was a brutal reminder that this was real.

It wasn't just some silly story I'd tell when I was older about that time I had to pretend a vampire was my boyfriend slash foreign exchange student slash whatever. He was a *vampire*. He drank people's blood. He'd made me drink *his* blood, and some insane voodoo magic bond was forcing me to feel like I couldn't bear to be ten steps away from the guy.

Reality apparently couldn't care less if this all seemed too off the wall to believe. Here I was, and there he was.

To complicate things, I was increasingly sure I actually liked the guy, too. Even if he did bite people in darkened alleys and live in some twisted, creepy world.

Lucian led me down a few steps directly in front of a black-painted brick building. The steps turned a corner and led to an equally black door with a woman dressed like a goth sitting out front. She eyed us, showing a little flickering recognition when she focused on Lucian.

"Is that you?" she asked.

Lucian grunted in acknowledgment. "It's been a while. I know. But I'm here now, and I brought a friend. My girlfriend, actually."

The woman swung an incredulous gaze in my direction. She got up from the stool she'd been perched on and sniffed me. *She sniffed me.*

"Is she human?" asked the woman.

"If you don't mind, we need to go inside and speak with Alaric and Seraphine."

The woman folded her arms, then shrugged. "I guess the Coldwells are going to stop having their fun with Lucian Undergrove back on the prowl, hm?"

Lucian looked like he didn't want the woman to say anymore in front of me. He stiffly nodded, then pulled me inside.

"What did she mean?" I asked.

"It's nothing."

I narrowed my eyes. "Didn't sound like nothing."

He sighed. "The Coldwells were a particularly powerful clan who opposed something called The Pact. I was one of the vampires with the job of making sure they didn't do too much damage. That's all."

"So do you get vampire paychecks?" I asked with a grin. "You said it was your job, so I'm assuming you have a boss?"

"That's enough questions, Cara."

Nope, I thought. It was probably never going to be enough questions to get me up to speed on all the weird rules and history of his world. But I'd learned he would answer my questions as long as I didn't stack too many of them together all at once.

Lucian and I headed inside, and I was greeted with what was absolutely a bar full of vampires. They weren't all beautiful, but even the more "normal" looking ones still carried a supreme air of confidence, as if they could snap their fingers and change the world, and they knew it. The dress code included slightly dated formal wear, extremely dated suits, fresh expensive designer dresses, and even old puffy ball gowns. It was like a *choose your era* costume party, but all the clothes were well-made and, I suspected, originals.

The music thumping through the air was modern and some of the people—*the vampires*—in the place were enjoying it as they danced. Most were crowded around tables speaking in low voices or enjoying drinks at the bar. It was normal, and completely abnormal at the same time.

"What's with the clothes?" I asked Lucian quietly as we moved through the room.

"Status symbols. Old clothes mean an old vampire. Old means powerful."

Lucian seemed to know where he was going. He took us past the bar, where more and more of the other vampires seemed to be noticing him. They were turning in their stools, standing from their tables, or stopping mid-dance to stare. I saw some of them muttering angrily to their neighbors and others staring in a state almost like awe.

"You're either super popular with these guys, or super unpopular. Which is it?"

"That depends which end of my work they've wound up on, I suppose." Lucian muttered.

I chuckled. "Watch out. We've got a badass over here." I was teasing him, but the looks on the faces of a room full of what I assumed were very powerful, very scary vampires said he really wasn't just an ordinary vampire.

"Yes," Lucian said. "We do. Now come on." He pulled open a door at the side of the large room and led us into a private area with a sleek, glossy black table and leather chairs. A beautiful woman and extremely handsome man were waiting at the table inside. They both got to their feet and went to Lucian, hugging him like they'd been worried.

It wasn't long before their attention turned to me.

With the discomfort of knowing I was being studied, I sat down. Lucian took the seat beside me and cleared his throat. "Alaric, Seraphina, you remember Cara."

The man had a smooth forehead and slicked back dirty blond hair. His features were sharp and wolf-like, but the overall effect made me think of some long-gone roguish gentleman from a dead era. He showed a crooked smile that mostly confirmed my suspicion about his character. "We didn't get a chance to properly thank you," Alaric said. "So let me formally say thank you for being a klutz and crashing down the wall that had us so detained."

"Don't be rude, brother," Seraphina said. She had the kind of face I imagined most women would come up with if they got to go into a computer program and had years to personally design every feature. Perfectly bold eyebrows. Slightly slanted and narrowed eyes that gave her an effortless edge of seduction. Lips like puffy pillows, and sleek black hair that she wore just above her shoulders in a silky curtain. "For all we know, she is a conspirator who was trying to set us free."

"Well," I said. My voice caught and I had to clear it a few times. "Actually, I really am just a klutz. I had to pee really bad and there was this key on that shelf. I knocked it over trying to get to it."

Alaric laughed, clapping his hands together once with a loud *pop*. Seraphina dipped her chin, showing the faintest hint of amusement. I jumped when Lucian put his hand on my thigh beneath the table. He seemed to realize what he'd done a moment later and jerked it back, but it wasn't before all the constantly erotic visions of him in the back of my mind raced up to focus.

"Wonderful," Alaric said. "The nefarious plans of our rival were undone by a full bladder. I love it."

Lucian didn't appear to be in any hurry to fill the silence that followed. He leaned back in his chair and folded his arms.

"Am I allowed to ask what I'm in the middle of?"

The three of them all silently exchanged looks, then Alaric and Seraphina nodded to Lucian.

"You've unintentionally brought yourself into the middle of a centuries long feud. Bennigan is one of the most powerful vampires in the area. He has a strong effect on women, even other vampires."

Alaric jumped in. "He basically has a harem of sex slaves who will claw and bite anything he tells them to. Honestly, I've always kind of been jealous of *that* gift."

Lucian nodded. "Yes. He and I have crossed paths many times because of his outrageous goals for more power. But a certain incident about a hundred years ago ramped up tensions."

"Because?" I prodded.

Lucian hesitated, and Alaric jumped in again for him. "Because doofus over here killed his wife."

"You killed somebody's *wife*?" I asked, voice full of incredulity.

"That somebody's wife was in the middle of trying to tear apart an innocent human with her bare hands. So, yes. I intervened."

Alaric leaned in, grinning. "He didn't just intervene. He killed Bennigan's favorite. And he did it to save a human."

I took a steadying breath. "Okay, hold on. I'd like to think I'm doing a pretty good job of absorbing all this vampire stuff in stride. But I wasn't ready for the killer part."

Lucian turned a ring over on his pinky finger, eyes distant. "You don't need to approve of it, Cara. We both just need to outlast the bond."

I looked down. Lucian hadn't spoken to me like that before, and I suddenly felt like a scolded child at a table with adults. I didn't interject anymore when the conversation resumed and the three of them started talking about alliances and rivalries.

From what I could figure out without context, it sounded like the only thing stopping vampires from openly killing anyone they slightly disagreed with was a fragile network of alliances and the other vampires like Lucian who tried to enforce some sort of code of conduct.

When they were finished, my fuzzy understanding was that Lucian needed to re-establish contacts with old allies. Without support, he wouldn't be able to keep enforcing "the code," and if the code wasn't enforced, there was nothing stopping Bennigan from sending his she-army down on us. At least that was my best attempt at understanding it all.

When they'd all finished, I momentarily forgot Lucian's temper and spoke. "There's something I don't understand. How did the three of you get walled into a room, anyway? And couldn't you just yell for help or knock it down?"

Seraphina answered. "Most vampires find a human steward they trust. It means you can sleep safely through the day and know you'll be woken if danger comes. Our steward grew paranoid about the danger we faced. She..."

Alaric looked uncomfortable, but interjected, as if Seraphina was waiting to let him finish. "I may have broken a rule or two and formed a relationship with the woman. We were in love, and my sweet Emily decided the only way to save me from Bennigan's relentless hunting was to hide me and throw away the key, so to speak."

"Wait, I thought Bennigan was the one who trapped you?"

"No," Lucian said. "He was the reason Emily was frightened enough to lock us away. But he would've come and finished the job if he'd known where we were. We were forced into a state like hibernation. With nothing to feed on, we would've died if we stayed awake. So we slept until you disturbed us."

"And you couldn't just... you know, punch the wall down?"

Alaric looked uncomfortable again. "It's possible I may have revealed some of our weaknesses to my dear Emily. She... *took advantage* of that knowledge."

Lucian glared at the man. "Which is why long-standing traditions of not blabbering about the things humans can do to hurt or kill us exist."

Alaric waved his hand. "It was love. You wouldn't understand."

"Haven't you guys been alive hundreds of years?" I asked. "I'm sure Lucian has loved someone before, right?"

"Lucian is the oldest," Alaric admitted. "By quite a bit. He doesn't talk about what he did or didn't do before we came along."

"Wait," I said. "I thought you were all siblings?"

Seraphina interjected. "It's a vampire thing. Your family name is from the one who turned you. We were all turned by Dominic Undergrove."

"Where is this Dominic guy now? Couldn't he help us?"

"That's enough questions," Lucian said. He sounded suddenly grumpier. "The two of you will need to take charge of contacting the Whites and the Hemlocks as soon as possible. I'll look into reaching out to the Marsh children when the next fight occurs. I figure they'll be more amenable to talks of an alliance if they get to watch a little bloodshed in the process. I'll be *occupied* tomorrow, so I'll need you two to make sure to handle the Whites and Hemlocks yourselves."

"Occupied with what?" Alaric asked.

"He has to pretend to be my foreign exchange student and then my boyfriend so I can get through my classes, internship, and my job."

Seraphina raised a single, sculpted brow. "Pretending to be her boyfriend, Lucian? Does she mean you're day walking?"

"No," he said.

"Only a little," I said at the same time.

Lucian looked annoyed.

"That's far too dangerous," Seraphina said. "You need to stop at once."

"Out of the question," Lucian growled. "I won't sabotage her life because she had the misfortune of crossing paths with us."

"She's just a human," Seraphina said. She looked at me and gave a tight, apologetic smile. "No offense."

"Some taken," I said with a shrug.

"She's my responsibility," Lucian said. "Human or not, I'm going to see to it that she makes it through this unscathed. She'll get to return to her normal life when this is through, and if that means day walking, then so be it."

"Is it not normal to walk around in the sun?" I asked.

Alaric grinned. "What did he tell you? That we all can do that?"

"Something like that?" The truth was it all started to blur together. I was learning so much and so fast that it was hard to keep it all straight.

"Lucian is abnormally gifted. The bastard is practically unkillable. Expose a normal vampire to the sun and they are going to dry up and die within seconds. But if he's in the sun walking around, taxing his powers, he'll—"

"Enough," Lucian said. "This isn't up for discussion. And Cara, you'll need to take a hiatus from your job. I'll provide you a discretionary fund so you will be able to cover expenses in the meantime. It will allow me more time after nightfall to manage my affairs."

"I like doing ghost tours."

"And I like being able to feel prepared when a bitter rival who has wanted me and my family dead for centuries is planning to strike."

I lowered my eyes. "Fair point. I'll let the tour company know I need to take a break."

"Good," Lucian stood, then motioned for me to follow. "I need to take her home so she can rest. There's no way she will be able to stay awake during her classes if I keep her out much later."

Seraphina and Alaric exchanged a look.

"What?" Lucian growled.

Seraphina shrugged. "You don't typically care about anyone or anything except enforcing the code. You're not sounding like yourself with all this selfless talk. Are you sure you're okay?"

"No," he snapped. "I'm bonded to a helpless human when all of our lives are in danger. Instead of focusing on the problem at hand, I'm forced to spend half my time making sure I don't derail Cara's life to save my own. It's ridiculous, and by all rights, I should tie her to my back, bind and gag her, and go about my business."

"Now that you mention it," Alaric said. "Isn't that more or less what you did with that villager back during the yellow fever? Remember?" he asked, laughing a little wistfully. "You forgot she would need to use the bathroom eventually and wound up with piss all over your cloak."

A dark look passed over Lucian's face. "I remember all too well. That was my favorite cloak."

I took a deep breath; suddenly not sure I was going to survive the few weeks left of this bond with Lucian. But no matter what Alaric and Seraphina implied, I *did* feel like I'd been getting a different version of him when we were together. I hadn't even considered that he didn't *have* to sacrifice anything on my behalf. I also hadn't thought how insignificant something like my classes and my internship should've seemed to a man—if that's still what he was—in his position.

"Do vampires still have hearts?" I asked when we got outside. "Like does it beat, I mean?"

Lucian's eyebrows pinched together. "Yes. Of course we do."

"Does it beat though?" For some reason I suddenly needed to know he was at least human in that small way. It felt important.

Without hesitating, he took my hand and raised it up to his chest.

My breath caught. My palm was pressed against the hard, muscular plane of his chest. I could feel a strong but incredibly slow thump there. He must've had a resting heart rate of like ten, if my guess was right.

"Wow," I whispered. "I read once that super high endurance athletes have a resting heart rate of like thirty. When you're not biting people and sucking their blood, are you out cycling and competing in triathlons or something?"

"I'm a vampire," he said plainly.

He'd started walking again and left me to trail behind him. I rolled my eyes at his back but found myself grinning all the same. *I'm a vampire* I mouthed to his broad shoulders and perfect hair.

15

CARA

I couldn't shake the feeling that someone was following Lucian and I for the entire walk back to my apartment. He insisted he'd "sense" it with his mysterious powers, but I still couldn't shake the tingling on the back of my neck.

I let us in the front door, then paused. "You know, I never invited you in. Is that a myth, too?"

Lucian nodded. "Some of my kind have put great effort into misleading humans. The more weaknesses they think they know, the less able they will be to harm us."

I arched an eyebrow. "Scared of us little humans, are you?"

He flashed a cocky half smile. "We're outnumbered. And we do have to sleep, despite your attempts to keep me up at all hours of the day and night."

"That's fair."

I had just pushed the door open when something smelly, large, and hairy flashed past me and Lucian.

Vlad turned to face us both with his arms spread out wide. He was wearing one of his stained medieval king get-ups again and laughed loudly. "Finally. It has been ages since I've been inside a human's dwelling." He gave me a conspiratorial look. "Can't come in unless we're invited, you know." He dragged out all of his syllables like the perfect caricature of a vampire from some movie in the 1800s.

I planted my fists on my hips, trying not to grin. "Is that right?"

"Oh, yes," Vlad said. "And don't even get me started on garlic." He winced at the thought, hissing a little. "I promise you this. Put garlic in my sauce, and you'll get an introduction to my impaling room." He licked his lips, eyes going wider at the thought.

"You have an impaling room?"

Vlad looked suddenly sullen. "I *did*. It was unceremoniously taken from me by some asshole with high cheekbones and a tight ass."

Lucian put his palm to his forehead. I grinned, noticing that he *did* have nice, high cheekbones. I'd already noticed the ass about two seconds after meeting him, too.

I lowered my voice, partly because we were still standing in the doorway of my apartment and in danger of summoning all my roommates and because I didn't want Vlad to hear. "He's joking about all the torture and impaling stuff, right?"

Lucian hesitated a beat. "Yes."

I watched him, noting that he wasn't making eye contact. *Terrible liar*. But I couldn't imagine Vlad, who seemed like a bumbling, stumbling fool hurting anyone.

"Cara? Did you bring friends?" Zack called from the kitchen.

"Nope!" I said. "Just—"

A moment later, Parker and Zack both walked into view. Zack was chewing on something—probably something expired. Parker was running a hand through his patchy beard and looking at Vlad and Lucian with rapidly increasing interest.

"Who are these guys?" Zack said.

Vlad waved. "I'm Vlad. You may have heard of me. I once impaled ten thousand of my enemies in a single night. You should have heard the screams." He grinned, then cupped his hands around his mouth and let out a long, whispering hiss that I guessed was supposed to be an approximation of the sound.

"Uh," Zack said, looking at Parker.

Parker shook his head. "Where did you find these guys, Cara?"

"They are cosplayers," I said quickly. "It's like when people dress up as popular characters and pretend. Right, Lucian?" I asked, elbowing him.

"Yes," Lucian said. "I am Lucian Undergrove. A vampire. And I have successfully resisted the urge to feed on and copulate with your roommate, Cara Skies, for several days now. I plan to continue that resistance for as long as I'm able."

Vlad laughed, then burped. "I'll eat 'er if you're not gonna, Lucy."

Lucian stiffened. "I've told you not to call me that, you pig."

Vlad bulged his eyes, sarcastically pretending to be scared as he cowered. He slapped his own ass and wandered deeper into the apartment, ignoring the looks Parker and Zack gave him. A moment later, we heard the refrigerator open. There was a carbonated hiss of a soda bottle opening, swigging, then the sound of Vlad aggressively spitting it out—hopefully in the sink.

"Why did you bring cosplayers home, exactly?" Zack asked.

Vlad came back before we could respond. "Oh," he said, snapping his fingers. "Look here humans. You didn't see shit. You're tired, and you're going up to bed. Also, you have no idea who clogged the toilet."

Zack and Parker looked dazed.

"Vlad!" I said. "What is with you vampires and thinking it's okay to just re-write human brains whenever it suits you? Seriously, how long have you guys been pulling this shit?"

Vlad counted on his fingers, then appeared to give up with a shrug. "I don't know, a thousand years or so?"

"Have any of your kind ever done a study to make sure it's not harmful? No long-term effects? Cancer?"

He laughed. "Humans already suffer from a harmful long-term effect. They're mortal and they all die in the blink of an eye." He nudged Lucian, looking for support, but Lucian at least had the good sense to keep a straight face and study the ground.

"Well?" I asked, focusing on Lucian now.

"I'm fairly sure nothing bad happens after we manipulate the memories of humans."

I shook my head. "You guys are unbelievable. Vlad, no more memory wiping."

He barked a laugh. "You may 'ave Lucy Boy by the cock, but unless you're planning to let me poke you, I don't take your orders." As if to demonstrate the fact, he snapped his fingers at Zack and Parker. "Dance for me, humans."

Zack, for some reason, dropped into a squat with his hands on his knees and started twerking his ass at us. Parker did some sort of shimmying awkward combination between kick boxing ghosts and twitching that he must've thought was a dance.

I covered my eyes. "God. Vlad get out of my apartment. Lucian, let's get to my room before the others come down."

Vlad grabbed himself some more things from our fridge before agreeing to leave. Lucian and I were just closing my door when I heard Mooney start cracking up laughing. "Get it, Zack! Shake that bubble butt, baby. Yo! Niles! Bring me my phone, dude. You've got to see this!"

I put my finger to my lips, signaling for Lucian to be quiet.

He nodded, then walked silently to his spot in the corner of my room and laid down, crossing his arms over his chest and assuming his usual adorably cliché sleeping position.

I grinned, slipping into bed fully clothed. It wasn't comfortable, but I knew better than to take off clothes around Lucian. Our days were full enough that it was easier to ignore the thumping sexual need the bond always kept simmering. But in the quiet moments, the visions started rising to the front of my thoughts. Visions of his lips on mine and his hands tangled in my hair—pinning me to the bed and kissing my neck.

"How much longer will it be like this?" I asked. "The bond, I mean."

"It's impossible to tell."

"Does it make you... *see* things too? Like really vivid images or whatever?" I halfway muttered the question, not entirely sure I wanted to admit my brain was a constant porn reel of all the ways I apparently wanted to get my world rocked by Lucian.

"Yes," he said plainly. "Just a moment ago I was imagining how you'd taste."

"What?" I asked, touching my neck self-consciously. "Does it work like that for you? I mean, are you going to lose control and drink me dry or something?" I briefly considered throwing a pillow in his direction and running for it. But then I remembered he seemed to have the conditioning of an elite athlete. I, on the other hand, had the conditioning of someone who was elite at finding places to put just one more doughnut when my stomach was begging for mercy.

"No," Lucian said, voice stiff. "I wasn't talking about the way your blood would taste."

I felt myself sink into the mattress a little, eyes bulging. *Oh lord. Please help me to resist the overwhelming horniness that's trying to consume me.*

Change the subject. It's your only salvation, Cara. Change the damn subject.

"The whole thing is just extra weird for me because I've never been a very sexual person. I mean, the last serious boyfriend—" *Oh God, stop talking Cara. Stop talking.* I cleared my throat, compelled by the momentum of stupidity and poor choices to continue. "It's been a long time," I said plainly. "A long, *long* time. I probably wouldn't even know where to put it anymore."

I stared at the ceiling. Suddenly I knew what Hell would be. It would be reliving the last ten seconds over and over. It would be sitting in a control room with twenty camera feeds and ultra-high-quality microphones so I could rewatch every little detail of my embarrassment.

As slowly as I could, I pulled the covers up over my eyeballs, retreating to some childlike mentality where the things I couldn't see wouldn't reach me.

Lucian made a sort of choking sound. I risked a look and saw he was propped up on one elbow and watching me with a strained expression. He swallowed, then laid back down, visibly making an effort to relax.

My eyes darted from him to the ceiling and back to him again. *What was that? Did vampires get indigestion?*

"You okay?" I whispered when he hadn't made a sound for a few minutes.

"I require silence," Lucian snapped. "I'm concentrating."

I squinted. "On what?" I asked, expecting him to tell me he was using some magic vampire powers to fight off Bennigan's attempt to reach his mind.

"To stay here on the floor. To stop myself from reminding you where 'it' goes."

Neither of us spoke after that, and I couldn't say for certain, but I didn't think either of us slept.

Lucian stayed in his place all night with his arms crossed over his chest. I stayed under my blankets, where I hoped he didn't have a supernatural sense of smell that could pick up on how hard my hormones were raging or how embarrassingly wet our blundering conversation had made me.

Eventually, the sun rose, and I lifted my tired, horny ass out of bed feeling like I'd been hit by a truck. Repeatedly.

I had a full day of classes ahead of me, my internship, and whatever seedy vampire establishments Lucian needed to drag me around to after dark ahead of me. *Woo freaking hoo.*

16

LUCIAN

By the time night came, Cara was practically sleep walking. We were in one of the graveyards of Savannah where I was supposed to meet the vampiress who fancied herself the head of the White family.

Cara was shaking her head as we weaved around gravestones. "I give tours of this place, you know. Well, *gave*. Are you seriously telling me you guys are *that* cliché? Meeting in graveyard crypts? It's almost disappointing."

"The safest places for us are the ones most thick with superstition. How likely would your kind be to believe a claim of supernatural beings lurking around a graveyard or a haunted house?"

Cara seemed to consider my question, then gave a little shrug of admittance. "I guess there's some logic to that." She punctuated her sentence with a huge, jaw-cracking yawn.

"You can sleep once we enter the crypt, if you prefer."

"Somehow I think I'll have a hard time sleeping while you have a clandestine meeting in the middle of a burial ground."

"Suit yourself."

I pushed back the latest frenzy of explicit images that flooded my mind. I saw brief snapshots of Cara waiting for me on her bed while she wore nothing but a thin t-shirt. I could see the soft skin of her thighs exposed, could sense how only the faintest movement would lift her shirt enough to show me everything. I could imagine the full weight of her breasts in my hands and how I'd enjoy taking her lower lip between mine.

The bond was not supposed to stay this strong for this long, but all I could do was endure.

We arrived before the White sisters. The place we were meeting was an underground crypt. It was a single room that wasn't very large with four benches and the polished stone coffins lying behind them.

I expected Cara to choose a bench opposite me, but either the bond, her sleepiness, or her fear of what would happen when the White sisters arrived compelled her to sit beside me. The bench wasn't very large, and her choice to sit beside me pressed our legs and shoulders together.

After only a minute or two of silence, I felt her slump against me. I grinned to myself, then put my arm around her.

When she was awake, it was easy to forget how fragile Cara was. Her personality was full of fire and spunk. But asleep, all I could see was how easy it would be for Bennigan to take her from me.

That last thought replayed in my head again, gaining significance as the meaning sank in. *To take her from me.*

I had to shake my head, trying to re-write the script I seemed to be creating. Cara was not mine. I'd bonded her out of necessity, and as soon as it was physically possible, the two of us would go our separate ways.

Besides, if I really cared about her, the best thing I could do for her would be to get her out of my life as soon as I could.

Mortals who became entangled with my kind rarely lived long, full lives. They either wound up turned to vampires themselves or a casualty of the crossfire.

Kira and Violet White arrived silently. They were a rarity among vampires because they'd been turned at an older age. Both women had stark white hair and wrinkled skin. They still carried themselves upright and proud, reminding any who might get ideas that they were just as powerful as any other vampire their age would be.

Kira was the shorter of the two with the shrewd eyes and expression of a businesswoman. She was always angling for a better deal or a way to put her own twist on any arrangement.

Violet was permanently frowning and suspicious. She was also known to lose her temper and start wars for the Whites. The fact that their family was still standing despite Violet's warlike nature was a testament to their strength—and to why I needed their support to help keep Bennigan at bay.

"Who is that?" Violet asked. She wasn't making any direct threat to Cara, but I found myself holding the small woman closer all the same.

"She's—" I cut myself off. *Mine. I was about to say mine.* "She's a human who had the misfortune of crossing paths with me. Don't worry about her."

Kira tapped her lips thoughtfully. "You said you were coming alone."

"I came as alone as I could."

"Ah," Kira said. "So you've bonded yourself to this one?"

Idiot. There were a dozen ways I could've chosen my words and I'd stumbled into the combination that told Kira exactly what I'd meant to hide. The fewer who knew about the bond, the safer Cara would be. I certainly hadn't wanted the Whites to know about it before we struck some sort of arrangement. "Yes. For now."

I could see her calculating the possibilities. But if she tried to blackmail me, I'd tell her that Bennigan almost certainly knew about the bond. They'd used her as bait to draw me out in the first place. I'd expected them to make some sort of move by now, but there had been nothing.

I wished he *would* show himself so we could sort this out like men. All the hiding and games were grating on my nerves. But that was how Bennigan operated. He hadn't lived as long as he had by being reckless or taking risks. He'd wait until he thought he saw an opening and then strike. And when he did strike, he'd make sure he had an army of support so he wouldn't have to put his own neck on the line.

"Am I correct in assuming you want my family's protection?" Kira asked.

"No. We don't need protection, but you can ally yourselves with us. With the order."

Her smile was crooked, but Violet's was sinister.

"There are three remaining Undergroves. Much has changed since you were last roaming freely. The order and its support are growing as thin as your family tree." she said flatly. "I don't particularly care how old or hard to kill you supposedly are, Lucian. You need us. We don't need you. It's that plain. Why should we ally with you and risk war with Bennigan?"

"Because we've already gathered allies," I said. It wasn't precisely true, but it was the line we'd been going with. The full truth was that I hadn't even gotten in contact with leadership yet, and Kira's warning that support of the order was growing thin came as news to me. "Bennigan may not be on the winning side of this war he insists on pursuing."

Kira considered, then waved her hand in dismissal. "We will think on it."

"You mean you'll wait to see which side will come out on top and join at the last minute like a coward?"

Violet bared her canines, which had already elongated. I ignored her. She was half my age, and she should've known her attempts at intimidation were wasted.

Kira's smile was self-satisfied. "I mean we will think on it. And if you do find yourself tipping the scales in your favor, we'll be happy to press our thumb down in your aid. But I would suggest you avoid losing ground, Lucian. Our history isn't a spotless one, and the Whites have a long memory."

I watched the two women go, feeling like that had gone about as well as I'd expected.

But the conversation was a reminder of the kind of danger I'd already put Cara in. She was a target for Bennigan. A chink in my armor.

I didn't know why he hadn't tried to exploit it yet, but I thought it was only a matter of time.

And if what Kira said was true, the order had already been on shaky ground before I'd been gone. If the vampires who opposed it had gained momentum, it meant we were all in far more danger than I'd even known.

17

CARA

I covered a yawn while I sat with Lucian in his dilapidated manor house. The fire was going beside the couch I sat on, which I suspected was for my benefit. By every indication I could gather, Lucian didn't feel the heat or the cold.

I had to admit I found him to be incredibly considerate and sweet when he wasn't focused on being a sarcastic, surly grump of an immortal.

Lucian sat across from me with one ankle resting on his knee. He was sitting perfectly straight with a focused look in his eyes, watching the fire. I'd helped him shop for more "casual" wear, but the most casual I'd convinced him to dress was what he had on now—a blood-red button down and dark gray slacks that hugged every line of his long legs.

It was dark outside, which meant Lucian was recovering from the long day of being dragged around in the daylight with me. It seemed to take him a couple hours after dark to get back to normal. Those were also the periods of time where he was most likely to do and say sweet things. My guess was that he made a conscious effort to keep me at arm's length when he was at full strength, but when he felt sun-fried, he lacked the willpower to pretend to be as much of an ass.

"Did they say when they would be here?" I asked. Seraphina and Alaric were supposed to be arriving any moment for a 'technology briefing' I'd arranged. The three vampires were absolutely hopeless, and I'd begun to worry about their complete lack of understanding when it came to all things modern.

Lucian shook his head. "They'll be here."

Alaric kept buying new cars and crashing them because he insisted he knew how to drive horse drawn carriages and shouldn't need to "suffer the indignity of some pimply teenager judging his worthiness to receive a driver's license." Seraphina apparently was quickly gaining a reputation with the police for her tendency to steal anything she wanted. She hadn't quite grasped the concept of security cameras or the idea that she couldn't use her powers of suggestion to convince them to pretend they hadn't seen a thing.

Then there was Lucian. I'd caught him composing a dorky handwritten letter with a fountain pen to some vampire in New York who was a higher up in his "order" the other night. He had a stack of supplies and was planning to "work through the night if need be." He looked completely baffled when I explained the concept of cell phones to him.

So I'd set up a sort of intervention. The plan was to familiarize my ancient, temporary friends with the world they'd woken up to. I'd considered including Lucian's wild, strange roommate, Vlad, in the intervention, but he had been awake this whole time. There was no reason the man should've needed my help navigating technology.

Both vampires were late, but I eventually had all three of them sitting in the living room. With the help of Lucian's bank account, I'd dragged him sunglasses, hoodie, gloves and all to a phone store and set up three phones for them. I handed one to each vampire and watched them turn the devices over with curiosity.

"I've seen the humans staring at these," Seraphina said. "Vampires as well."

Alaric nodded. "Yep. I was too embarrassed to ask anyone what they were, but the one time I got a look at someone's screen there was a moving picture of two turtles. It looked like they were having intercourse. The turtle in the back appeared to be enjoying it quite a bit."

Lucian and Seraphina looked disgusted, but I was grinning.

I spent the next half hour giving them all a crash course on everything from the internet to texting.

Seraphina was typing something on hers with an intense look of concentration once I finished. A moment later, an excited voice started talking from a video she'd apparently pulled up. "So you want to see some virgins? Let's bring 'em out!"

Seraphina smiled to herself, then walked off to another room.

"Okay," I said quietly. "I guess that shouldn't shock me."

Lucian frowned. "It's shaking itself in my pocket."

"Check it," I said.

Alaric was at the other end of the room with a shit-eating smile on his face.

Lucian picked up the phone, then looked away, half-shielding his eyes. "God. What is that?"

"It's my penis," Alaric said, laughing.

I shook my head. What was it with men? Give three ancient immortal beings phones, and within an hour one of them literally discovers the art of the dick pic? I guessed there really was no hope.

"How do I get it off my electronic device?" Lucian said, holding the phone at arm's length like it was poisoned.

"Press the home button," I said. "And Alaric, you should not send people pictures of your penis. Also, you've been standing here this entire time. When did you even have time to—"

He looked smug. "I'm very fast."

Doesn't really answer the question, but okay. "Alaric. There are instructional videos on driving cars with no horses on the internet. If you're not going to take the test, you should at least watch them."

He gave me a suspicious look, then nodded to Lucian. "When did we start taking orders from a human, exactly?"

"The human has a good point. You've already ruined several vehicles. It's only a matter of time before you destroy a human and bring the attention of the police on us."

I stared at Lucian. "Really?"

"Tragically destroy a human?" he tried.

Vlad wandered into the room wearing what looked like a medieval king's robe and only a pair of questionably yellow boxers beneath it. His hairy belly and chest were on full, horrifying display. It appeared he was growing out a pointy mustache on top of his five-o-clock shadow, too.

"Oh, quite nice," he said. "A little tech demo?" he threw an arm around Alaric's shoulder and spread his palm in the air in front of both of them, eyes going distant. "Sex, my friend. You must try it. That little thing in your hand can bring you all the sexual excitement you could ever wish for."

Alaric looked at the phone in his hand, turning it over with pure concentration. "Vlad, I don't know how small your dick is, but there's no way mine is fitting in here."

"Your tiny dick fit on my device," Lucian said.

Vlad cackled with laughter, slapped Alaric on the back, and wandered out of the room.

Alaric lifted his phone toward me. "Do people really fuck these things?"

18

CARA

Of all the things I expected to be doing with my night, watching three vampires unpack a suitcase full of expensive looking pistols was not one of them.

We were out in the fields beyond the city by a line of trees. Lucian had driven me, and we'd met up with Alaric, who was carrying the case. It was my first time riding in a car with Lucian. He thankfully was a faster learner than Alaric and already seemed to be a completely competent driver, even if he had a little bit of a lead foot.

Alaric, on the other hand, had arrived in a dented, formerly nice-looking luxury car that was making a sad clunking noise and spewing smoke from beneath the hood. Alaric had sworn he hadn't "tragically destroyed" any humans on the way, but I'd made sure there was no blood or hair on the car all the same.

"What's this?" I asked, pointing to the growing arsenal of weapons in front of us.

"Guns," Alaric said. "You point them in the direction of a thing you don't like and pull the trigger." He hefted one, then started clumsily handling it and pressing random buttons.

I flinched back. "Do you know how to use that?" I threw my hand over my face when he swung the pistol in my direction briefly as he turned it around and started banging it on a rock.

"Of course I do," Alaric said.

Lucian pulled one out of the box and inspected it by looking straight down the barrel. I slapped it out of his hands and gave him a look of utter disbelief. "What the hell is wrong with you two? Those are *guns*. You aren't supposed to point them at anything you don't want to kill. Even if they aren't loaded."

Alaric's rock banging technique managed to knock the clip free of his pistol. He pursed his lips, as if impressed with himself. Then he aimed it in Lucian's direction, squinting one eye shut.

"Hey! What did—" I started, but was cut off by a deafening *crack*.

I blinked a few times, stumbling backward and then realizing what had happened after a short delay. Lucian and Alaric were both staring in fascination at Lucian's arm.

A high-pitched ringing was blaring in my ears, making everything else sound muffled and unnaturally quiet.

"You shot me," Lucian said, voice deadpan.

Alaric frowned, like he was trying to think of an argument to state otherwise. "In a sense, the gun shot you."

"No," Lucian said, anger rising in his voice. "There's no in a sense about it. You fucking shot me, you idiot."

Lucian had been standing by a tree, which he was now resting his elbow on and leaning forward, clearly in a bit of discomfort.

Alaric walked behind him and let out a low, impressed whistle. "Went straight through."

"Of course it did," Lucian snapped. "Don't touch it," he said, slapping Alaric's prodding finger away.

I could barely breathe. The gun was still in Alaric's hand and smoking. He lifted it to look down the barrel in confusion, giving me my third heart attack of the last ten seconds. "I don't get it. I saw the bullets all come out in that little package. What did I even shoot you with?"

"There was a bullet in the chamber," I said. My voice sounded a little muffled. I put a finger in my ear and wiggled it around, trying to silence the ringing. "Last time I used a pistol, it didn't work like that. Or maybe it did... It has been a while, I suppose."

Lucian looked up. "You're familiar with these weapons? Can you show us?"

I pointed to his arm. "You have a freaking bullet wound, Lucian. We need to take you to a doctor or something. Are there vampire doctors?"

He smiled, flashing that gorgeous dimple of his. "Do I detect concern?"

"Are you seriously going to fish for a complement when there's a bullet hole in your arm?"

Lucian fell to one knee, groaning. "It hurts."

I got down beside him and tried to help him up, but he weighed as much as a granite statue. "God," I said, groaning with effort. "What are you made out of?"

"Bullshit," Alaric said, kicking Lucian in the side lightly. "He's fine. I once watched him regrow an entire arm in a couple hours."

I looked at Lucian, who was grinning like a rogue.

I made an annoyed noise, then pushed off and planted my hands on my hips. "Are you serious?"

He got up, dusting off his knees. "Sorry. You're cute when you worry. But yes, I'll be fine." He rolled his shoulders back and looked focused. The wound in his arm started to hiss faintly and smoke rose from it.

I watched in fascinated horror as the wound bubbled and sealed up, leaving nothing but dried blood and smooth, flawless skin beneath a torn hole in his suit.

"Wow," I said, walking closer and touching it. "Does it hurt?"

"Yes. Being shot hurts," he said. "And fixing it burns."

"Oh, get over it," Alaric said. He was already banging another weapon against a rock. "Can't get these damn bullets out."

"What do vampires want with guns?"

"What do you think?" Alaric said.

"Don't you guys have powers or something?"

"I don't know what your movies imply," Lucian said. "But it's more effective to shoot people than it is to try to punch them very hard. And it's not as if we can fire lasers from our eyes."

I shrugged. "I guess that makes some sense. So why do you two look so clueless with those things, then?"

"Because the last time we were free, there were fewer buttons." Alaric brought the gun up high and slammed it down on a rock, shattering it in a very expensive sounding way. He glared at the pieces. "Impossible," he groaned. "This stuff isn't all that effective against us, anyway. It's mostly an annoyance. But if you put enough holes in a vampire, he'll at least need to go rest. If you really want to kill one, though, you have to—"

"Alaric," Lucian hissed. "Haven't you learned your lesson about explaining our weaknesses to humans?"

I wasn't sure why I felt a little emotional blow from the way he lumped me in as just another human. I guessed it was a sign of how desperately detached I was from any romantic attention from the opposite sex. A few nights of talking and getting to know Lucian and I already thought he should trust me with the secret to ending his immortality.

Stupid.

"Okay, so you have guns so you can put holes in the bad guys if they come after us? Basically, just to slow them down... Am I keeping up?"

"Pretty much," Alaric said.

"Alaric was also the worst shot I'd ever seen in my life the last time I saw him handle a weapon," Lucian added. "And I've lived a long life."

"He's exaggerating," Alaric said. "I'm perfectly capable of—" The gun in his hand went off, jolting it out of his grasp and sending it in a crazy spiral toward the ground. He whistled, then picked it back up and started banging on the rock like nothing had happened. "I can handle myself just fine."

Lucian sighed. "What will we do?"

"Did either of you consider looking at the directions?"

The men were still poking and prodding the weapons when a truck pulled off the road in the distance and started coming our way.

"Were you two expecting someone?" I asked.

Both men looked alert.

"No," Lucian said. "Get behind me."

"Why? What does that mean?"

All the light-hearted carelessness of a moment ago evaporated in an instant. Alaric and Lucian looked like dogs with their hackles raised, and my stomach was suddenly ice cold.

"Get her to the trees, I'll provide a distraction," Alaric said.

"Why do you guys look worried? I thought the guns were just an annoyance? If those are bad guys, what are they going to do?"

Lucian ignored my question, picking me up with such a lack of effort that I felt my breath catch. He scooped me up like I was a child and started hauling his beautifully crafted vampire ass toward the trees with me in tow.

"What are we going to do? Is he going to be okay?" I asked, bouncing wildly in his arms.

"Most likely," Lucian said. "I heal quickly. Alaric runs quickly."

"Faster than a truck?"

"No," he said.

I chewed my lip, watching as Alaric gave the weapon in his hand a few angry bangs on the nearest rock. I wanted to scream some advice to him, like to maybe stop smashing the guns against rocks like a caveman, but we were already too far away for him to hear me clearly.

Alaric straightened and tucked the gun behind his back when the truck stopped in front of him.

I saw Bennigan get out of the truck with the two women from before. Bennigan approached Alaric and yelled some things I couldn't hear. Alaric spoke back, then he hurled the gun at full speed toward Bennigan's head. The man dodged with supernatural speed, and then Alaric was running toward us.

It all happened so fast I didn't even see the three rival vampires pull out weapons and start firing.

Alaric *was* fast.

It felt like my eyes were playing tricks with how fast he was eating up the distance between us. Clumps of grass were flying away from his feet with every step and his legs were practically a blur.

I flinched down when I felt something zip through the air near me.

Holy shit. That was a bullet.

My heart couldn't beat any faster if it tried. I was going to die. I was going to get shot in the head by a vampire.

We reached the trees and Lucian started weaving between them, holding me tight. Bark exploded from a tree near us, showering me with splinters. I could hear the truck engine in the distance and the constant peppering thud of gunshots. The worst sound was the whistle when the bullets were close.

All I could do was curl up and make myself as small as I could. Every second, I felt like I was about to feel the thud of a bullet punching through me, but the impact never came.

It felt like an eternity until the shooting slowed and nearly stopped.

"They have horrible aim," I said once I thought we were deep enough into the trees to be relatively safe.

Alaric appeared at our side, easily keeping pace with Lucian, who was ducking and weaving through the undergrowth in the thickening forest. "Give me that gun," he said.

"Why? So you can hurl it at Bennigan's head?" Lucian asked. His voice didn't even sound strained despite the fact that he was probably running faster than an Olympic athlete at the moment.

"Give *me* the gun," I said.

Both men hesitated, then Alaric shrugged.

"You'll be careful?" Lucian asked.

"More careful than you two."

He handed it to me, and I fiddled with it for a few moments, calling up every relevant scene in a movie I could think of. Eventually, I figured out how to pull the top part of the gun back until it made a clicking sound. I aimed behind us at a random tree and pulled the trigger, then realized the safety was on. The next time I tried, the weapon practically jumped out of my hand as it fired.

"Got it," I said.

"Go see if they're still following," Lucian told Alaric.

Alaric nodded, planted a foot that skidded in the dead leaves, then rushed back toward the way we'd come from.

"Are you hurt?" Lucian asked.

The rational thing to do would've been shut up and take the craziness unfolding as deadly serious as I probably should've. Instead, I felt hopped up on adrenaline and nerves, which apparently just made me sassy instead of quiet. "Am I detecting concern?"

Lucian's grin was wildly hot. "You really are quite the woman, aren't you?"

"I think it depends who you ask."

Alaric caught back up with us a short while later. "I think we're good. They were heading back to the truck, and there's no way it's getting through these trees."

Lucian slowed his mad sprint through the woods and eased me down. He scrutinized me for apparent damage, running his hands up and down my legs and my arms.

I grinned. "I think I'd know if I was shot."

"You would be surprised what adrenaline can do to inhibit pain," he muttered, still surveying me.

"You're sure this isn't just an excuse to put your hands all over me?"

Lucian seemed to realize that he was currently pressing his fingertips against the bottom of my butt cheek as he searched for bullet holes. He straightened, flashing a slightly guilty smile. "You appear intact. Though I would prefer to do a more thorough search."

I raised an eyebrow. "I bet you would."

Alaric cleared his throat. "Not to be the bearer of unfun news, but I should mention the bond tends to amplify under the effects of adrenaline. You two may want to be careful, assuming your plan is still to avoid fucking, that is."

I took a half step back from Lucian, which prompted the ever-present throb in my chest to urge me back toward him. "Wonderful," I said. "As if this wasn't hard enough already."

Lucian's eyes didn't leave mine. "Yes. It's quite hard."

I titled my chin to the side. "Is it?"

Alaric laughed. "Do I need to separate you two?"

I felt myself snap out of the hormonal haze long enough to catch where my thoughts were going. I may not survive the next few days. I may end up riddled with bullet holes or getting sucked dry in some back alley. Worse, I may even end up giving in to the unrelenting tug of the bond making me want to jump Lucian in all his gorgeous glory.

But...

If I survived this, I was absolutely going to crush my thesis paper. I could already imagine the looks of pure hatred and loathing on my professor's faces when I walked in with a sample of the magic, curative blood. Of course, I'd need to do some fiddling to figure out the sexual side effects, but that was the only thing standing between me and a discovery that could literally change the world.

Lucian was breathing heavy, even though the breakneck sprint through the forest hadn't seemed to wind him. He tore his gaze from me and looked to Alaric. "What did Bennigan say to you?"

"You mean before I threw a pistol at his head?"

"Yes. Before that."

"He said he wanted to 'tear your little human's throat out and feed it to his dogs.'"

"Vampire dogs?" I asked.

Lucian waved my question away, still looking at Alaric with growing concern. He grimaced. "She's too vulnerable. We need to convince him that I've sealed the bond."

"Easy enough. I could send him a *phone video* of the way you two look at one another. I'm sure he'd be convinced within moments that you've been ravenously fucking at every opportunity."

I looked away. *Rude.* Not exactly untrue, but rude.

Lucian moved closer to me, taking me by the shoulder and waiting for me to look up.

"We need to convince them that you're one of us."

"You want me to pretend to be a vampire?"

"Yes," he said. "More specifically, you need to pretend you're an Undergrove. *My* Undergrove."

I narrowed my eyes. "You're saying that like it has some kind of magical significance but I'm not sure I follow. Weren't we already pretending I was your girlfriend?"

"There is a very big difference between a human plaything and a bonded human who is newly turned."

Alaric nodded. "One is hardly worth a raised eyebrow. The other is something of a rarity."

"There were so many of you. I'd think you guys were turning people to vampires all the time."

Lucian shook his head. "It was already not common before we were locked away. It's less common now. The power balance has grown so delicate that turning new vampires is seen as an act of aggression. It's also something that requires a certain degree of strength. There aren't as many elders as there once were, it seems."

"So what makes it a good idea to pretend we're doing the thing that other vampires see as an act of aggression?"

"I don't believe Bennigan was telling the truth to my brother. I also know he is a much better shot than he displayed during our brief chase. He didn't want to risk shooting you."

I felt my stomach clench. "He wanted me alive?"

"Yes. And if he believes I've already turned you, he won't think he can torment me by doing it first."

I swallowed, throat clicking noisily. "You think he wants to… what? Make me drink his blood and then sleep with me?"

"Possibly. Bennigan's grudge runs deeply enough that I wouldn't put it past him. He might even hope to train you to be the one to put me down. There's really no telling what he intends, but I want to protect you from it. I brought you into this mess, and I'm going to make sure you survive it."

Lucian had his hand on my cheek and there was a lingering moment. I thought I could feel some sort of gravity tugging us together that didn't feel like the bond. He could kiss me, and I would let him. It wouldn't be because of some silly vampire trick. It'd be because nobody had ever made me feel as important as he did. As *safe*. Maybe that was a stupid thought, considering he was the whole reason I was in danger.

Our faces were inching closer, his lips poised to take mine. I wanted it so badly it felt like a physical pain thudding away in my head.

"Ahem," Alaric said. "I advise you not to kiss the woman you're trying to avoid sleeping with."

I jumped back from him, feeling like the temporary spell had broken. "You know," I said, speaking to break the awkwardness of the near kiss. "It's kind of a convoluted argument, anyway," I said. "You saved my life, which put me in danger. I'm going to go ahead and absolve you of any guilt from this point forward."

"That's kind," he said. "But I won't forgive myself if any harm comes to you. When I saved you, I took you under my protection. I intend to keep you safe, no matter the cost."

"Objection," Alaric said. "I propose that if *I* am the cost, we sacrifice the human we've known for only a few days. No offense," he said, showing me a straight-toothed smile. He cupped a hand on his cheek and mouthed the words *thanks for the phone, though*, then winked.

"As long as she's bonded to me, nothing is more important," Lucian said.

Alaric looked like he was about to argue but seemed to think better of it. "We should probably find a way home before Bennigan decides to get creative."

"Agreed," Lucian said. He took my hand in his and pulled me closer.

I didn't know what exactly had changed, beyond the brush with death. But I could feel in the way he'd effortlessly taken my hand that something between Lucian and I had evolved. He really would do anything to keep me safe. Despite some tiny feministic part of me that cried out in defiance and wanted to claim I didn't need some asshole to protect me, I had to admit his protectiveness made me feel warm, fuzzy, and gooey on the inside.

I wasn't developing feelings for a man, let alone a vampire.

It wasn't happening.

And if it was, I hoped my talents of self-denial were powerful enough to pretend it wasn't.

19

CARA

Ever since Lucian wiped the memory of my roommates, we'd managed to avoid another confrontation. The morning after the gunfight in the woods, we weren't so lucky.

Zack was standing in the kitchen when I came down. Of course, I was also trailed by a pale, breathtakingly gorgeous man in a suit. Lucian amusingly went to sleep fully dressed in his suits and ties, but he managed to keep them wrinkle free by some mysterious magic as well.

I had to admit some of his adherence to vampire clichés *was* a little bit adorable. I'd even caught him trying to talk to a bat he "mistook for a friend of his." When I pressed him about whether he could actually turn into a bat, he claimed the whole thing had been a joke.

"Uh," Zack said. "Is this your lawyer or something?"

I was getting used to introducing Lucian to Zack for the first time, over and over again. Maybe this time he'd survive with his memory intact.

"Yes," I said. "I keep a lawyer in my bedroom. Just in case."

Lucian walked up to Zack. Zack was an inch or two taller than Lucian, but somehow Lucian still seemed like the bigger, more intimidating man. I guessed it was that Zack was thinly muscular and boyish while Lucian was still well over six feet tall and more thickly made. He also had that rough edge of manliness that came with a few hundred years more experience, I guessed.

They shook hands, and I could see the suspicion on Zack's face. "How do you know Cara?"

"Quite well," Lucian said.

I wanted to face palm, but the dynamic of the conversation left me standing several feet away and feeling unable to effectively jump in. It was up to Lucian and his total lack of vampire charm to navigate this one.

"How did you *meet* her?"

"She approached me in a cafe."

Zack looked past Lucian, who I was already suspecting I was going to want to punch when this was through. Zack's eyebrows were rising. "Cara approached you? Since when does she care about anything but school and blood?"

"She told me I took her breath away and she wouldn't forgive herself if she didn't at least make introductions. She also mentioned she very much admired my blood," he added as an afterthought.

Yep. I was going to punch him. I could see the faintest shadow of a smile threatening to reveal Lucian's dimple. The bastard was doing this on purpose, and it made me wonder how much of his supposed bumbling and awkwardness was actually just a well-hidden technique to tease and antagonize me.

"Cara said that?"

I knew I couldn't deny anything Lucian was saying without casting more doubt on an already doubtful situation. I swallowed, then nodded my head vigorously when Zack looked my way. "Yes, but—"

"But," Lucian said, cutting me off with his deep voice. "She said it had been far too long since she'd known the touch of a man. She wanted to feel alive again. *Free*," he added in a mysterious whisper.

Zack's eyes went unfocused. He backed up to the counter and idly picked up an apple that looked far too squishy to be edible and took a bite. "That's, uh. Yeah. That's pretty wild."

"It was great for you two to meet," I said, taking Lucian's hand and tugging him toward the door. "We really have to go, though."

"The other guys will want to meet him."

"Later," I said. "Gotta get to class though."

Once we were outside, I punched Lucian in the shoulder. He smiled openly, letting out a deep, resonant chuckle.

"What was that?" I demanded.

"Enjoyable, by my estimation."

"For who?"

"Whom. And I like seeing you worked up. You're quite the woman, you know."

I stood still, but Lucian kept walking with his obnoxious long strides. I had to half jog to catch up. "What kind of person were you before you got turned?"

"Why do you want to know?"

"Because I need help understanding you."

"It has been a very long time since I was turned. Nobody cares about the man I was anymore. Anyone who knew that man is long dead. *Almost* everyone," he added with a twist of his lips.

"I care who you were."

He stared ahead, not speaking for a while. "I don't make a habit of talking about the time before I was turned."

"Why?"

"Because it's better to accept my fate. Dwelling on what I've lost only brings pain."

I hadn't considered that. "You didn't want to be this way? A vampire, I mean."

"Would you?"

"No," I said, not hesitating. "Maybe. I don't know."

He looked down at me, eyes intense. "There's a cost to this life I can't put into words, Cara." Lucian seemed to search inside himself for the right explanation, then simply shook his head. "I wouldn't wish this on you. The loneliness."

"What about other vampires?" I said. "You're not completely alone. And couldn't you fall in love with a vampire, or something? Vampires can have kids, right?"

"I think it would be better if you didn't ask so many questions."

I groaned. "I know you say knowing is dangerous for me. But don't I already know enough to put myself in danger as it is? I don't see why you can't just help me understand exactly what is going on. Maybe I could help if I knew more."

Lucian's jaw flexed. He already looked strained from the minute or two we'd spent in the sunlight. He pulled out the sunglasses I'd got him and put them on, even though I doubted it helped much. "Because every minute we're together, I'm putting you in danger. Every time I tell you more than you need to know, I'm putting you in danger. If the wrong vampire finds out the things I've told you, they will not show mercy. The more you know, the crueler they'll be."

He stopped in the shade of a tree and blew out a breath. "Cara, I'm going to make this as plain for you as I can. It doesn't matter if I have feelings for you or not beyond the bond. There can never be anything more between us. I won't turn you, and a mortal is a glaring target to my kind. It's a weakness others will exploit to hurt me."

"You could give me a gun." I smiled, firing off a shot or two with my finger gun in his direction.

Lucian's smile was sad. He lifted his hand and pushed my hair behind my ear softly. He appeared to realize what he was doing and jerked his hand back like he'd been petting a snake. He took another steadying breath. "We're dangerous for each other, Cara Skies. The sooner we can part ways, the better."

I chewed the inside of my cheek as we walked, searching for some argument. It wasn't that I wanted to convince him to be my boyfriend or something. I just... I didn't like the idea of an external force telling me who I could and couldn't care about. I guess it ignited a stubborn part of me that wanted to chase after exactly who I supposedly couldn't.

I also was dying to get that magic blood of his under a microscope to see if I could do any good with it.

"Can I ask you something?" I said when we had nearly reached my school.

Lucian looked tired and irritated from our walk in the sun, and he regarded me from under his shades. "I thought I said no more questions."

"This isn't about that. Not exactly, at least. I was wondering if you'd let me look at your blood under a microscope."

"Out of the question."

I sighed. "Nobody would have to know where it came from. It's not like they'd believe me if I told them. I was just thinking there might be a way to kind of reverse engineer it. I mean, do vampires get diseases? Do they get sick? Because your blood could be the answer to all kinds of suffering out there. We could help people. I've been looking at my own blood with the bond, but those little black things in my samples keep dying. I'm guessing they don't in your blood, or maybe there's something else entirely."

Lucian hesitated, then shoved the door to the science building open. "I'm not here to help people."

I followed after him, noting how that wasn't exactly true. He may want to see himself as a knight of the darkness. But I saw him as the man who put himself at considerable risk to save me. The man who subjected himself to a bond he knew was going to put him in danger. He was the man who promised to protect me, no matter the cost.

Lucian Undergrove may not want to be honest with himself about it, but I had a sneaking suspicion he was a good person. He was a *funny* person, when he wasn't trying to play the role of the dangerous vampire.

And day by day, I was starting to fear the point when our bond loosened enough that he wouldn't be stuck by my side.

20

LUCIAN

I'd been away from my duties for far too long, but I needed to wait until my bond with Cara had faded enough for me to meet with my former employers in private. I was putting her in enough danger as it was without reaching out to the order again.

So there wasn't much to do but wait out the bond—to pass the days with two critical objectives: do not let Bennigan harm Cara Skies, and do not sleep with Cara Skies.

I was under the sink in her smelly apartment kitchen, cranking a wrench to fit the new pipes I'd cut.

Cara sat on the counter eating little brown crunchy sticks she called pretzels. "A vampire plumber. I like it."

"You need more than a plumber. This apartment is a hazard to any mortal who lives here."

"Yeah," she said. "But it's the best we can afford. And plumbers cost a lot of money."

I got up from the sink and tested it. "No more leak. But this cabinet is ruined. It'll mold soon."

Cara shrugged. She was wearing a particularly rebellious outfit today. Her short hair was braided and tucked behind one ear, where she'd tied it in place with a rainbow-colored ribbon. She had on a leather jacket and a short skirt, which I could nearly see up if I caught her at the right angle.

"I don't think I've ever seen someone fix a sink while wearing a suit and tie. It's kind of hot." She popped another pretzel in her mouth, smirking.

"I'm glad you enjoy it. Now you're about to see someone fix your cabinet in a suit and tie."

She raised her eyebrows. "You know how to do that?"

"Yes. Where can I purchase tools?"

A few hours later, I was in the parking lot outside Cara's apartment with a stack of wooden sheets, saws, screwdrivers, glue, and cabinet hinges.

The sun had set while we shopped, which mercifully meant I could work outside and feel my strength recover in the moonlight. Cara sat cross-legged and closed one of her academic books on her lap. She glanced up as I was arranging my materials. "You're sure you know how to do this?"

"Yes," I said.

I started setting up the wood and making my cuts.

"Don't you need to make measurements of the spot below the sink?"

"I used my vampire powers to estimate the size of the cabinet."

"Wait, seriously?"

"Yes," I said, turning my back so she couldn't see me grin. I'd already measured it before we left, but she hadn't been paying attention.

It felt good to do work with my hands again. I couldn't say how long it had been since I'd worked with wood, but I was glad to find the techniques were still fresh in my mind.

Cara eventually curled up in the grass and fell asleep while I worked. I drew looks from the young college students who came and went from the building while I worked, and I gave my best glare to any who decided to look too long at Cara's sleeping form.

Seraphina appeared a few hours into my work. She leaned against the building, watching me work for a short while before she spoke. "Have you contacted the order, yet?"

"After the bond passes."

"We could use their protection," she said. "Assuming they still have the strength to offer it." Seraphina held up her phone limply. "This device is useless for things about our kind. That, or I have no idea where to begin my search."

"We will have to make our own way for now. Did you make any progress securing alliances?"

"No," she said. "Nobody wants to get on Bennigan's bad side. It also seems more and more vampires are leaning into the old ways. They think the pact should be abolished, and any who support it should be left in the sun to fry."

"We've been gone too long." I hammered a few nails, then stepped back to admire my work. "What do you think?"

"I think the three of us may have had some power before we were detained, but Alaric's ill-advised romance with a human robbed us of that power."

"No," I said. "I mean the cabinet."

Seraphina sighed. "It's great, Lucian. But I fear you're walking in the same footsteps Alaric walked. You're losing sight of the bigger picture because of a human." She motioned to Cara, who had rolled to her back so her mouth was hanging open and she was snoring in a very un-ladylike, but adorable way.

"I don't only enforce the pact because it pays well," I said. "I believe in what it stands for."

Seraphina cocked her head, looking annoyed. "And you think I don't?"

"I think you enjoy having The Order's authority behind you when you enforce the pact."

She grinned. "You do know me well. But believe it or not, I don't look down on them." Her gaze slid to Cara again. "But if I have to choose between us and them, I'll choose us. I'll choose family."

"And I'll make the choices I can live with," I said, picking up the cabinet. "Cara," I said softly. "It's finished.

She sat up suddenly, slurping in some drool, then wiping her mouth with the back of her hand. As I expected, Seraphina had already left before Cara was done blinking the grogginess from her eyes. "What time is it?"

"Time to get you inside and get this cabinet installed."

I was relieved that none of her roommates were in the kitchen to bother us while I removed the previous, water-logged cabinet and installed the new one.

Cara appeared to gradually be waking up. She rubbed her eyes, yawning. "So do I get to have your number and call you for household repairs when this is all over?"

"When this is all over," I said, getting on my back to reach up and screw in the fasteners. "We will never see each other again."

I couldn't see Cara's reaction, but there was a long pause. "You keep saying that. You're really just going to disappear?"

"I have to."

"What if I don't want you to?"

I set the screwdriver down and sat up, looking at her. She was watching me intently, eyes focused. She kept pushing her lips over to one side, an expression I'd come to learn was her way of showing she was nervous—maybe even a little embarrassed.

"I don't *want* to leave. I must, though."

"You could protect me from the others, couldn't you?"

"Not if things are as bad as they are starting to appear. Before we were locked away, my... *employer* was very powerful. My position enforcing the pact made *me* powerful. It meant Bennigan and anyone else with a grudge couldn't move openly against me."

"What is this pact thing you keep talking about?"

"A dangerous topic you don't need to know about."

"Spare me, Lucian," she snapped. "I'm tired of you telling me what I should and shouldn't know."

I bit back a smile. I really did like this woman. "A very long time ago, some of the most powerful vampires decided we shouldn't have to hide. They wanted to reveal themselves openly and take their 'proper' place as the masters of this world. But there were others who saw what their idea would truly look like. It would be master and slave. Humans subjugated and treated like cattle. It would be hell on earth, and there was a large group of us who formed The Order and helped resist any efforts of an uprising. Over time, The Pact was formed. It was our commitment to co-existence. We live our lives in the shadows, you live yours in the light. It also means we don't harm humans beyond what's necessary to feed."

"And now this pact thing isn't as widely supported?"

"That's what we're gradually coming to realize. Yes. It doesn't seem as though my kind have embraced the technology available, so our ability to learn more is limited at the moment. So far, we're only encountering vampires who are too afraid to openly support the pact, and I have no way to contact The Order."

"So where does that leave us?"

"Outnumbered and on the wrong side of a centuries old debate."

"How did you used to contact this order place?"

"Through agents who have either fled, changed sides, or been killed while I was away."

"No wonder you have such a grumpy streak. But what are you going to do? I mean, after the bond is gone and you're free to do your own thing?"

"I'm going to do what I've always done. Enforce The Pact, whether or not I have The Order behind me. I'll make sure I do what I can."

"That sounds like suicide."

"I'm not easy to kill."

Cara crossed her arms. "I don't want to think about people trying to kill you."

I got up and moved to stand in front of her. I took her hands in mine, watching as she raised her eyes to meet mine. "That's because you're kinder to me than you should be."

"You're a good person, Lucian. I don't know why you don't see that."

"Because nobody who lives as long as I have can still be a good person."

"You're good enough for me," she said, chewing her lip. Cara's small hand took my tie and tugged me toward her.

I could have resisted the pull. I could've fought it easily, but I let myself be brought down toward those waiting lips—toward her closed eyes and upturned face.

And I kissed her.

Warmth exploded through me. It woke a vivid memory of the sun on my skin as a youth before I'd been turned, of closing my eyes and looking up toward a beaming ball of light until I felt the heat sinking through every pore.

My body was on fire.

Alive.

Her lips were soft pillows of heat, sharing their wetness with mine as I cupped her cheek and let my fingers circle around the back of her head and in her hair.

My other hand took the side of her thigh and tugged her closer, pressing our lower bodies together in a delicious collision of sensitive flesh against sensitive flesh.

I wanted to devour her. To take her now and never let her go.

I could feel my fangs elongating, but she showed no sign of breaking away from the kiss, even though she surely must've felt them. I could feel the temptation to be carried away with passion. Letting the moment proceed from inevitability to inevitability would've been as easy as breathing. But I knew what would happen.

We were still bonded.

If I slept with her, I'd turn her.

I'd be dooming her.

So I started to pry myself away from her, even as her hands cupped my face and her thighs wrapped around my waist, tugging me into the heat of her panties and her pushed-up skirt.

I put a hand on her shoulder, removing myself from the embrace with the wet release of our lips. She leaned forward toward me, eyes beseeching, and hand still outstretched.

"We can't," I breathed.

"Why? Let me be like you. It doesn't have to be over when the bond ends. We could be together. You wouldn't have to be so alone all the time, I could—"

"No," I said. "You don't understand what you're volunteering for. You could never understand. Come. We need to rest for tomorrow."

I rushed upstairs, ignoring the maddening tug of the bond urging me to stay closer to her. I only had to endure it for a few moments, because Cara quickly followed after me.

I took my place on the floor and crossed my arms over my chest, lying down in my place as I always did. I heard her slip into the blankets of her bed, still breathing heavily. I could *smell* her arousal, and it was intoxicating enough that I was almost compelled to get back up and forsake everything I believed in just to feel the relief of plunging myself into her. Of having her. *Fucking* her.

But I closed my hands into fists and clenched my jaw until mortal teeth would've cracked. I was going to stay here, and I was not going to drag her down to my hell because I was selfish and lacked the self-control to do what was necessary.

"Lucian, I—"

"Sleep, Cara," I said. "We both need to sleep."

21

LUCIAN

Cara had on a simple outfit of a white shirt and tight-fitting, stretchy black pants. She was sitting in one of the antique chairs in my home in front of a mirror. It was nightfall, and Seraphine was prowling behind the chair, her bare feet padding on the thick red rugs splayed across the living room.

Cara let out a huge yawn, then shook her head, blinking and opening her eyes a little wider as if trying to wake herself up. "Okay. So the goal here is to make me look more like a vampire, right?"

"Somehow," Seraphina said. She was studying Cara like an artist might look at a solid block of stone.

I was as tired as Cara looked. My healing capabilities served the double benefit of always keeping me feeling completely fresh and energized. *Usually.* It seemed walking around in the sunlight every day was tapping my reserves of power to their limits, and certain discomforts and annoyances I thought I left behind centuries ago were coming back.

I stretched my lower back, trying to relieve some tension there.

I covered my own yawn as I watched Cara from the far wall. She looked perfect as she sat there straight backed and amused.

She stole a look my way, then smiled. I found myself smiling back before I wiped the look from my face.

Be strong. Don't make this harder than it already is.

I'd felt the gradual slip of resistance melting away between us. My willpower could only withstand so much temptation, and day after day of being by her side and enduring her charmingly innocent personality was taking its toll. It was also causing me to be loose lipped with information I was supposed to protect. I knew I'd told her far more than I should have about our kind already. I thought Seraphina and Alaric were only acting like they didn't care was because they assumed I'd wipe her memories when this was through.

Others wouldn't care what my intentions were. They'd want to make an example out of her to show anyone else who wanted to reveal our secrets to mortals.

I focused instead on my desire to keep her safe, because I needed to funnel all the built-up energy inside me into some action. Otherwise I would burst.

At least obsessing about keeping her safe would keep me out of her pants. I knew if I let my mind wander, it would go back to the kiss, to that tantalizing taste of life. Kissing Cara was like being alive again. Being mortal. I could close my eyes and forget what my existence had become. I could embrace the warm explosion that had spread into every fiber of my body at her touch.

And yet I couldn't let myself hope to feel that again. The same taste of life for me was a taste of death for her. A taste of the endless void that was immortality. I'd be true to my namesake if I let our desires come to fruition. I'd feed on her very lifeforce and leave her empty—sucked dry.

Seraphina walked a slow circle around Cara, tapping her chin in thought. "You're sure I can't just snack on her?"

"Seraphina," I warned.

Cara gave me an uncertain look. "Is she joking?"

"No," Seraphina said.

"Yes. You swore you would be helpful," I growled.

Seraphina sighed. "Well, it's not as if there's a dress code for our kind. What this little human needs is more confidence." She tucked a finger under Cara's chin and pulled her head up straighter. She put her finger tips behind Cara's shoulder blades and urged her to puff her chest and pull her shoulders back. "You need to look like you've had decades to cement your own superiority over the human race. And you need to not appear intimidated in front of our kind."

"Okay," Cara said.

"Also, eyeliner. I will admit we have a little bit of an unhealthy obsession with it." She plucked a tube from a bag on the counter and bent down to apply it to Cara's eyes. "And you may borrow some of my wardrobe, but if you ruin my clothes, I will bite you."

Cara was perfectly still, but I could sense the fear radiating off her.

I moved closer, allowing the bond to get what it wanted. "You won't lay a finger on her with malicious intent."

"No," Seraphina said. "But I may lay a few teeth on her."

I bared my teeth. "If you want to lose them."

"Is this like playful banter, or are you guys actually serious right now?"

"You smell fantastic," Seraphina said. "So, no. I'm not joking. I would like to feed on you. You wouldn't even need to remember a thing, and you'd be completely fine. Just a little tired."

"Seraphina," I warned.

She gave me a dangerous look, but resumed applying the eyeliner to Cara, who appeared too scared to so much as flinch.

"So, uh, do different people taste different?" Cara asked.

"Yes," Seraphina said. "You can tell how they'll taste by the smell. And you smell particularly good."

"Thanks," Cara said lightly. "I really like pineapple juice. Maybe that's why."

"No," Seraphina said. "I find the more innocent and virginal the human, the more delicious."

Cara cleared her throat. "Virginal isn't strictly accurate. I've been sexually active before."

Seraphina paused with the applicator in her hands. "You're sure you are mortal, then? Judging by how faint the smell is, I wouldn't think you've been sexually active in centuries. Was it an exceptionally brief encounter? Maybe a particularly unrewarding one?"

"We don't really need to go into the details," Cara murmured.

"Yes, well if the way you smell is any indication, it has been long years since any man so much as came near you with a penis."

I stifled a laugh. Cara's cheeks were turning red.

"Do you beat them away with heavy objects?" I asked. I'd noticed the same peculiarity in her scent as well. She nearly smelled like a virgin might, and despite her claims it was hard to imagine she'd really spent any significant time with a man. "I know I've been away from the world for a long time, but you appear to be perfectly breedable and in good health."

Cara gave me a long suffering, dry look. "I can't even tell if you're being serious anymore."

"Lucian suffers from delusions. Particularly, the delusion that he's funny. Don't mind him."

"At least he doesn't want to eat me," Cara noted.

Not exactly true, I thought.

"I want to *drink* you," Seraphina said. "And I'd leave enough for your little heart to keep beating. You wouldn't have to worry."

"She won't need to worry," I said, "because you will not feed from my human."

"*His human,*" Cara said in a mockingly deep voice. "For somebody who talks like I'm basically a rental, you can be very possessive."

I moved back to the wall, feeling myself fume on the inside. She was right, of course. The things I said didn't match with the conflict raging inside my chest. I didn't want to give up Cara when the bond collapsed. I didn't want to be responsible and let her grow old and live her own life outside my world.

She was a connection back to a time when my life was brighter. She reminded me of what it felt like to be human. And even though I knew I was a fool for thinking so, I thought that quality in her would still remain if she was no longer mortal.

I clenched my fists at my side. *But I was not going to discover that truth.* Because I was not going to be selfish and reckless. I was going to do what I said. Protect her, then return her as safely as I could to the life she'd lived before we crossed paths. That was the only way it could be.

22

CARA

The dress Seraphina gave me was itchy and hot. I was wearing what felt like seven layers and it was nowhere near chilly enough outside to call for it. But I admittedly enjoyed the way Lucian kept sneaking glances my way. I wondered if the puffy, old-school dress reminded him of the girls he'd chased before he was a vampire.

I tried to picture that.

I pulled up a mental image of Lucian and then tanned his skin. I tried to remove some of the icy intimidation that seemed to radiate from him. I imagined that dimple and easy laughter. I thought of him teasing a girl in a small chapel classroom over a hundred years ago.

"Why are you smiling?" Lucian asked.

"Was Lucian the name you were born with? Or do you guys get to choose kind of like a superhero name when you get turned? I think I'd want to be something cool. You know? Like, *Opal Waterfall.*"

Lucian let out a spurting laugh. He pressed a fist to his mouth. "Uh, Opal Waterfall would be quite the name. But, no. We keep our names. We only take the name of the family that turned us."

"Did you say what ever happened to the guy who turned you? Dominic, right? How did he die?"

"You don't need to know about things that happened before you even existed."

I folded my arms, which pressed my cleavage up into the little square window cut down from the neckline of the dress. Lucian's eyes drifted in that direction, and I naughtily didn't uncross my arms.

He teased me at every opportunity, and it was only fitting that I return the favor when I could manage it.

"Will Bennigan be at this place?" I asked a little while later. We were arriving outside another decrepit looking bar downtown. A tall man in a dark suit waited out front—a vampire, I assumed.

"That's another question."

"Questions are how you get to know people. Excuse me, but if I'm forced to be stuck at your hip and constantly visualizing wild, kinky sex dreams about you, then I want to at least know if you like crunchy or smooth peanut butter."

Lucian stopped me suddenly. "Wait. The sexual dreams. You said they are kinky. What is unusual about them?"

"Uh, I don't think it'd be appropriate to really recount the details with you."

"It is important. It could mean you're in danger."

"What?" I asked, heart starting to pound. "I mean, I just had one where you kind of... you know, bit my neck while we were, *you know*. And then there was one where you kept saying 'I'm gonna fang you so dirty, little human. I'm gonna fang you so hard.'" I could feel my cheeks blazing with red heat, but figured I'd gone this far, and I might as well tell him everything if it was important. "And there was also one where you were wearing a cape and had your hair slicked back. You came in through my window and you said…" I trailed off. My throat went completely dry and shut itself in self-defense. *Do not finish that sentence. Surely he doesn't need every little detail.*

"Cara," he said. "It's important that you tell me everything. Your life could depend on it."

I blew out a shaky breath. "You said… *'I 'vant you to suck my cock.'* Then you opened up your cape and you were butt naked underneath. And very erect," I added.

Lucian stared at me for several long seconds, leaving me to wonder if he was about to reveal whatever my dreams meant was some sure sign of danger. Finally, his lips shook and then broke into a smile. Then he was bent over laughing.

"What?" I demanded. "What is so funny?"

"I'm sorry," he said when he finally calmed down. "I didn't think you were actually going to tell me so much."

"What do you mean?"

"It's possible I over-stated the danger of what your dreams could mean. I was mostly just curious what the 'kink' you spoke of was."

My nostrils flared. I was going to kill him. Slowly.

"Come on," he said. "I vant you to come with me."

I punched his arm a few times. "I hope that bruise doesn't heal."

"It will," he promised, grinning with that obnoxious dimple on full display.

Asshole.

23

CARA

The place Lucian brought me to was some sort of smelly, loud, poorly lit fighting ring. There was a caged arena in the center and cushy leather seating surrounding the ring.

"Please tell me this isn't what it looks like."

Lucian showed me to a seat near the back. It was a long, pleated leather couch in a semi-circle facing the ring. There was a menu on the table, which made me shudder at the thought of what would be on a vampire menu, considering I hadn't seen Lucian eat anything except the blood of the two women in the alley.

"This is probably what it looks like," he said. Lucian was dressed in one of the suits I'd helped him select, and I had to say he wore it well. The whole suit was a deep shade of crimson with accents of charcoal gray. The effect was striking against his pale, sculpted features and dark eyes.

"Why are we here?"

"The Marsh children used to be members of The Order. I'm hoping I can convince them to come back to the side of The Pact.

But they also have an unhealthy obsession with the fighting pits," he said, gesturing to the ring in the center of the room. "So I thought I would diplomatically bring up the topic when they were somewhere they loved."

"And you think this will stop Bennigan from coming after you?"

"It will be a step in that direction. Hopefully. The more alliances and strength we can show is on our side, the more reasons he'll have to think twice."

"Having a perverted old vampire living in your house who likes to reminisce about the good ol' days when he tortured virgins also didn't seem to stop Bennigan. Are you sure things even work the way they used to?"

"Bennigan was hoping to take you. It wasn't a true attempt on my life or Alaric's. Vampires don't die easily or by accident. It's quite common to send a message through violence, but a true *killing*. I don't think it matters how much things have changed since my captivity. Killing without cause would start a war."

"Wait. I thought you killed Bennigan's wife? Alaric made it sound like it was an accident, but—"

"Some acts justify a true death," He said curtly. "I don't regret what I did."

I raised my eyebrows, then looked down, feeling like I'd just touched a forbidden topic and needed to change the subject. "Not that you aren't charming," I said with a touch of sarcasm. "But why would killing you start a war?"

"Because a true death is already a serious crime. But the true death of an elder is considered a high crime. Whether a vampire believes in The Pact or not, nobody wants us to neuter ourselves by wiping out the most powerful among us."

"So you're saying you're old, even for a vampire? You mean I've been having kinky sex fantasies about a bloodthirsty geezer?"

Lucian grinned wickedly. "This bloodthirsty geezer only has so much patience for being insulted."

"Is that so?" I asked. "What happens when I test your patience? Are you going to bite me?" Tauntingly, I stretched my neck to the side, exposing the flesh there. I'd meant it as a joke, but Lucian's eyes flickered as he stared down at my neck. He swallowed, then ran his teeth over his lower lip. I hadn't ever noticed his canines look quite as large as they did then. Although I remembered how long they'd felt while we were kissing.

Just the flash of memory from the kiss made my skin flush even hotter. I assumed it was the bond's fault, but I had hardly been able to stop thinking about that brief kiss. I'd kissed guys before, but nothing I'd ever done made my body react the way it had from a few stolen moments of contact with Lucian.

I cleared my throat, trying not to think about it anymore, especially as Lucian was looking at me like he was now.

I straightened my neck, feeling stupid. "Do your teeth get bigger when you are thinking about drinking blood?"

"Yes."

"Like an erection of the mouth. That must get awkward."

Lucian's canines were protruding just below his upper lip. He lifted the menu, covering his mouth. "Would you like me to order some food for you?"

"I'll pass. Virgin's blood isn't really my style. Besides, I thought the whole point of getting dressed in this getup was to convince people I was a vampire. Won't eating food tip them off?"

"No. Newly turned vampires still need to eat regular food for a few weeks while they transition."

I shook my head. "It's okay, I'm fine."

"I'll order you something." Lucian got up and went to talk to a woman who was circulating the room. I still couldn't tell at a glance who was a vampire and who was a human. But it seemed strange that some vampires appeared to operate like medieval kings and queens while others worked menial jobs like being bodyguards, bouncers, and bartenders. I assumed his world was organized into social classes based on age. Except I didn't quite understand why someone apparently as old as Vlad was lurking around like a drunken college student in Lucian's house. Maybe there were exceptions.

Even with Lucian only traveling a short distance away, I could tell that little by little, the bond seemed to have loosened its stranglehold on us. At first, going to the bathroom had been like torture, even with Lucian waiting just outside. Now I could be in a different room than him and mostly handle the never-ending tug of magnetism that drew me toward him.

Watching him stand even a little farther away still dredged up a pathetic kind of sadness in me. It reminded me that this strange, mostly terrifying adventure had an expiration date. Someone like Lucian wouldn't keep putting up with the hassle of being in my life any longer than he had to. Maybe he was a bit of a flirt now, but it was probably the bond doing the talking, not the real man beneath the fangs.

I wasn't sure I actually believed that. The truth was, my heart told me the real Lucian did care about me and he did like me. All the grumpy moments and stiff words were just him trying to keep me at arm's length to protect us both. But I didn't want to be protected. I just wanted him to let me in. The more I got to know him, the more I felt heartbroken to see how alone he made himself. Being his someone felt good, and I wished he would just let me be that for him.

I looked around the room, endlessly fascinated to be glimpsing the hidden world of vampires that I'd apparently been living on top of without knowing. I thought I recognized many of the same faces from the bar the other night, which led me to believe there weren't hundreds of vampires in the city. Lucian had declined to answer any questions on the topic, like most of the things I asked about.

But if there weren't even a hundred vampires in Savannah, there must be thousands across the country. Maybe tens of thousands.

I guessed it didn't exactly matter. But if I could find some way to extract the healing properties from vampire blood and turn it into some sort of miracle drug, there was no end to the number of lives that could be saved. It was strange to be thinking about academics as rarely as I seemed to lately. Even in class or at Anya's, I felt like I was just going through the motions. My mind was racing with this world and all the impossible things I was learning.

Still, I knew this would all end, and when it did, I'd be holding a tantalizing piece of knowledge. The question was whether I'd have the ability or the resources to do anything with it.

Before Lucian returned, I spotted a familiar, curly haired, mustached, five-o-clock shadowed face. *Vlad.*

He saw me from the other side of the room and took a celebratory sip of the beer in his hand. Of course, he immediately turned his head to the side and spit it all over the floor. *I still needed to remember to ask Lucian what the hell that was all about.*

"Human!" Vlad shouted for the entire room to hear.

I made a *shush* face, pressing my finger to my lips.

He was still approaching from halfway across the room, but he widened his eyes, then gave me a knowing wink and tip-toed the rest of his way to me.

"Bonded human with no vampire?" Vlad said, sitting across from me and spreading his arms wide. His pose had the unfortunate effect of popping a button on his vest, which released the lower half of his round, hairy belly. "How'd you do it?"

"Do what?" I asked.

"Kill Lucian. You know, he can be alright. But If I'm being honest, I thought about killing him a few times, too. Just never got around to it."

"I didn't kill him. He's right over there?" I pointed, wishing Lucian would sense my discomfort and hurry back.

"Oh," Vlad said easily, laughing. "Just fucking with you. Besides, I haven't killed anyone in a long, long time." He made uncomfortable eye contact with me as he sipped and spat another mouthful of his drink.

"Why do you do that, exactly?"

"It brings back memories. Can't swallow it though or I get horrible indigestion."

"Are you really as old as you say?" I asked.

He wiggled his eyebrows playfully. "You won't get answers like that out of me unless you're playing poke the vampire with some sharp objects." Vlad leaned forward suddenly, elbows now on his knees and eyes lit with fiery excitement. "Do you want to play that with me?"

I swallowed. "No, thank you though."

"Your loss. Anyway, I've got to go. And don't mention to old Lucy that I said I'd considered killing him."

I grinned. "Why, are you scared of him? I thought the older the vampire, the more powerful."

"I am a man of peace. Besides, I only torture and kill humans. I have no interest in getting involved in messy vampire conflicts. Too much work."

"You said you haven't killed anyone in a very long time."

Vlad hesitated. "Right. Yes, like I said. I *have tortured* and *killed* humans. A very long time ago. Maurice!" Vlad yelled suddenly, dropping his drink to double-point at a nervous looking man with elongated fangs hanging over his lower lip. "Where the hell have you been, you fucker?"

Vlad mercifully rushed off. Lucian came back a short while later, looking toward Vlad. "Did Vlad come speak to you?"

"You could call it that," I said.

Lucian nodded absently.

"Are you sure he's... You know, safe?"

"Vlad is harmless. Here," he said, handing me a glass of wine in a fancy crystal goblet. "Go ahead. Enjoy yourself."

I looked suspiciously at the drink.

"It's possible that you might wish to be slightly inebriated before you witness the fight."

"Are the Marsh people you mentioned still coming?"

"The Marsh children should be here any moment."

"Children?" I asked.

A waitress set down a sandwich for me. One look and I realized I *was* actually hungry, and I gratefully picked it up and started eating.

"Well, they are nearly a hundred years old," Lucian said. "Maybe two. I can never remember. But they were turned as children. So they are small."

"It hardly seems fair. Getting stuck at whatever age you are, I mean."

"Yes. When some cosmic force thought up the rules to this whole feeding on the blood of humans in exchange for immortality, they must've forgotten a detail or two that would've made it all much more 'fair.'"

"Well," I said, looking for a way to cheer him up. Lucian always seemed to get gloomy and pessimistic when he talked about being a vampire. "I've seen more vampire movies and read more vampire books than I'd care to admit. People's imaginations are a lot crueler to you guys than reality, apparently. Because in books vampires burst into flames the moment sunlight hits them. They usually have to kill the people they feed on, too. Or feeding turns people into vampires. The list of ways popular media has made being you guys shitty is endless, really."

"What a comfort," he said. "And every other vampire I've met *does* need to mortally fear the sun. But at least we can eat garlic."

I bit back a smile. "You're like a sexy vampire. It's funny how they leave that part out of the movies. One sip of your blood and it's like the world's most ridiculous aphrodisiac."

"Needing to feed on humans is also an inconvenience, if we're keeping score. And younger vampires have to do it daily. Only my age and particular gifts let me go weeks between feedings."

"Hm," I said. "Tell me something... Is it weird being a million years old and wanting to sleep with someone my age? Doesn't it make me seem like a child to you?"

"No," he said. "I was only a few years older than you are now when I was turned. I think the real difference between the young and the old is the betrayal of the body. A human at seventy usually possesses an almost identical mind to a younger person. The difference is their failing body makes them weary."

"That sounds exactly like something a super old, crusty geezer would say to get into the pants of a young human." I grinned. *Young.* I had to admit a vain part of me liked this world where thirty wasn't already the beginning of the end for being considered "young." To these vampires, I was practically radiant with youth. I also enjoyed teasing a man who looked like the picture of someone in the prime of their life about his age.

Lucian had seemed distracted for most of our conversation, but he finally looked at me with the edge of playfulness I'd caught brief glimpses of from him. "I wonder if it's stranger for you to be so hopelessly attracted to an old, crusty geezer such as myself."

"Yes. It's strange."

We were making some scorching eye contact when a small child approached our table. He looked about eight and had shock white hair cut into a perfectly strange bowl cut.

"Good of you to come, Adam," Lucian said.

Adam inclined his chin, looking from me to Lucian with a hint of curiosity. There was a strange vibe to the little boy. I knew Lucian must've been talking about him when he mentioned the hundred or two hundred year old kids, and I believed it. I'd never seen a young boy who looked so confident or carried himself quite as the boy did. He had coal black eyes and little touches of malice on his small face that I couldn't put my finger on. All I knew was I felt nervous around him.

"Where are your brothers?" Lucian asked.

"My brothers aren't as willing to listen to your words as I am. They think you'll just bring Bennigan down on us all."

"And you disagree?"

"*I* wasn't willing to miss the fights. And I enjoy hearing powerful people beg. So, please, let's hear why I should convince my brothers to support you and not Bennigan. Is this your human?" he asked, pointing to me.

"No. She is one of us. Newly turned, of course," Lucian said.

I nodded, then remembered a vampire wouldn't look wide-eyed and confused. I tried to put on my best smoking hot, *I'm a badass who bites people for fun* look. Adam's frank disinterest as he regarded me made me feel immediately silly.

"It's true," I said. "I love blood. I spread the stuff on my toast, even."

Lucian slowly turned his head toward me, giving me look that clearly said *please stop talking*.

Adam completely ignored my dumb comment and started listening to Lucian's attempts to convince him to come back to The Order.

I lost track of the conversation between Lucian and Adam because the seats around the room had filled and the fighting ring was now occupied by two very muscular, sculpted men wearing no shirts. There was no announcer and no ceremony. Both of the men in the ring just charged at each other and started clawing, biting, and punching.

I immediately averted my eyes, but I could still hear the violence. When I tuned my ears back into the conversation between Lucian and Adam, they were talking about the ways Bennigan would eradicate their entire family lines if they crossed him. It was hard to follow some of the references the two men made, but I poured as much of my attention into it as I could. It was better than focusing on the fight raging while the room full of vampires cheered.

I'd thought of this whole experience with Lucian as a dangerous, wild adventure more than once already. I'd even felt sad just minutes ago to see him cross the room without me and demonstrate the bond was weakening. But in a rushing, overwhelming moment, I was reminded how serious it all was.

These creatures were dangerous, different, and deadly. One of them wanted to use me to hurt Lucian, and after that, he wanted to wipe out anyone who so much as dared to support Lucian.

Half of me wanted to scoot closer to Lucian and cling to him for protection. The other half wanted to run as far as I could and try to forget I'd ever learned vampires were real.

24

LUCIAN

We were in Cara's cramped little room while I put the finishing touches on a dresser I'd built her. I'd seen the way she had to lay the majority of her clothing on the floor in a neat pile and then carefully dig through it when she wanted to find something to wear. The rest was stuffed in an extremely small closet that barely had room for a few jackets.

I had a chisel in one hand and a mallet in the other as I fine-tuned the joinery for the dresser doors.

She was sitting on her bed, watching me while she twirled a barefooted toe in idle circles. Cara had on a fuzzy, oversized sweater and a pair of the "leggings" she liked to wear on lazy days. Some of her short hair was pulled up into a very small topknot while the rest hung at the back messily.

I kept forgetting to focus on my work because I was stealing glances at her, and she had noticed. She was wearing her patented knowing smirk as she sat there, toe endlessly circling.

"I can't believe you built me a dresser," she said. "Fixing the sink was nice, but this might be the most manly thing a guy has ever done for me."

I grinned. "The ones at the stores were not suitable. It appears they build furniture out of wood dust now. Those things would fall apart on you in months. And besides, they were too large for the space. It made sense to build something specific for your room."

"It made sense to you because you're the sweetest vampire I've ever met," she said with a raised eyebrow.

I chuckled. "I'm one of only a handful of vampires you've ever met."

"Still the sweetest," she said.

I looked up, pointing the chisel at her. "Do me a favor and don't spread that around. It wouldn't be good for my reputation."

She mockingly zipped her lips.

I tested the fit of the drawer I'd been working on, found it satisfactory, and moved on to the next. "The bond should be weakening any day now."

There was a thick silence before Cara finally spoke. "And you'll go when it does?"

I looked up. "I have to."

"You don't," she said. She got off the bed and moved to sit beside me on her knees, taking my hand in hers. "I could learn to be safe in your world. With you. I don't want you to go, Lucian."

"That's my fault for sheltering you from the worst of this. You still can't fully understand what you'd be getting into."

"I've been around you ever minute of every day since that night. How different could your world really be from what I've seen?"

I took my hands from hers and started hammering the dovetail I was working on but rushed the cut and mangled it. I clenched my teeth, staring at the wasted wood before looking back up to her. "You wouldn't survive being with me. It might not happen today, this week, or even this month. But eventually someone would come for you. The work I do makes me a target. That would make *you* a target."

"I don't care," she said.

I sighed. "I do. I'm not willing to let you throw your life away."

"It's not your decision." Tears were welling in her eyes, but she got on her hands and crawled closer to me, pulling the chisel from my hand and then the mallet next. I was sitting cross legged, and when she crawled closer, our faces were just inches apart. "I don't want this to end," she said, voice a hot whisper against my lips.

"It has to."

She kissed me suddenly. I nearly fell back from the burst of warmth that spiraled through me. My skin tingled and my hairs stood on end. My hand was cupping the back of her neck before I knew what I was doing, and my tongue was swirling with hers.

She let out a soft moan in my mouth, and I tried to pull back. She shook her head fiercely, eyes blazing into mine. A hot tear pattered from her cheek to my arm.

"No," she said. "I care about you, Lucian. If the only reason you want to get away from me is for my own sake, then I'm telling you *no*. You don't get to choose that for me. It's my life to risk, and I'll risk it for you. To be with you," she added, punctuating her words with a kiss that nearly shattered me.

I kissed her back, mind racing for some excuse—some way out. Every caress and touch felt like I was writing her death sentence.

She climbed into my lap, letting me envelop her in my arms. She wrapped her legs around my waist, pressing herself against the pulsing need between my legs. I groaned into her mouth, taking her hair in my fist hard enough to make her gasp.

"We can't," I said. "I've told you what this would mean."

"I don't care," she said. "I don't care."

I was kissing her again and letting her lean me backwards. I was on my back and she was sitting on top of me.

Her small hands were holding fistfuls of my shirt and my own were greedily exploring her. She was letting out the sexiest, breathy moans every time she grinded her hips into me, fucking me through my clothing.

This is okay. So long as we keep our clothes on. We can both get it out of our system and have a rational conversation about this later. So long as—

Cara sat up on me, tugging her sweater over her head and releasing two beautiful breasts that were briefly lifted and then fell heavily when the fabric was peeled away. Her nipples were erect, and my hands and mouth were all over her before I could think better of it.

She arched her back into me, hips digging against my erection as she did in a wonderful rush of friction and heat.

Cara's chin was resting on the back of my head while both her hands wildly ran through my hair, her body pulsating with her need. "I want you to take me," she whispered. "Make me yours."

I was waging a war inside myself. A thousand years couldn't have prepared me for the temptation to do exactly that—to throw her on the bed, peel away her leggings, and bury my face between her legs before I plunged inside her. I wanted to see her face while I filled her with my seed. I wanted to feel her curl into me as she came for me, gasping and whispering about how she'd always be mine.

Selfishly, I wanted it all.

But I did the hardest thing I'd ever done and shook my head then, taking my hands away from her breasts and looking away. "I can't, Cara. I would never forgive myself."

"Lucian, please," she said, cupping my face and trying to turn me to look at her. "Please. I want this."

"You don't know what you're asking for. And I can't give it."

"Please," she whispered.

With a growl of frustration, I flipped her over to her back, then plunged my hand down the front of her pants. I found her clit and started to circle it, locking my eyes on hers. "I won't make you like me," I whispered even as she squirmed, eyes clenching shut against the rush of pleasure.

"I won't sacrifice you for my pleasure."

She gasped, hand gripping my arm as it circled her more feverishly.

Because I love you, I thought. *I love you, and that's the only reason I'm strong enough to stop this from happening.*

"Lucian," she said, eyes seeking mine. "I—"

I put my mouth on hers, silencing her as I used my fingers to drive her to orgasm. She moaned into my mouth, hands desperately clutching at me, trying to pull me on top of her to give her what we both wanted.

But when she was through, I moved away from her and went back to my work, trying my best to ignore the long period where she watched me, her shirt still off. Finally, she put her shirt on and went to her bed.

I didn't say anything, because I didn't trust myself not to say something stupid. Something that would make this harder for both of us. I suspected the only thing stopping her from continuing to press me to continue was not knowing my feelings. If she knew how I really felt, she'd know it would've only taken one more nudge. One last ounce of pressure and I would've completely caved in.

But I thanked whatever deity allowed my miserable existence that she just went and put her head on the pillow, then rolled to the side so her back was facing me.

Good. Be mad at me, if that's what it takes. Hate me, if that's what you need.

Whatever is necessary to keep you from being dragged into my hell.

25

CARA

The first sign of the bond weakening was that I woke and didn't see Lucian on his usual spot in the floor. I also didn't feel a panic-inducing level of thudding in my chest at his absence.

I manufactured that sensation on my own, bond or no bond, and rushed out of bed. I tripped over some of his woodworking tools he'd left out from working in my room the other night and thudded down the stairs without an ounce of grace.

In the kitchen, I found Parker and Lucian at the kitchen table. Parker was explaining something about night terrors to Lucian, who was listening with a surprising amount of interest.

I had a few moments to look at him before he noticed me. Lucian had a way of looming in a space, like a dark, pale shadow. He looked supremely out of place no matter what context I saw him in, even among other vampires.

He was too impressive. *Too* beautifully different.

My thoughts went to last night and my stomach sank all over again. I'd laid everything out. I'd put my feelings in front of him and stripped away any sense of dignity. I told him *exactly* how I felt, and he'd pushed me away. The only thing keeping me from feeling completely crushed was knowing his motivations.

Lucian thought he was protecting me.

I'd seen enough to know that if he thought it was that dangerous for me to be involved with him, the threat was real. Except no matter how many times I tried to talk reason to myself, I still wanted to be with him. The bond weakening hadn't so much as chipped away at my resolve, either. This wasn't some vampire magic of his. It was just him.

"Oh," Parker said, looking up at me and waving dorkily. He was wearing a faded blue hoodie that was too small. He had the hood up and was hunched over his laptop. Lucian was standing behind his chair, bending his straight back to look at whatever Parker was talking about. "I was just telling Lucian about the man with the hat."

"The what?" I asked. I expected Lucian to give me a *save me* look, but he actually jumped in and explained for Parker.

"He's speaking of the Fae."

"Huh?" Parker said. "No, it's not fairies. It's like—"

"Yes," Lucian said. "Shadowy figures who loom in your bedroom at night? Your body is completely paralyzed. All you can do is watch?"

"Yeah," Parker said. "But it's a chemical thing. Like your brain gets you halfway to a dream state and immobilizes your muscles. The problem is you're still awake, so it lets you see into some version of reality you're not supposed to see."

"Yes," Lucian said plainly.

Parker was looking at Lucian with the startled eyes of a conspiracy junkie who had never met somebody who tried to one-up his conspiracy with something even crazier. Lucian just looked deadly serious.

I covered my mouth, smiling a little. Knowing Lucian, he was either screwing with Parker, or I needed to add the existence of shadowy fae creatures to my growing list of "shit that isn't supposed to be real but actually is real."

I waited patiently while Parker grilled Lucian with questions, which Lucian answered. When the two of them were through, Lucian joined me on my walk to campus.

We didn't talk for most of the walk to my morning classes. I'd learned not to really bother Lucian when he was in direct sunlight. Even being indoors when sun was filtering through windows was hard for him, I'd discovered. He wouldn't answer any direct questions about it, but I was fairly sure it was getting harder for him every day, like he wasn't able to completely recover from being in the sun because he was having to do it so much. Or maybe it was because he was having to steal little bits of sleep during my classes and on Anya's couch while I fiddled with samples of my bond-rich blood.

He started walking more slowly when we were about two minutes away from reaching my building. Then he slumped, falling to one knee.

"Lucian?" I said, crouching beside him and putting my hands on his shoulders.

His head was hanging, and when I looked closer, I saw his skin looked blistered.

"Oh, God," I whispered. "We need to get you out of the sun."

I tried to tug on his arms, but he was heavy. *Ridiculously heavy.*

"Come on!" I hissed.

Lucian shook his head. He tried to say something, then winced in pain.

We had walked the back way through campus, which meant we were on a seldom used path that cut over a bridge and through some trees. I looked around for anyone who could help me drag him inside, but there was nobody.

Lucian was just grunting and breathing heavy, apparently unable to even speak.

I pulled out my phone and decided he could get pissed at me later, but I was calling in help. I sent a group text to Zack, Niles, Mooney, and Parker asking them to come as soon as they could and told them where to find us.

Zack and Mooney were already on campus and only a couple minutes away in the gym. I waited by Lucian's side, trying to use my body to shield his face from the sun as he writhed, and the blisters grew redder and more numerous.

"Please hang on," I said. "The guys are coming to help me move you."

I got up a few times and uselessly tried to yank him toward a patch of shade that was only a short distance away, but he might as well have been solid stone for how much I could move him. All I accomplished was getting myself sweaty and out of breath and he hadn't moved an inch.

Zack and Niles finally came pounding heavy-footed up the path toward us.

"What's wrong with him?" Zack asked between heavy breaths.

"He needs to get inside," I said.

Mooney and Zack could see that Lucian was in trouble, even if they didn't have any idea why. They thankfully decided to hoist him up between themselves with Mooney taking his shoulders and Zack taking his legs. They jogged with him toward the closest building, drawing concerned looks from students on their way to class.

"This guy is fucking heavy," Zack groaned as they backed their way through the doors leading inside to a long hallway lined with doors on one side and big windows on the other.

"Anything would be heavy with those twigs you call arms, bro," Mooney laughed.

"He needs to be away from windows," I said, trying a few doors until I found one that was unlocked. It thankfully opened to a dim, unoccupied lecture hall.

The boys put Lucian down, then stepped back to look at him. "Uh," Zack said. "Is he allergic to sunlight or something?"

Lucian's eyes were squeezed shut and his teeth were showing as he winced in pain. I cringed when I realized his canines were elongated. *Shit.*

I'd only seen him feed one time, and he'd seemed healthier and more energetic after he did. How long ago had that been?

"I think he needs food," I said shakily.

Mooney rooted through his backpack and pulled out a crushed ham sandwich. "I was looking forward to this, but I guess he could... Hey, what's with his teeth?"

Zack leaned down, hands on his knees. "Uh, yeah. Those look really fucking real."

I took a deep breath. Lucian could yell at me later, but I needed the guys to help right now and the simplest way I could think of was to tell the truth.

"Lucian is a vampire, okay? I accidentally broke a wall where he and these two other vampires were trapped. There were some asshole vampires who want him dead, and they tried to kill me to lure him out. Then he saved me with his blood, which meant we couldn't be more than a few feet apart for the last few weeks. You don't remember much because he kept wiping your memories until I convinced him to stop."

Mooney and Zack didn't say anything at first, then they both laughed. "A vampire?"

Zack knelt down, then tugged on one of Lucian's teeth as if he expected it to pop off. The amused look on his face faltered. "What's this thing stuck on with, superglue?"

"Funny," Mooney said. He got down and tried as well, grunting with effort.

Lucian, who was still blistered, squirming, and very much in pain, flinched. It happened so fast that none of us moved.

One moment, Mooney was tugging on Lucian's tooth, the next, Lucian's teeth were clamped around his wrist and a thick droplet of blood was pattering from Mooney to the ground.

"What the fuck!" Mooney yelled. He tried to pull back, but Lucian's other arm shot up and gripped his upper arm, locking him in place.

Zack tried to kick at Lucian, but Lucian effortlessly swung his arm to the side, sending Zack literally tumbling through the air several feet to crash into a row of seats.

"Lucian!" I screamed.

Only a few seconds had passed, but Lucian's blisters started to bubble and fade. His eyes opened. The look in them was wild, like a cornered animal. Like something dangerous and unnatural.

Then he blinked and I saw the man I'd started to fall in love with.

He released Mooney, who scurried back, clutching his wrist and looking at Lucian like he might look at a lion who had just wandered into the room. Zack was groaning and trying to pull himself up from the seat, which had broken under the weight of his fall.

Lucian closed his eyes, let out a long breath, and then his whole body let off a rush of steam. He sighed with relief, and got to his feet, rolling his neck. "I feel much better. Thank you for the blood, Mooney."

"The—fucking—you—" Mooney stammered. He looked around, saw a lectern, and hoisted it up, holding it like a baseball bat. He started inching toward Lucian with it. "You fucker. You *bit* me."

"You were pulling on my teeth, if I recall," Lucian said.

Mooney swung the lectern toward Lucian so hard that I flinched. I expected to see Lucian crumble to the ground with the force of the heavy object being swung at his head. Instead, he lifted his forearm to shield himself. There was a gruesome crack.

Lucian glared, nostrils flaring. His forearm was bent at a strange angle, then there was another faint hissing sound and it straightened itself.

Mooney dropped the broken lectern, taking a few staggering steps back.

Zack was on his feet now, rubbing the small of his back. He picked up a piece of the chair and launched it at Lucian. It bounced off Lucian's head with a comically quiet *thud*.

"Stop!" I shouted. "Vampire. He's a vampire. Okay? You were tugging on a freaking vampire's teeth. Of course he bit you a little bit!"

Mooney shook his bleeding wrist around, spraying bits of blood on the carpet. "A little bit? The fucker tried to take my hand off!"

"It's a flesh wound." Lucian, who currently had a blood mustache, was already completely healed of blisters.

"Any wound is technically a flesh wound," Zack said shakily. He was backing up, not taking his eyes from Lucian. "I mean, like, if you get cut in half that's a flesh wound. And then some."

"He's going to live. Unfortunately," Lucian said. "I barely took any blood."

"Be nice, Lucian." I moved to put myself between Lucian and Mooney, just in case Mooney tried to charge him. "They helped me drag you in here. You were boiling alive out there. What the hell was that?"

He shook his head. "I don't know. I pushed my ability to heal to its limits. I've been quite hungry as well, but I was hoping to wait until you didn't need to watch me feed."

"Oh how fucking sweet," Mooney groaned. He waved his wrist around limply. "Looks like that plan backfired, huh, Dracula."

"Dracula?" Lucian laughed. "He has been dead for centuries. Quite the asshole, if the stories are true."

Zack wagged a finger. "If you're really a vampire. Prove it. Do something only a vampire could do."

Mooney squinted. "Yeah. If you were really a vampire, you'd have some kind of power, right?"

"I plan to, but you won't remember it." Lucian moved toward Mooney with that look he got when he was trying to get into people's minds.

"Lucian!" I warned. "I told you. No more memory wiping."

Lucian sighed. "Then it would be easier if they believed what you've told them and stopped screeching like scared children." He rolled up the sleeve of his suit and dragged a fingernail down his wrist, drawing blood.

Zack looked gruesomely entertained, but Mooney winced. "The hell, man," Mooney muttered to himself.

Lucian's wound bubbled, hissed, and sealed itself in an instant. "There. Convinced?"

Zack and Mooney weren't convinced until Lucian patiently went through about five more demonstrations, including healing more wounds, lifting both Zack and Mooney up off their feet at the same time, and a close-up look as his canines.

"Okay," Mooney said slowly. "So your boyfriend is a vampire."

Zack folded his arms. "And some bad vampires want to hurt you because of it?"

I nodded. "That's mostly the situation. Yeah."

"How can we help?" Zack asked.

"By telling no one," Lucian said.

"Wait." Zack looked up at the ceiling, then snapped his fingers. "Werewolves. Are they real, too?"

"No comment," Lucian said.

"He's stingy with answers," I explained. "You're lucky you got this much."

Lucian took my hand and started pulling me toward the hallway. "Come. We need you to get to your class or you'll never pass the test on Friday."

I gave Mooney and Zack a wave before I was out of the room, then grinned at Lucian. "How do you know about my test on Friday?"

"I meant what I said about not wanting to ruin your life. This school work is important to you. I've been making sure you keep on track with your studies."

I pulled his arm toward me and gave it a little hug. "Normally I'd make a joke about how you probably just wanted to get in my pants. But..." I trailed off, remembering all too vividly how the disaster of last night had gone.

Lucian stopped me in the hallway, bending his neck to meet my eyes as he cupped my cheeks. "I'm attracted to you, Cara." His jaw flexed and his eyes blazed. "I would do things to you..." He wet his lips, and I could feel the barely contained desire practically radiating off of him like heat. "There's almost nothing I wouldn't give to have you all to myself, even for one night. But the price is too great. I wouldn't sacrifice *you*. You're the one thing I wouldn't give up."

I lowered my eyes, smiling a little sadly. "I'm the one thing you wouldn't give up to get... *me*. I'm not sure that entirely makes sense."

"Sleeping with you while we're bonded would be unforgivable."

I chewed the corner of my lip, looking back up into his dark, penetrating gaze. "So what are the technicalities? What happens if you don't, you know, go inside me?"

"The bond is only consummated through vaginal intercourse, if I feed on you, or through an obscure ritual I haven't heard of anyone performing in a very long time."

"So we could do other things, is what you're saying."

"Well, yes. But I don't—"

I got on my tiptoes and planted a kiss on his lips. He staggered backwards until we bumped against the window sill. I took two fistfuls of his suit, trying to keep him from running away again or pushing me off.

Lucian didn't kiss me back at first, but then he seemed to relax into it, kissing me back as he hooked his arms around me, pulling me tight to his hard, lean body.

I gasped when he finally pulled back from the kiss. "You really need to get to class. Your test on Friday will be a quarter of your grade."

"People post notes online," I said, kissing his neck.

"These notes are good enough to get you through the test?" he asked.

"Yes, Dad," I laughed.

Lucian smiled crookedly, revealing his vertical slash of a dimple. "I only want what's best for you."

"Right now, I'm so wet that I think I'm going to need to throw these panties away," I whispered. "And I think your hand between my legs is what would be best for me."

Lucian's eyes widened. "You make a compelling argument for skipping class."

I nodded. "Zack and Mooney are probably out of that lecture hall by now. We could see if it's still empty."

I giggled when Lucian scooped me up and carried me toward the door. He opened it with his knee, then kicked it open and locked it behind us.

26

LUCIAN

I pressed Cara against the door as soon as it was closed. Her flirtations might as well have broken a dam inside me to release a torrential flood of hunger.

I kissed her ravenously. My hands found the soft warmth of her stomach and pushed her shirt up. I struggled with her bra, which drew a laugh from her.

"I guess these are different than the last time you had to unhook one," she said, reaching back to help undo the clasp for me.

It fell to the ground between us and I took a handful of her breast, feeling her nipple harden instantly against my palm.

I pushed my hand down the front of her jeans and inside her panties. She *was* wet. She was soaked, and my cock was stiff within moments. I slid my finger inside her, using my palm to circle her clit while my fingers glided in and out of her.

She arched her back into me, rolling her head back and exposing her neck.

I stared at the flesh there while she gripped my finger with her walls and rhythmically ground her hips into me. One of her hands had drifted to my cock, which she was rubbing through my pants in clumsy but hungry movements.

The vein in her neck thumped subtly against her skin, reminding me how hungry I still was. I closed my eyes, kissing her there to prove to myself I was above my desires. I wasn't ruled by them.

"Oh, God, Lucian," she gasped into my ear.

Her body thudded against the door as she shook with an orgasm. I felt her warm entrance tense and grip my fingers as she came, her whole body vibrating for the first few seconds of it.

She took my cock in a death grip, which I wasn't sure I would survive.

I held my breath, riding out her orgasm until she finally loosened her grip on me.

I grinned down at her, planting a kiss on her full lips. "We shouldn't make a habit of this."

"Why not?" Cara asked. She looked achingly beautiful. Her face was flushed, and her hair was just messy enough to make it clear what we'd been doing. Her eyes were heavy-lidded, and her lips were parted.

"Because it can't last. And we're playing with fire—doing this."

She shook her head. "You keep talking like you can get rid of me. What if I refuse to let you go?"

I smiled, feeling a pang of sadness inside me. *Then I'll still have to go, but it'll just hurt both of us that much more.* "We should get you to class."

I lifted up her bra from the ground and handed it to her with a half smile. "I'm going to need you to put those beautiful breasts back in their holsters before your classmates get any ideas."

Cara tauntingly lifted her shirt, flashing me with a view of her chest that made me rethink everything for a heartbeat. It made me want to rip her pants down and free my cock, to—

I blinked, forcing myself to focus. What mattered was keeping her safe. Nothing else.

27

LUCIAN

The bond eventually weakened enough that Cara and I could separate for a few hours at a time. It was still difficult, but if I waited until she was sleeping at night to go out, she could mostly sleep through the cravings for closeness. I knew Bennigan couldn't strike at her during the day, so I was also able to let her get back to some degree of normalcy in her life. I'd asked Zack and Mooney to keep an extra close eye on her while I rested, which they'd eagerly agreed to.

On my first few nights of separation, I hadn't dared travel too far from her. I mostly lurked around outside her apartment, testing the limits of the bond and ensuring Bennigan or his harem weren't lurking nearby, waiting to strike the moment I left.

After I'd become reasonably certain it was safe, I started a methodical search of the city for information. I was able to investigate some of the more dangerous contacts I had, knowing I didn't need to drag Cara along to the meetings anymore.

I met Vlad outside a place called Head Fangers, which was a sort of hardcore music scene for vampires. Of course, the sign outside claimed the place was a mattress store. My kind had discovered a very long time ago that mattress stores were the perfect front for any kind of vampire hangout. All that was needed was a human or two to appear to run the place and a healthy dose of daily memory wiping. Other than that, the average human seemed to think it was perfectly normal for several mattress stores that never had any customers to exist on the same street.

Vlad had his curly hair slicked back and he was actually wearing a nice—albeit ancient—set of embroidered finery. He shook out the ruffles on his sleeves and checked his collar. "How do I look?" he asked.

"Like a greased pig," I said.

Vlad snorted. "You fucker. I look fantastic."

"You're sure Jewel knows you're coming?"

"Of course she does," he said. "I've been telling her for decades that I was going to come visit any day."

I nodded. I should've expected as much when Vlad told me he already had a meeting set up with Jewel. She used to be one of the top agents for The Order, but everything I'd heard lately said that was in the past. At the very least, I hoped I could find some answers from her.

Vlad licked his fingers, then slicked back his eyebrows and wiggled them at me. "Should I show her my bat form?"

"No," I said firmly. "*No.*"

We moved through the mattress store, casually wiping the memory of the human salesman who approached us. Vlad lifted a mattress in the back of the store to reveal a staircase leading down to the main building. After a few steps, we could hear the thumping sounds of fast music and screaming vocals.

The room was low-ceilinged and cave-like. The air smelled damp, with faint hints of blood. There were a few human virgins on display for feedings, but most of the clientele were gathered around a small stage where the band was currently playing.

We found Jewel sitting in a corner booth with a young, mostly naked human virgin in her lap. Her lips were red, and her fangs were elongated. The human was pacified and motionless in her lap.

"Vlad," Jewel said easily. "I was expecting you." Jewel was a large woman who looked like she very likely could have walked through a brick wall if she put her mind to it. She had the thick neck of a football player, broad shoulders of someone who was no stranger to manual labor, and the ruddy cheeks of a farmer. Vlad also had an aggressive crush on the woman, which supposedly had simmered for centuries, ever since they met on a farm in the French countryside.

He grunted, then sat down and patted the table. He stuck his hand up like he was hoping to arm wrestle. Instead of looking confused, Jewel rolled up her sleeve and planted her elbow across from his, then clasped his hand in hers.

The two vampires held each other's stares for several long seconds until I finally sighed and moved closer.

As unenthusiastically as I could, I counted down for them. "Three. Two. One."

They both started grunting and groaning immediately, but Vlad's hand was the one getting pushed toward the tabletop.

"You giant wench," he gritted through clenched teeth.

"You hairy ball of grease," she groaned back, but with a faint smile.

I discreetly looked around the room, hoping nobody was observing me be a part of their nonsense.

Jewel finally slammed Vlad's hand down to the table, thumping the wood and making her human lift his head. She shushed him and pushed his head back into her lap.

"Damn it," Vlad said, massaging his wrist. He looked annoyed at first, but then his expression grew lecherous. "You always were strong."

Jewel leered right back at him.

Disgusting.

"I was hoping we could talk," I said, interrupting what was quickly becoming a private moment between the two large vampires.

"We're talkin'," Jewel said.

Vlad laughed too loud at her sarcasm. He was currently doing an undignified scooting maneuver to get himself around the circular seat and the table so he could sit beside her. I took a spot at the edge of the bench, resting my elbows on the table.

"I need to know how to get in contact with the elders. Marcell. Lilith. Demeter. I just need a location."

Jewel sniffed dismissively. "Dead. Boots up."

My stomach clenched. "What do you mean?"

"I mean The Order has been gutted, Lucian. Why do you think so many of us got out of the business?"

"Demeter was over a thousand years old. Who could even kill someone that powerful?"

"Someone older, I reckon," she said. "You didn't ever think maybe the oldest ones of our kind have been out there the whole time? That maybe they were among us, figurin' it was better not to be known than known?"

The idea made my skin feel colder than usual. "It occurred to me."

Jewel nodded. "Word is out that you've been tryin' to re-establish contacts with The Order, Lucian. That's not the sort of word you want getting' out in these times."

"You want me to hide, then? Like you?"

Jewel slammed her fist on the table, leaning toward me. "I'm waitin'. Coming out right now in support of The Pact is puttin' a target on your back. I suggest you do the same."

"I won't hide. You know as well as I do what will happen if The Pact isn't honored."

"Enslavement of the human race?" Jewel asked. "So what? Maybe it's time we stopped lurkin' in the shadows, anyway."

I got up, feeling disgusted. "There's nobody left?" I asked. "Not a single contact?"

She looked annoyed, but her shoulders slumped, and she let out a sigh. "If you're insistin' on gettin' yourself killed by whoever this old ass vampire is that's beheading the order, I reckon that's your business, 'innit?"

"It is," I said.

"There's a rumor about some idiots in the city trying to round up resistance. I heard they operate out of a place called *Bloody Harry's*."

"Does this group have a name? The ones trying to oppose The Pact?"

"They're calling themselves Shadow Force."

Vlad spurted with laughter. "Shadow Force? Do they wear tight little brightly colored suits and helmets? Do sparks fly out when they punch things?"

Jewel crossed her arms beneath her considerable bosom, clearly unamused. "You wouldn't be laughin' if you knew the things they done."

Vlad grinned. "Nope. Pretty sure I'd still be laughing. What a horrible name. *Shadow Force*," he said, muttering to himself then barking with more laughter.

"The name is quite silly," I admitted.

"I'll make sure to pass your complaints on to the ancient, deadly vampires that are gonna want you dead come tomorrow."

I motioned for Vlad to follow me, but he bulged his eyes and shook his head, then tipped his chin toward Jewel.

I needed to get back to Cara before I could check out the place Jewel mentioned, but at least I had a lead for the first time in weeks. Whoever these vampires resisting "Shadow Force" were, I had a sinking feeling it wasn't going to be anything close to the organized strength The Order I'd known had.

Worse, if there *was* an ancient vampire out there with an agenda and a terrible ability to name organizations, Cara was in more danger than I'd thought.

I could lay low and wait until the bond was completely gone to make a move, which would avoid the risk of drawing any more dangerous attention on Cara than I already had. But doing that would mean letting my enemies continue to gather strength. If their end goal was the enslavement of the entire human race, I couldn't exactly pretend I was protecting Cara by waiting to act. Could I?

28

LUCIAN

I opened my eyes on Cara's floor, noting that sickening yellow sunlight was seeping through her window. I could already feel the now-familiar fatigue it brought. I got up, rolled my neck more out of habit than necessity. Sometimes, I irrationally wanted to wake up feeling stiff and in need of stretching like I had when I was a human.

But the body of a vampire didn't experience discomfort like a human's. I could lay on stone and feel no urge to shift around my position or roll to my side. I could sit for hours in the same spot and be completely at ease. I only grew truly hungry for blood every four to five days, and I didn't get cold or hot.

My recent over-exposure to the sun had brought back some hints of those old annoyances, but it was still nothing but a dull reminder.

I was nearly a void of physical sensation, except all the carnal senses seemed amplified.

It only made my constant lust for Cara harder to ignore. She was the single pulse of light in a dark room. The flickering temptation to step closer, to explore more. She was the thing I wanted to reach out and put my fingertips to so I could remember what warmth felt like.

I'd already let myself slip too many times with her. In the kitchen and then in the empty classroom. Both moments were on constant repeat in my mind, driving me ever more mad with the hunger for more. She was more than a physical craving, though.

Cara's innocent curiosity was refreshing. She didn't treat me like some immortal, terrifying being. She acted like I was any other man, at least as much as that was possible in our situation. She made me *feel* normal for the first time in ages.

And now the bond was fading. I should've felt immense relief to be free of her. After all, she was a glaring weakness all my enemies would love to exploit if they got the opportunity. The sooner we were out of each other's lives, the better it should've been for both of us.

Except I worried I'd reached a point where I would've traded my own safety just for another day with her. I'd grown irrational. Sentimental. *Weak.*

Cara sat upright, stretching her arms overhead in a way that pressed her thin, pale pink t-shirt against her breasts. I told myself not to look, but I saw the hardened points of her nipples pressing through the fabric.

It was all I could do not to go to her then. To throw the blankets off her bed and push her shirt up to her neck, taking her nipple between my teeth and letting out all the suppressed need I'd barely been bottling.

She saw me, then pulled her covers up a little with a curious little smile. "Morning, Lucy."

"Do *not* start calling me that."

"Vlad calls you Lucy."

"Vlad is potentially thousands of years old, mentally unstable, and probably impervious to any of my attempts to harm him. *You, on the other hand...*"

"What are you going to do?" she asked, raising a taunting eyebrow. "Bite me?"

"You'd be surprised what methods of punishment I could imagine."

Stop making this harder than it already is. I tightened my hands into fists, willing the urge to tease and flirt with her down. It was only going to lead to more kissing. More pleasure. More bad ideas that would make the coming moment when I needed to leave that much worse.

Cara tilted her head and smiled with a touch of mischief. "I thought Vlad was the one who was into torture."

I was on her bed before I knew what I was doing, looming over her. "Touch yourself for me."

Her smile was crooked—amused. She pressed her fingertips to her wrist and mockingly arched her neck, moaning.

I grabbed her hand and pushed it between her legs. I saw she was only wearing a pair of black panties beneath her oversized t-shirt. The playfulness in her features dropped away, leaving only a startled, red-cheeked look of innocent arousal.

"Come for me."

She moved her hand away, reaching for mine. "I want you to do it."

"And your punishment is that you have to do it yourself. While I watch."

She stared longingly at me, but I moved away from the bed and went to the wall where I could see her clearly. "Do it," I commanded.

Cara hesitated, but her slender fingers started to move against the fabric of her panties eventually. She was silent at first, body stiff. She kept looking at me, then swallowing hard.

Her knees were bent, and her fingers kept circling, but I could tell she was too self-conscious to let loose and really enjoy herself.

I didn't just want to see her go through the motions. I wanted her to come. I reached down to my cock and started to rub it through my pants. The next time Cara glanced at me, her eyes went a little wider. She chewed her lip, then pressed her head back into the pillows. A few seconds later, she let out a soft gasp and pressed her hips up against her own hand, knees coming together.

Fuck.

I'd only intended to give her a little encouragement, but she was too damn sexy. I unzipped my pants and freed my throbbing cock, stroking it as I watched. She lifted her head, regularly checking to see what I was doing between her heavy breaths of pleasure.

Cara slid her hand inside her panties, occasionally moving in a way that gave me tantalizing glimpses of the slick skin there. She started pressing her fingers into herself so they made a soft, wet sound that made me want nothing more than to plunge myself inside her and feel her warm wetness pressing against my length.

Her body tensed and her legs rolled to the side so she was curled up, fingers motionless. Quakes of pleasure ran through her for several long seconds until she finally laughed softly, then looked at me with a dangerous glint in her eyes.

I was still hard and had my hand on myself, and I knew I wasn't going to have the willpower to tell her not to do what she was about to do. I was only moments from coming when Cara got her long legs off the bed and walked toward me, then sank to her knees.

She looked up at me, lips twisted suggestively, then gripped me in her small hand and took the head of my cock in her mouth.

She felt like silk. Wet, warm, absolutely perfect fucking silk.

I groaned, resting my head against the wall, then bending my neck again to watch her short black hair rock back and forth with the movement of her head against me.

It could've only been seconds before I felt the rush of my orgasm come thundering through me. I gripped her hair, surprised to see she wasn't pulling her mouth away from me even as I came.

Cara waited, making sure I was finished, then I saw her swallow.

She pulled back, wiped her mouth with a delicate fingertip, then sucked it clean and wiggled her eyebrows at me. "Do I get credit for that orgasm, or did you do all the work?"

I chuckled. "You get extra credit."

"Well," she said, hopping to her feet and giving my still-hard cock a playful bop with her palm that sent it bobbing up and down ridiculously. "That was a great start to my morning. I've got to get showered and go to class. Are you coming today, or are you going to make me go alone?"

I looked at the sun streaking through her windows. "I need to rest and gather my strength. You'll be safe, though. The others can't even be near windows during the day."

She nodded. "I know. If it wasn't safe, you wouldn't let me do it."

I smiled at her but felt a pang of immense sadness in my chest. She trusted me completely and utterly. She already knew I would do anything to keep her safe, but I wondered if she knew that meant I still needed to leave when I could.

"I will meet you at Anya's after the sun sets."

"Okay," she said. "Sounds like a date."

I WAS ON THE COUCH THAT SMELLED OF CATS IN ANYA'S BASEMENT. Cara had her eyes in a machine while the Anya woman muttered nonsense to herself and sorted through small glass vials of blood.

I usually felt completely drained by the time we reached Cara's internship because I had endured a full day of the sunlight by this point. Now I was uncharacteristically alert, and I decided to get up and go see what Cara was doing.

"What do you see through those eyepieces?" I asked.

"You want to look?" Cara asked, eyes bright and excited.

I bit back a smile. She was cute when she talked about blood. I figured there was some amusing irony in that. I drank blood out of necessity and resented it. She willingly chose to devote her life to blood. I took blood to prolong my own existence, she hoped to use it to help others live better, longer lives.

She really was a good person. It only reminded me that I needed to do everything I could to protect her from my world. *From me.*

"Sure," I said.

She scooted her rolling chair to the side and let me bend down to look in the little eye-pieces.

"See those little puffy balls? Those are red blood cells. That's what blood looks like in a microscopic level. And see those little black spikey things?"

I nodded.

"Those are not supposed to be there. But ever since..." She lowered her voice, sneaking a glance toward Anya. "Ever since I drank your blood, they have been absolutely loaded in my blood. They repair damage, fight off invasive diseases and viruses. They are absolutely incredible. It's basically like having tiny little super-smart medical machines crawling through my blood at all times. I've been calling them Lucio's," she added a little guiltily.

I glared. "Really?"

"Just to myself," she said quickly. "But they are incredible, aren't they?"

"Yes. It's very interesting," I said, and I wasn't just patronizing her. *It really was.* I wondered how many of my kind knew this. I hardly knew of any vampires who so much as attempted to lead normal lives and masquerade as humans, even a hundred years ago. I imagined it would be much more difficult now. Maybe nobody had seen this or understood it for what it was. "This was why you wanted to look at my blood, I assume?"

"Mhm," Cara said. "See how some of the Lucio's start shaking and then dissolve? The ones in my blood are dying. When I looked at this the first time, there were ten times as many. I guess that's how we know the bond is almost done, right? Once there are no more Lucio's, I won't feel so pulled towards you."

"Yes," I said. "That does make sense."

"Have you made any progress finding a way to distill these and use them to treat other humans?"

Cara's instant smile told me she'd been waiting for me to ask. "Watch this." She scooted her chair over to a container of blood vials and a clear plastic container with a transparent fluid in it. She set both down, then put on gloves, a face shield, and a white suit. "I'd tell you to suit up, but I'm assuming you can't get sick, right?"

"Correct."

"Okay, so this is healthy human blood." She applied a drop of the clear fluid to it. "And this is a sample of a pretty new blood disease called Palto-2. It's mostly harmless, but it's extremely aggressive and it fools red blood cells into taking itself on like little hitchhikers."

I put my eyes to the lenses and watched little globules of fuzzy material approach the red blobs. Within seconds, it clung to the sides of them and seemed to stay put.

"Okay," I said. "So it sticks to the cells?"

Cara nodded. "Yep. But watch what happens if I add a modified sample of my blood to this. I spun it down and found out I could extract just plasma and the Lucio's. And when I add that..." She took the top off the slide, dropped the new liquid on, and covered it before sliding it under the microscope again.

"I watched as the same, black spikey balls rushed through the sample and converged anywhere there was one of the viral hitchhikers. They'd shake against it and turn it to dust, then move on to the next.

I looked up at her. She was beaming, but all I felt was dread. "This is dangerous," I said.

"No. Well, I mean, yes, we'd need to do clinical trials and get all kinds of approvals to get permission to treat patients. But it's incredible. Do you realize what this could mean? Imagine if these things could attack cancer like that. Or freeze the aging process?"

"It's dangerous because if my kind discover you're working on this, they will stop you."

"What?" Cara asked, face draining of color.

"If your world finds out about us, they will never allow our existence to continue. Not as it does. And worse, if they find out our blood is a super cure to fix all their problems, they'll use us. Shove us in cages and siphon our blood when they need more."

Cara lowered her eyes. "It wouldn't have to be like that."

"It would," I snapped. "You're toying with things you can't even begin to understand. And there are already extremely dangerous, powerful forces trying to convince the rest of my kind that humans should be our servants. Something like this might push vampires to their side who weren't sure yet."

"Sounds like boyfriend having bad day," Anya said, laughing deeply. "If my boyfriend mad like that, I make him happy. You know," she added, twirling her finger as she tried to find the right word. "In pants. I touch his—"

"Thanks, Anya," Cara said. "We're fine, though."

"Can we talk in private?" I asked.

Cara followed me upstairs where we didn't have Anya eavesdropping. "I think you're being selfish. So what if it puts me in danger?"

"What do you mean 'so what'? Bennigan would kill you if he knew you were working on something like this."

"Last time I checked, Bennigan wanted to kill me anyway, right? I might as well try to do something honorable if he's going to want to kill me either way."

I gritted my teeth. "It's not that simple. I can't let you risk it."

"You can't stop me," she said, eyes blazing with defiance. "This is more important than me or you."

"No. It's not. I swore I'd get you through this in one piece. I'm not going to let you risk your life."

"Maybe you forgot what it's like to be human, Lucian." Her tone was harsh, and I immediately felt the sinking sensation of knowing I'd crossed the line. "But humans have to deal with pain, sickness, diseases, and losing the people we love. And we have to know there might eventually be a cure for all those things, but that it didn't come in time to help us. I could change that for all those people with this."

My nostrils flared. "You're not thinking carefully. How will you save anyone if you're dead?"

"That's what my big, selfish bodyguard is good for. Isn't it?"

She gave me a little shove to emphasize her point. I caught her wrist, locking my eyes on hers.

"I need to know you're safe, Cara," I said through clenched teeth.

"And I need to do what is important to me. *This* is what matters most to me, and you can't change my mind about it."

She was breathing heavy and I could see her pulse pounding beneath the warm softness of her neck. Cara was watching me from behind thick eyelashes, her full lips parted slightly. She was so beautiful it hurt.

I was about to say something when the phone she'd given me buzzed in my pocket. I picked it up and saw an image had been texted to me from Alaric. He and Vlad were flashing peace signs with their fingers from what looked like a rooftop view of the building just outside Anya's. Then I noticed a black car parked in front. Bennigan, Jezabel, and Leah were getting out with weapons in their hands.

Shit. I'd gotten complacent. I'd started thinking Bennigan was waiting for me to slip up and leave her alone, but apparently, he was tired of waiting for an opportunity and was hoping to make one.

"We need to go," I said.

"Where?"

"Out, quickly."

I briefly considered trying to hunker down in Anya's basement, but we'd have a better chance on the street than we would trapped inside this house.

"What's happening?" Cara asked.

"Bennigan."

29

CARA

Lucian took me by the hand and pulled me outside into the street. It was dusk, and there was a healthy amount of foot traffic. But when I looked to my left, I saw Bennigan in a heavy-shouldered fur coat that dragged behind him on the pavement and flared out. In the dark, the profile made it look like a high collar and a cape—almost like the picture of a vampire from some old movie in the 1800s. At least if I ignored the gun in his hand. On either side of him, Jezabel and Leah were following with guns in their hands, too.

There were mostly college aged kids out on the street at this hour, and they were used to seeing enough strange things that Bennigan and his women were only drawing an occasional curious glance.

"Can I just say the whole vampire with gun thing is still weird?" I asked as Lucian pulled me in the opposite direction.

"We can talk about it another time."

I flinched when a gunshot rang out like a rogue firecracker. Except it wasn't from behind us. It was from high above and on the other side of the street. I looked up and saw Alaric holding a pistol sideways and firing wildly. If the little puffs of dust exploding from buildings and the glass bursting from cars was any indication, he had inhumanly bad aim.

Next to him, Vlad was holding a crossbow. He aimed, fired, and I heard one of the vampire women call out more in annoyance than pain.

I glanced over my shoulder and saw our pursuers had ducked behind a car and started firing toward the rooftop.

Within seconds, the streets were full of people running in either direction, which thankfully meant Alaric was less likely to take out an innocent bystander with his horrible aim.

We had covered quite a bit of ground when I heard Alaric let out a frustrated grunt. "Fuck. I really liked this shirt, assholes!" His voice was drowned out by a flurry of gunfire.

"Are they going to be okay up there?" I asked once we'd reached the end of the block and turned a corner. I could still hear gunshots in the distance and the wail of approaching police sirens from all directions.

"Yes," Lucian said.

"How can you be so sure? What if those three go up to the rooftop to get them?"

"They won't want to wait around to deal with the police. In small numbers, they could charm them. If they get surrounded in the streets, it would be a much lengthier ordeal to charm their way out of captivity."

"How will Alaric and Vlad get away from the police, though?"

"Vlad… He has a unique talent. They will be fine."

I squinted. "A unique talent? Like what?"

"He can turn into a very large bat."

I stopped, forgetting the gunshots. "You're serious? Vlad can turn into a *bat*?"

"Yes. But don't ever ask him to do it. When he changes back, he's completely nude. He loves to show it off at parties."

"I'm sorry I asked," I said, resuming our half jog away from the carnage. "So what does that mean? Bennigan and his people keep coming after us with guns. I thought all your diplomacy was supposed to be protecting us, or something."

"That hasn't gone as well as I'd hoped. We may end up having to deal with Bennigan more directly to resolve this."

"Directly? Like what, killing him?"

"That's one option on the table."

"You still haven't even told me if it's possible to kill you people."

Lucian's smirk looked like it belonged more in a darkened muscle car parked above the city instead of the aftermath of a firefight. "Keep asking how to kill us, and I'll start wondering if you're a vampire hunter."

"Wait," I said, jogging to catch up with him as he continued walking. "There are really vampire hunters? What about werewolves?"

Lucian's grin told me he wasn't going to answer me and that he was highly entertained to get to leave me hanging. It seemed like deadly gun fights and ricocheting bullets weren't enough to stop him from enjoying a little casual teasing.

Asshole.

30

LUCIAN

Once I got Cara back to my house, I gave her a very thorough look. I ran my hands down her arms and turned her by the shoulders, all while she watched me with a wry, amused smile.

"I'm starting to wonder if you are staging these gunfights for an excuse to feel me up," Cara said.

"I need to make sure you're not hurt."

"The benefit of dealing with humans instead of animals is you can just ask them if they're hurt. Have you tried that?"

I gave her a slight smile. "I considered it but preferred the hands-on approach when it comes to this particular human."

Cara's eyes twinkled with innocent shyness and mingling fire. It was a devastatingly effective combination on my libido, which was pounding in time with my heart.

"I'm sorry I've dragged you into this. It's far too dangerous for a human. And if anything happened to you, I—"

"Hey." Cara put a hand on my arm. The slight contact was making shockwaves of heat roll through my cold body. "You're taking better care of me than anyone ever has. I mean, my roommates are super protective. But this is different. I guess because I feel like you actually *can* keep me safe."

"That's a ringing endorsement for your roommates."

She laughed. "They mean well. But they're basically over-sized puppies. And they are typically trying to protect me from things like walking home at night or dating guys they don't approve of. Nothing serious, I mean."

"Yes, well. I will need these oversized puppies to learn to do a better job of keeping you safe when this is over."

Cara looked sad for a moment, but she recovered quickly. "You think they'll leave me alone when the bond is done?"

"I think this will be over when I find a way to make sure they know you're off limits."

"How will you do that?"

"I haven't decided yet. But death and dismemberment for anyone who dares to touch you is on my list of options."

The door to my house flew open as Alaric and a very naked Vlad came in. Alaric had a wound on his neck that didn't look too serious but appeared otherwise as casual and unconcerned as usual.

Cara threw her hands in front of her face and let out a terrified little scream. "Oh, God," she said, averting her eyes from Vlad. "He's so naked."

"I know," Vlad said, smiling like a pirate. "Impressive, isn't it?"

"So the bat thing is real?" she asked nobody in particular, still turning her head and squeezing her eyes shut.

"Oh," Vlad said deeply in his thick accent. "She wants to see my bat. She can touch, if she wants to see how it feels in her grip."

"Vlad," I warned. "Go find some pants so we don't have to keep looking at your... *bat*."

Vlad waved me off, then clutched his lower back as he walked up the stairs. "Alaric," he said over his shoulder. "You're fucking heavy, man. Next time you want a ride, you are going on a diet. Virgin blood only," he said, wagging a finger and laughing from his belly as he left.

Alaric gave Vlad's hairy ass the middle finger, then looked Cara and I over. "You two appear to be alive."

I nodded. "You as well."

"You're welcome."

"What does Bennigan think he's going to accomplish like this? If he really wanted me dead, he'd stop charging at us with guns in the open. He'd get the supposed army of charmed women in his harem to surround us. Something about these attacks feels wrong, like he's not really trying to accomplish what it looks like he's trying to accomplish."

Cara looked thoughtful. "Maybe he's trying to make it look more like a war and less like an assassination."

"What do you mean?" I asked her.

"You said it's all political with you guys, right? What if he's not really trying to get the revenge he wants on you yet? Maybe the others will just start hearing about all these times you two were fighting and they'll lose track of who was starting it."

Alaric gave Cara an impressed look. "She sounds like she understands this better than I do." He pulled out his phone then took a picture of himself and the wound on his neck.

"What the hell are you doing?" I asked.

"There's this place called Instagram. As soon as I post pictures of myself, swarms of women try to sleep with me. It's wonderful."

"I'm glad you're devoting your full attention to Bennigan and the threat he poses to us."

Alaric shrugged. "You worry too much, Lucian."

"And you don't worry enough." The truth was I might not have cared as much as I did if I hadn't tied Cara up in the mess with us. To a lesser degree, I also cared about keeping Seraphina and Alaric safe. I was the oldest remaining Undergrove as far as I knew, and that put the responsibility of the family on my shoulders.

Cara's stomach rumbled, reminding me once again that humans needed to eat actual food on a regular basis. I'd dragged her straight here and completely forgotten she most likely wanted dinner.

"Let's go get you something to eat."

Cara smiled a little shyly. "Are we going to get shot at if we go outside?"

"No," I said. I paused briefly. "I don't expect we will, at least."

"Good enough. I'm starving."

31

CARA

I woke in the morning and looked to the floor, where I expected to see Lucian in all his hot, ridiculously cliché vampire glory—arms crossed and gorgeous pale face at rest. Except there was just an empty place on the floor. He wasn't even looming in the corner as he liked to do sometimes.

My heart jumped in my chest and I sat up suddenly. "Lucian?" I hissed. "*Lucian! Where are you?*"

I looked around the room and didn't see him anywhere. I didn't even feel the tug I'd become so used to pulling me toward him. He was just gone, and apparently, so was the bond.

We'd both known it was growing weaker for days now. I'd been on my own during the daylight hours and back with him at night. But we hadn't had a real conversation about what would happen when the bond was completely gone.

Except that wasn't entirely true. Lucian had made it clear from the beginning that he was going to do anything to keep me safe. His disappearance meant he thought I was safer with him gone, and I wished he was here so I could tell him what an idiot he was being.

It felt like something deep inside my chest had been scooped out and left hollow. All I could think for those first few seconds was about filling it back up to stop the rushing emptiness from eating me inside out.

I went downstairs, not bothering to tame my hair or change out of my pajamas.

All my roommates were scattered around the kitchen and dining table in various states of morning bleariness like nothing had ever changed. Parker had some website pulled up on his phone that looked like it was made in the early 90s, complete with pictures of UFOs and poorly rendered aliens in the borders.

Mooney had a freshly cut head of hair, a well-put together, trendy outfit on, and a smug expression on his face as he read something on his phone. *Probably a sext.*

Niles was lurking in all his ten foot whatever of lanky, shaved-headed glory as far from the mess on the kitchen counter as he could.

The only one who seemed to notice me was Zack, who had his arms crossed and was watching me from beneath a ridge of curly brown hair. There was an unusually perceptive glint in his eyes. "Missing something? *Or someone?*"

"Have you seen him?" I asked.

My voice garnered the attention of my roommates, which lead to a barrage of accusations—some playful and some serious—about how they hardly saw me anymore and how I was avoiding them.

I knew Zack and Mooney knew the real truth, but Parker and Niles were still out of the loop. It meant I couldn't just blurt out what was wrong, even if I thought Zack and Mooney suspected something from the way they were watching me.

I twirled my hand in the air, hoping some convincing near-truth would pop out of my mouth if I started talking. "It has been a really long time since I liked a guy," I tried. "I just got carried away. We don't need to turn this into an interrogation. All I want to know is if anyone saw Lucian leave?"

"You mean the vampire?" Parker asked. He had half turned in his chair and had one arm thrown over the backrest to go with the crooked, cocky smile on his patchily bearded face.

Niles normally gave Parker's conspiracy theories about as much attention as Zack gave to expiration dates on food. But he was watching me with interest now.

"Am I supposed to even dignify that with a response?" I asked.

Parker scoffed. "Come on, Cara. *Lucifer*? What kind of name is that? Wait, what was his last name again? Bloodsucker? Crossburner?"

"Lucian. His name is Lucian."

"Last name!" Mooney chanted in an exaggerated deep voice.

I wanted to punch him. The asshole *knew* what was going on and he was still trying to make this worse? Although if I wanted to give him the benefit of the doubt, I guessed it would've been weirder if he didn't help antagonize me.

The other guys chimed in, pounding their fists on whatever they could reach like a frat-guy drum beat. "Last name! Last name!"

"Undergrove," I muttered.

All four guys cupped fists in front of their mouths and let out low, immature "oooh" sounds. Suddenly this was a group project, it seemed. Even Zack was joining in, hopefully for the sake of not being suspicious and not just to torment me.

"And the pale skin?" Parker noted. "I've never seen someone that pale. I mean, if you looked like that guy, would you really be avoiding the beach?"

"It sounds like you have a crush," I said, hoping to change the subject. My comment earned three cupped fists and more "oooh"'s.

"Okay," Niles said. "You do have to admit the way he dressed was super weird."

"I helped him pick out those clothes," I said.

The guys all threw their fists up again, bulging their eyes and whooping like I'd just revealed some big secret.

"Oh my God," I groaned. "You are all children. Oversized, ridiculous children."

"And even we can see as clear as day that your boyfriend was a vampire," Parker said. "Let us see your neck."

Mooney discreetly covered his wrist by crossing his arms at that moment.

I took a step back. "My neck is right here, doofus. Look all you want."

Niles approached me and gave me a once over. "Maybe he's got really small teeth."

Another round of whooping laughter and jibes. "Cara's boyfriend had small fangs!"

I rolled my eyes. "If you're all done having fun with this, can someone please just tell me if you saw him or not?"

"Nah," Niles said. "Sorry, Cara. I didn't see anything."

The others, who were still wearing smiles from their last round of immaturity gradually sobered up and shook their heads. "Sorry," Mooney echoed. "Nope."

I left the apartment and ignored the fact that I was going to miss my morning classes. At least I knew I wasn't missing any tests, but I was going to have to beg somebody for their notes in advanced biochem if I would have any hope of keeping up.

I went straight to Lucian's house and knocked. Nobody answered, so I had to charge through the darkened mansion until I found a gloomy, crypt-like room with a single coffin. I rolled my eyes. Were these people serious? They actually slept in coffins?

I kicked open the lid of the coffin, hoping to find Lucian.

Instead, Vlad rose up in the darkness supernaturally, as if a rope attached to his shoulders jerked him up to his feet. He hissed and showed me his fingertips, then relaxed.

"Oh, it's just you," he said. His belly was on display in his rich purple and yellow embroidered coat that was wide open and fluffy dark red pants that didn't exactly match. "Come by for some morning poking?"

"No, Vlad," I said. "Is Lucian here?"

He waved his hand in front of my face, twinkling my fingers. "You don't know anybody named Lucian."

I stared. "Where is he?"

"Where is who?" Vlad asked.

"Lucian!" I shouted. "Where is he?"

"Oh. It didn't work?" He tried the same hand wave again.

I put my fists on my hips. "Vlad. I swear to God. I will fight you."

He raised an eyebrow. "Please, don't tease me, little human. But really, why isn't it working on you? Vlad is the most powerful vampire he knows. This is supposed to work." He tried waving his hand again. "You really don't know anybody named Lucian."

"I really do. Let me see him."

He pursed his lips, then sighed. "Well, Vlad tried. Lucian is trying to extract himself from your life. He thinks he's being noble or some shit. He has also asked Alaric and Seraphine to help keep an eye on you when he can't during the night hours." Vlad checked his hairy wrist, which was not equipped with a watch. "Which means you've still got a few hours before they start spying on you, by Vlad's calculations."

"When did you start talking in third person?"

He waved his hand in front of my face, twinkling his sausage-like fingers. "Vlad has always talked in third person."

"You've always talked in third person," I said, making my voice monotone.

Vlad smiled triumphantly. "Jesus. Vlad was starting to worry he'd lost the touch."

"Where can I find Lucian?"

"You can't. He's going to keep avoiding you until you give up. He thinks he's doing what's best for you."

"Then he's an idiot. I'm an adult, and I deserve to be part of decisions about what is best for me."

Vlad held up his hands. "Vlad just delivers news. He does not cook it. Go complain to the chef."

I sighed and left, having no idea where I was supposed to find Lucian but knowing I needed to try.

Then an idea struck me. It was a stupid idea, but Lucian had done a stupid thing, and repaying him with an act of equal stupidity only seemed fitting. At least that was the line I was planning to use to convince myself to go through with it.

32

LUCIAN

Being away from Cara was harder than it should have been. I'd woken in the night and felt the last of the bond evaporate. She was free of me, and I'd worried I wouldn't have the conviction to do it, but I did. I left immediately, promising I would keep her watched over until I knew for certain that Bennigan wasn't going to try to use her to hurt me.

It was easy to fall into thinking I was keeping her safe by being in the same room, but I knew that was just a lie I was telling for the sake of my own weakness. She'd be no safer that way than if I watched her from a distance. She'd be able to get back to her normal life without me lurking in her shadow, and I'd hopefully be able to go back to focusing on my own preservation. Cara was dangerous for me in more ways than one. With her, I'd been ready to throw myself in harm's way to prevent her from the mere suggestion of danger.

Without her distracting presence, I could start focusing on the bigger picture—on finding a way to re-connect with The Order or maybe even rebuild it from its fragmented state, if necessary.

This was better for both of us.

I'd asked Alaric and Seraphina to help me keep an eye on her when I couldn't. I'd planned to rest during the day but found myself creeping after her all morning as she went to my house from her apartment and then skipped class to go to Anya's. I had suspected she might move off schedule when she found that I wasn't there.

It pained me to see how badly she wanted to find me, especially when she'd told Vlad that she deserved to be part of the conversation about what was best for her. I knew I couldn't have trusted myself to make the choice I needed to make if I was looking into her eyes. I would've stayed.

I'd listened to every word of the conversation from a safe distance, then followed her when she left and went straight to Anya's.

She had been inside Anya's building nearly all day. Despite the sun constantly taking its toll until I felt fatigued and my thoughts grew sluggish, I couldn't make myself leave. She hadn't been truly on her own since I met her, and the idea of just walking away and trusting she would be okay felt unconscionable. Reckless.

Cara was the most important thing in my bleak world, bond or not.

Maybe she couldn't be mine anymore—if she ever had been—but I would at least make sure she was safe. *Happy. Protected.*

A few minutes before sunset, I felt something strange. It was like the bond waking up inside me. There was a slight pull in her direction at first, then it grew stronger until I knew I wasn't imagining it.

What the hell?

I was sitting on the roof across from her building when Seraphina appeared at my side. She was wearing an oddly human assortment of clothes—a black skirt, white t-shirt, and sneakers.

I could still feel the growing sense of bond between Cara and I, but I hoped to distract myself from the confusing question of how that was possible. "Why are you dressed like that?" I asked.

"You told me not to let the girl out of my sight. I thought I might be less suspicious like this if I had to follow her into a building."

"Oh," I said, then I grinned. "The look suits you."

Seraphina stared straight ahead. "Shut up."

There was a clatter of footsteps behind us on the rooftop. I stood, spinning to face the sound.

My stomach sank.

It was a small army of vampires. All female. All beautiful. *Bennigan's charmed army*, I thought.

They were all standing in a row across from us, eyes loaded with hostility. Even more joined them, some climbing up from the wall of the building and others emerging from the staircase. I noticed the Marsh children, the Whites, and several others I'd recently tried to win to our side standing there as well. "What is this?" I asked.

"This is a compromise," Adam Marsh said. "We keep you here while Bennigan takes what he wants."

"You all agreed to this? Don't you have any backbone? Any self-respect?" I asked.

Kira, who was standing just in front of Violet White, shrugged. "I told you where we stood, Lucian. The power is on Bennigan's side. I don't want to cross The Council, so I'm crossing you."

"Wait," I said. "Who is The Council?"

Adam answered. "It was Shadow Force, but they changed their name."

I shook my head. "This 'council' is behind shattering The Order? For what? To pretend none of us ever swore to The Pact?"

Kira stepped closer. "Most of us swore to The Pact because people like you would hunt us down if we didn't, Lucian. Now you're just a memory. A dead man who hasn't gotten around to getting dead yet."

I was also unfortunately severely weakened from so much sunlight. My thoughts were coming sluggishly, and my body felt taxed to its limits already. "Why now?"

"Because someone powerful wanted it this way. I don't know, and I frankly don't care," Kira said. "All I know is we have to keep you here while they take your little human."

I jerked my head down toward Anya's, where I saw Bennigan and his vampiresses kicking in the front door.

Shit, shit, shit. I'd let Kira distract me from watching Anya's and given Bennigan a chance to get to her door while I was still here.

I'd only taken one step toward the ledge of the roof to jump when I heard a rush of approaching feet, some much faster than my sun-weakened efforts.

Countless hands grasped me just as I was leaping away from the roof and yanked me back, slamming me to the ground and pinning me there. To my side, I saw Seraphina biting and scratching, but ultimately being overwhelmed and pushed down as well.

"Let me go!" I roared.

But it was hopeless. Bennigan had made sure he had more than enough help to keep us contained. I strained against the hands holding me, swearing revenge on anyone I could see.

The sound of gunshots rang out and the hands holding me relented.

Alaric was running toward us with a pistol in either hand, shooting wildly. The idiot still hadn't learned to aim, and one of his bullets thudded into my own thigh. I groaned in pain, then rolled off the edge of the building, vaguely hoping the few minutes of starlight had been enough to heal me through the incoming impact.

The wind screamed in my ears and my stomach lurched from the brief fall. I hit the ground hard, bouncing up from the impact and landing a second, much less violent time.

For a few seconds, everything was black, and my body was wracked with pain.

I tried to get up, but muscles and bones weren't working like they should. Every impulse just sent a fresh explosion of white-hot pain through me.

I thought of Cara and how scared she would be to see Bennigan coming for her—how she would be wondering why I abandoned her and let this happen. I gritted my teeth, forcing all the energy I had into my broken body until I could sense the growing pressure moving through me, knitting broken bones and weaving torn muscles back together.

Within moments, I was limping toward Anya's, then walking, then running.

I heard more gunshots from the rooftop above but couldn't afford to stop and worry about them.

Seraphina and Alaric would be okay. This was Bennigan's game. He knew he couldn't actually kill any of us without more justification, but he could hurt me. He could take Cara from me, and all anyone would hear was that he'd toyed with my human. They wouldn't care, and the world would go on.

I wondered if the bastard actually preferred this to killing me. I'd taken his wife, but he was taking the woman I cared about and making me live with the shame of knowing I hadn't been able to stop him. He probably hoped he'd turn her into one of his disgusting little harem, too. It was his gift, after all. He charmed women into following him blindly, vampires and humans alike.

I saw Bennigan shoving Cara into a car while she kicked and screamed for him to let her go. There was a little metallic ping on the ground when the bullet in my leg was forced out by healing flesh.

I broke into a run, wishing I had Alaric's speed, even though I knew he couldn't even keep up with a car. I followed them for a block until I lost sight and had to stop to think of a coherent plan.

I didn't know how, but I was going to find her and get her back.

Then I had stopped long enough to feel the growing sense of separation in my chest—the familiar pulsing throb of the bond.

It was a bond that shouldn't have been possible.

A bond that made no sense and defied all my understanding.

But right now, it was also the bond that was going to lead me straight to Cara, even though Bennigan likely thought I'd have no way to find them.

I'd get Cara back, and this time, I wouldn't leave her side unless Bennigan was in the ground.

33

CARA

I threw my legs and arms out wildly, kicking or punching anything I could reach. My fist found something squishy and earned me a tighter grip from the two women in the back holding me.

Jezabel let out a low, irritated grunt. "Punch my breast again and I'll drain you of every drop of blood in your pathetic little body, human."

They adjusted their grip, twisting my arms and forcing them behind my back so all I could do was sit there and fume. "You kidnapped me," I grunted. "Am I supposed to start writing thank you notes?"

"You're supposed to cooperate if you don't want us to hit you until you stop resisting."

With effort, I managed to stop squirming and trying to break free from the women. I felt myself calm enough to try to take stock of the situation. I could see Bennigan's huge shoulders and shaved head in the driver's seat. An old, dignified looking man in an expensive suit was in the passenger seat, too.

"Who's that?" I asked, nodding my head—which was the only part of my body that wasn't being pinned down by the women on either side of me.

The man turned to look at me. There was a cold depth to his eyes that made me want to flinch back. *Definitely a vampire.*

"I am here to make sure this goes smoothly." He had a faint accent that sounded vaguely European, but I was hardly an expert. His hair was dark with flecks of gray and he wore it pushed back from his forehead. His nose was slightly hooked, and his eyes were hooded and dark.

"*What* goes smoothly?" I asked.

"The pawn doesn't need to know why it's being moved. It only needs to know it has no choice."

I wanted to be defiant and try to dig more information out of the men, but I had a feeling it didn't matter how much I knew. I could gather the obvious, critical clues about my situation easily enough.

They were taking me, and they weren't killing me. They'd already used me as bait once and it worked. They wanted Lucian, and I was their ticket to drawing him in.

I knew I had really gone over the deep end when my first thought was to hope he didn't come. It wasn't that I didn't want to see him again or feel his touch. I didn't trust these vampires not to hurt him—to *kill* him, if that was even possible.

I didn't want to be the weak link that got him hurt, and I also didn't want these cocky, snide assholes to have everything go according to their plan.

But I could feel that same magnetism inside my chest rising up even now. Worse, I thought I could sense Lucian's presence, and unless I was confused, I thought he was following us.

I still couldn't believe I'd been reckless enough to do what I'd done at Anya's. I'd barely had time to let it all register because Bennigan and his people had come bursting in just moments after I discovered what I'd done.

I spent all day spiraling like an addict yanked away from their fix, except my drug had a dimple and fangs. I'd concocted the desperate idea to take some of the little black, spikey Lucios and inject them into my blood. If the bond was just my blood plus those, I reasoned I could re-ignite the bond and draw Lucian back to myself if I re-introduced them

Except there had been one problem. The only way to keep the Lucios in my samples from decaying just like the ones in my blood had been to regularly introduce new blood. The little black balls would absorb the red blood cells of the newly introduced blood and start multiplying until they'd absorbed all the cells from the new sample.

It was fascinating, and it meant I'd been able to keep my stores stocked with plenty of Lucios.

And *that* was what I'd injected into myself just minutes before Bennigan kicked in the door at Anya's to take me. I knew it was reckless, and I knew there was a very real possibility I could've introduced diseases into my own blood or any number of other risks. I also knew I didn't care. I just wanted him back. I wanted one last chance to convince him we were better off together, danger or no danger.

But there was another strange feeling beneath the tug of the bond. Something new.

I couldn't put my finger on what it was, exactly, so all I could do was sit and wait while we drove in silence.

Eventually, Bennigan pulled the car up to a shipping yard full of shipping containers.

"What are we doing here?" I asked.

"Shut up, human," Jezabel said.

"She doesn't smell right," Leah noted. Her poreless model's nose twitched as she leaned in toward me.

"Sorry," I said. "Getting kidnapped may have made me sweat past my deodorant's capabilities."

"No," she said, nose still twitching. "Why does she smell like a vampire?"

Oh no. Why do I smell like a vampire?

Bennigan turned in his seat, face a mask of annoyance. "You're losing your touch, Leah. Lucian never turned her." A slow, lecherous grin spread on Bennigan's face. "But we'll fix that, won't we, darling?" He reached for my face and I bit his finger before he could touch my cheek.

He pulled his hand back, eyes curious. He looked like he was trying to solve a mystery instead of being mad that I'd bit him. I noticed both women and the man were looking strangely at me too, but I didn't think it was just because I'd tried to fight back.

Within moments, the car was stopped outside a rusty blue shipping container. Jezabel pulled me out, hugging me tight against her muscular body as she yanked me from the car. Just for the sake of being difficult, I flailed around a little to make her life more difficult. I even let out a few ear-piercing shrieks. All it earned me was a knee in the back of the ribs, which stopped my resistance.

They took me inside the container and sat me in a chair, which they tied me to.

"Really?" I asked. "Tying me to a chair? You're sure you guys can't just tell me the plan at this point? Is it going to even make a difference if I know?"

The old mysterious man made a dismissive sound between a snort and a laugh. "You are the method of our revenge, little human. That's all you need to know. Now be a good girl and stay put until we need you."

They yanked the heavy metal doors of the container closed and left me in complete darkness.

It took about one minute of total darkness to reconsider my thought from before about hoping Lucian wouldn't come for me.

Maybe part of me hoped he would find some way to come, as long as it didn't involve getting himself hurt or killed. If nothing else, I wanted a chance to say goodbye—the chance his stubborn ass had robbed me of when he decided to slip out of my life in the middle of the night.

Come on, Lucian. Come save me. Just don't do anything crazy like showing up by yourself.

34

LUCIAN

There was no time to wait for the others.

I could feel Cara through the bond, and I could sense how afraid she was. She needed me, and I needed to do whatever I could to save her now. Not later.

I wished I hadn't spent all day letting the sunlight sap my strength. Even after close to an hour of starlight, I still felt weak and drained.

I managed to borrow a car from a screaming woman shortly after Bennigan drove off with Cara. I'd told her I would probably bring it back, but she'd still screamed and sprayed me with some sort of liquid that had smelled horrible.

I knew I was close when I arrived at a sort of shipping yard. There were huge rectangular boxes in various colors stacked across the huge concrete space. I couldn't see any sign of activity, but my sense of Cara's location was clear as day.

The phone she'd given me vibrated in my pocket. I pulled it free, then answered.

"Who is this?"

Bennigan's laugh came from the other side. "I didn't quite believe they'd taught you how to use a cell phone. I guess it's true."

"Give her to me now and I'll consider showing you mercy."

"You're sure you wouldn't rather let me handle her? She seems too feisty for you, Lucian."

I gripped the phone tighter at the thought of him going anywhere near Cara. *My Cara.* "If you touch her..."

Bennigan laughed. "I plan to. And once I've had a little time, she'll be begging to touch *me*. Do you know how video texts work? I'll make sure to send you one."

"Give her back and I'll consider letting you live."

"No. I think I'd rather let you watch me take the human for myself. She was stubborn, but my charm worked on her just like all the others. She has been begging me to let her at my cock, and I think if you keep irritating me, I may give her what she wants soon."

I clenched my teeth. I knew he was lying—just trying to push my buttons. Maybe it was because I knew the bond should've protected Cara from the worst of his abilities. But Bennigan was strong enough to charm other vampires, which meant she wouldn't be immune forever. "What do you want from me?"

"Nothing, Lucian. That's the best part. There is absolutely nothing you can offer me. This isn't a negotiation. I just want to see your misery. I want you to feel a fraction of what I felt when you took Emily away from me."

"Emily took herself away from you when she—"

"*Don't speak her name,*" he hissed.

I gripped the phone until I could feel the fragile machinery threatening to break between my fingers. "Give me Cara. This is your last chance."

"Or what? You'll *make* me? Please, Lucian. *Please try.* I would love nothing more than being able to look the others in the face and telling them you gave me no choice. That the only thing I could do was remove your pretty little head from your body."

I bared my teeth, even though I knew he couldn't see me. "You can try." I turned off the call.

I walked forward, trying to head toward the source of the pull in my chest. Toward Cara.

I'd left her on her own, and now she was paying for my mistake. I'd told myself she would be better without me in her life, but I'd been a fool to think I could keep her safe from a distance. Hell, I'd been a fool to think I could handle the constant ache of being away from her, with or without the bond. It had only taken minutes before I'd longed to see her again.

I knew there was no future for us, but I was going to get her back. I'd keep her safe. And this time, I'd take as much time as I could possibly get with her. I'd let *her* decide when it was time to part ways, because I knew I couldn't willingly walk away from her again.

I'm coming, Cara.

35

CARA

I couldn't see a thing.

The darkness seemed to make the first sound of struggle feel amplified. There was grunting, shouting, the scuffing of feet, then several gunshots.

My heart was pounding as I imagined what was coming for me. I pictured the old man with the dead eyes deciding he wanted to torture me for fun, or Bennigan letting Jezabel have me to do with as she pleased.

There was shouting, muffled thuds like someone getting punched.

Laughter.

Scraping like feet being dragged across gravel that was getting closer.

Then the doors of the container were yanked open. Bennigan and Jezabel were dragging Lucian between them. He was covered in blood and I could see at least three obvious bullet wounds.

Lucian.

Despite what should have been mortal wounds, the man actually shot me a roguish grin as they dragged him and a chair to sit beside me.

"Looks like he was dumber than I anticipated." Bennigan said to me with a crooked grin. "Came alone and unarmed."

"You should see the other guys," Lucian muttered.

"What are you doing?" I asked.

"Coming for you."

"Yeah," I hissed. "You clearly accomplished that. Did you think it might be a good idea to figure out how you were going to leave with me, too?"

"Didn't get that far," he admitted.

"We'll be back shortly," Bennigan said. "There's one small matter to tend to before I can have my fun with you two."

I had a second to see Lucian's pale, blood-streaked skin glimmer in the moonlight just before they closed the doors again and left us in darkness.

"I wasn't sure if you'd come," I admitted. It was probably stupid and definitely sentimental, but I felt like I could face whatever was coming for us now that we were together. I hated that I was selfish enough to be glad he was here with me, but I was.

"I shouldn't have left in the first place," Lucian said.

"Yeah. I had an entire angry speech planned to give you about that. But I'll save it for when we get out of here."

"You have a plan for that?"

"No," I said. "I was hoping you did and just weren't going to say it in front of them."

He lowered his voice. "I did text Alaric, Vlad, and Seraphina. But the last time I saw them, they were in a gunfight on the rooftop outside Anya's."

"How would they even find us?"

"Vlad may not look it, but he's immensely powerful. He could follow our scent if he was properly motivated."

"Properly motivated? He needs more motivation than knowing we're both going to get chopped up by maniacs?"

"I may have promised I'd let him re-open his torture room if he got us out of this. But I didn't say for how long."

I stared into the darkness. "He really tortures people?"

"He doesn't usually kill them," Lucian said with a touch of uncertainty.

"We'll talk about that later. If there is a later."

"Do I want to know why I'm sensing the bond again?" Lucian asked after a few seconds of silence.

"About that... I may have taken some drastic measures when you disappeared. Like injecting some of those little Lucios back into my blood."

I could feel his disapproval radiating through the darkness. "That was reckless."

"And you left me without even saying goodbye."

Another pause. "That was a mistake I won't repeat."

"No," I said. "You won't. Also," I added with a little less confidence. "Leah said I smelled like a vampire. What does that mean, exactly?"

I heard Lucian sniff deeply. He didn't speak right away. "Did you alter the blood you injected into yourself?"

"Sort of. I mean, I spun it down and extracted pretty much just the little vampire balls. But they kept dying and I figured out the only way to keep them alive and reproducing was to inject new blood into the sample."

"You mean you vampirized blood and then injected it into yourself."

I narrowed my eyes, turning that concept over. "You know, when you phrase it like that, it makes it sound like the consequences would be super obvious. But it didn't feel that way at the time."

"Cara..."

My stomach was doing all sorts of summersaults. Little by little, the glowing neon signs that I had inadvertently turned myself into some sort of vampire were becoming impossible to ignore. "I thought you said it would have to be you feeding on my blood to seal the bond? I just used random samples of blood."

"That shouldn't have caused you to turn, no," he said. "A bonded human could drink as much blood as they wanted with no consequence."

"Maybe it's different when it's all done in test tubes? I also added a few random chemicals here and there to try to help keep the Lucios from dying so quickly."

"You are a very determined woman, aren't you?" he asked. I wasn't sure if he was impressed, annoyed, scared, or all three.

"You didn't even let me say goodbye."

"And that was a grave mistake. So was underestimating your determination to make me regret it."

I grinned in the darkness. "Well, at least if we die gruesome deaths, we learned a little about each other in the process. But seriously, what are we going to do? Those psychopaths want to torture us, and now you're trapped in here with me."

"I'm not trapped," Lucian said. "I can get out of these chains."

"With super strength?" I asked.

"No. Vlad isn't the only one who can transform himself."

I waited. "You were serious about the bat thing?"

"Yes. But if you speak of this, I will deny it to anyone."

I smiled. "Why, is it like a taboo to be able to turn into a bat in the vampire world?"

"Because the less my enemies know about what I can do, the more likely I am to catch them by surprise. Also, because my bat form is very small, but that has no bearing on the size of my manhood, despite some silly sayings among my kind. *Just a moment.*"

For a few seconds, I heard nothing. Then I felt a subtle shockwave in the air that made the hairs on my arms stand on end. The sound of chains clinking to the ground followed, along with a high-pitched chirp. Then I heard two heavy feet land on the ground beside me, shaking the container.

"Uh," I said, still not sure I trusted the story my ears had just told me. "Are you still bleeding from multiple gunshot wounds?"

"Yes," Lucian said. "I'm also completely naked. Please try not to stare when we open the doors."

I laughed. "Wait, if you turn into a small bat, what happens to your clothes? Shouldn't they be on the ground? And why did you make a bat noise when you turned? Did you try to say something?"

"I didn't make the rules, Cara. They just vanish. It's terribly inconvenient. And yes, I said 'fuck,' because the transformation hurts."

Lucian had just got me free of my chains when there was a deep screech from above us. Gunshots rang out along with the sound of bullets pinging off heavy metal containers. Raised voices shouted to look up or to get down. Someone started shooting and little circular holes of light burst through the wall of our container. Lucian covered me with his body, which I was confusingly aroused to find *was* naked. He crouched down, wrapping his arms around me.

"If that's you, Alaric," Lucian shouted, trying to be heard over the chaos outside. "You're about to shoot the people you're trying to save."

"Oh," Alaric called from outside the container. He yanked the doors open. "My fault. Was trying to shoot the bad guys."

The sound of screams and gunshots was still raging in the distance, but Alaric was staring at us with his head tilted to the side. "Uh," he said. "You didn't think it would make more sense to get her out of here before you got naked? Where are your clothes, anyway?"

"I didn't bring them," Lucian said curtly. He stood, taking my hand and leading me at his side.

I tried to be a gentlewoman and control my eyes, but I figured there was a fifty percent chance I was going to get killed by a stray bullet any minute. So I stole several girthy glances at Lucian, who was completely pulling off the naked with confidence thing. I'd already confirmed as much when I put it in my mouth, but I was reminded that he definitely wasn't lying. If vampires thought a small bat form meant a small penis, they clearly hadn't seen Lucian.

"What's the plan?" I whispered.

There was an ear-piercing, heavily accented screech in the distance. The sound was followed by a few gunshots, then exclamations about how hairy and naked whatever they were apparently shooting at was.

"We run," Lucian said.

I followed after him and Alaric, who were hunched over and rushing through the crates. Lucian ended up scooping me in his arms and carrying me with him. Over his shoulder, I saw lightning-like flashes of light as more gunshots rang out and pinged off the containers. There was an occasional shout, sometimes a thump, and always more gunshots.

"How many people came with you?" I asked Alaric. "it sounds like a warzone over there."

"Just Vlad," Alaric said. "Seraphina was busy."

"Vlad is by himself? There were four of the bad guys!" I hissed.

"Four?" Lucian asked. "Bennigan, Jezabel, Leah, and who else?"

"Some old guy with dead eyes. He seemed like he was the boss of Bennigan or something."

Alaric and Lucian shared a look as we made our way past the perimeter of the shipping yard.

"What?" I asked, jumping into the car Lucian must've driven and buckling myself in the backseat. "What does that look mean?"

"Nothing," Lucian said.

"Shouldn't you two get guns and go back in a blaze of glory to save Vlad, or something?"

Alaric got in the passenger seat and looked back at me while Lucian turned the engine over and started to drive. "You've got to understand this whole gunfighting thing for vampires doesn't carry the same weight it would for a human. We shoot each other, we bleed a little, it hurts, boo hoo. It's really more about the emotional message."

I narrowed my eyes. "You shoot each other with guns to send emotional messages?"

Alaric nodded. "Exactly. It's pretty brutal work to actually kill one of us. Not something you're likely to do by accident. So the whole gun part is like… Foreplay."

"I see," I said slowly. "I don't think I understand, but I see."

"Hey," Alaric said, looking over toward Lucian. "Were you planning to just keep being naked, or did you want me to see if there's something in here we can use to cover your cock with? I feel like it's trying to make eye contact with me and I'm being rude by not returning the favor."

"If you're having trouble keeping your eyes off it, it's not my problem," Lucian said dryly.

Alaric looked at me. "You know, that's the first time I've caught Lucian completely nude with someone before. He must really like you."

"Alaric," Lucian said. "As much as I appreciate the daring rescue, I need you to stop talking."

I turned to look behind the car toward the docks. I could still see brief flashes of light illuminating the containers sporadically. I could hear what now sounded like pops from distant fireworks. And...

I squinted.

I thought I saw a huge black shape rise above the containers and swoop back down again. I shook my head. *Nope. Did not just see that.*

Except the only thing I had to look at when I peeled my eyes from the gunfight was Lucian as he sat completely naked in the driver's seat of the car. The only slight mercy was that the center console was keeping me from having a full view of *everything*. But I could see enough to learn that my body clearly didn't care if it was in danger of being torn to shreds—hot naked guy was still hot naked guy, and all the proper internal alarms and procedures had been activated.

We had only driven a couple minutes when Lucian brought the car to a stop and nakedly got out to check the trunk for spare clothes. Alaric said something about going to make sure Vlad was okay, then sprinted off with his eye-defying vampire speed.

When Lucian came back in the car, I had trouble not laughing at what he was wearing. He had on some sort of faded polo with a company logo on the chest and slacks that were several sizes too small. Because of his freakish good looks, he managed to make mismatched, dated clothes look like a bold fashion-forward statement, though.

"Nice," I said. "I think those are women's pants."

"Not anymore."

He turned the car on and started driving.

"Aren't we waiting for Alaric?"

"He'll be fine. We need to find a place to lay low for a little while, and then we can decide what to do next."

Lucian's "place to lay low" ended up being a bridge overlooking the river. He pulled the car down a gravely incline off the road and brought it to rest beside the bridge. We both got out and I took in the view of the inky water reflecting the stars overhead. The night looked cold, but I was surprised to notice that I didn't feel it at all.

Once we were both out of the car, Lucian began running his hands up and down my arms, then kneeling to check my legs.

I smiled down at him. "This is the third time you've frisked me, you know."

"I'm aware," he said. "And I would appreciate if you stopped getting involved in gunfights so I could stop checking you for bullet holes."

"If gunfights mean you'll keep putting your hands on me, I may make a habit of getting into them."

He straightened, hands still wrapped around my waist. He tugged me a little closer until our bodies collided—my head only reaching to his chest. He hugged me then, holding me tight and rubbing my hair with one hand.

It was tender, and I closed my eyes, leaning into it.

"I was worried," he said, voice rumbling from his chest straight into my ear.

"I was, too. I thought maybe you would do something crazy like coming by yourself to rescue me and getting yourself caught in the process."

Lucian chuckled. "It wasn't my finest moment of planning. But I've got you back."

"Until the next time you disappear on me, at least," I said.

He cupped my face, pulling me back so he could lean down and look into my eyes. His gaze was like the blackness of the sky, vast and magnetic, full of the promise of an endless eternity. "I will always protect you."

"I don't just want your protection, Lucian. I want *you*. I want you to realize it's more important for us to be together than it is for me to be safe."

"I won't sacrifice you."

"It's not your choice." I punched my fist against his chest, frustration boiling over. "*I* decided to love you. Okay? That was my stupid decision. But it's too late to hope I'll change my mind, because I'm stubborn as hell and I'm not going to. Do you get that? I love you and your stupid fangs. I love you and your obnoxious but adorable quirks. And even when you're trying your hardest to push me away, I still love you enough that I don't care what happens, as long as we're together."

Lucian's nostrils flared and his eyes fell. He looked back at me and started to lean in for a kiss.

I put my fingers on his lips, shaking my head. "No. Nope. You do not get to just kiss your way out of telling me how you feel. Because I can already see it. You're thinking whatever you're thinking but knowing that you'll still try to get out of my life at the first opportunity because it's what's best for me."

His smile was slow and reluctant. "Maybe you really have begun turning into a vampire. Because you may have read my mind."

"It's not hard to predict stupid."

Lucian let out a surprised laugh, then his expression sobered. "I learned a long time ago not to love. The more my kind care, the deeper the eventual scars run. The more we love, the more we grieve."

"Then you really are dead. If you're too scared to love because you don't want it to hurt, then you're not living. You're just existing. I don't care if I am turning into a vampire or if Bennigan shows up in an hour and kills us both. I'm going to *live*. And that means loving you, whether you like it or not."

He didn't answer at first, but his fingertips ran a goose-bump inducing path down my cheek and neck. He looked lost in thought before he finally spoke. "I care more about you than I am willing to accept. Enough that it frightens me. Enough that I don't know what limits I wouldn't push past or what barriers I wouldn't break. You've become my everything, and the thought of someone taking you away or hurting you is too much to bear."

"Then let me promise you something. If you *ever* think about disappearing on me again or doing the honorable thing and leaving, I will recklessly come looking for you. I'll turn over every rock and ask every vampire where you are until I'm in so much more danger because you left than I ever would've been if you stayed."

He searched my eyes, then a half smile formed on his lips. "You mean every word of that, don't you?"

"All you have to do is look at what happened the first time you tried leaving. I went and turned myself into a vampire and got kidnapped within twenty-four hours. Imagine if you try it again."

Lucian nodded, smiling. "Then I have no choice. I do love you, Cara. More than I can understand. And it seems as though you've checkmated me."

I chewed my lip. "You promise to stop trying to run away from me?"

"I promise to stay right here. Loving you. Protecting you. For as long as we have."

"That's the sweetest thing a guy wearing women's pants has ever told me."

Lucian smirked, then hiked up his tight-fitting pants. "Maybe we'd both be more comfortable if I took these off."

I arched an eyebrow. "The backseat of that car was pretty spacious."

"I also noticed that."

36

LUCIAN

I kissed Cara, backing her toward the car as I awkwardly tried to free myself of the ill-fitting clothes. As much as her physical presence was all-consuming, I still felt the rush of excitement from our conversation—from telling her the truth and feeling her rip away my last thread of resistance.

She was right.

The only way to keep her safe was to stay.

She *would* put herself in more danger if I tried to do the honorable thing and leave.

It meant there were no more barriers. No more reasons I couldn't be with her in every way. And there was no denying what had happened to her. She may not be ready to hear it yet, but I could smell it on her and sense it through the bond, which had begun transforming, just like she had.

Cara was already one of my kind.

I lifted her shirt over her head, then pushed her into the backseat of the car because nobody but me got to lay eyes on her body. I was relatively sure we were alone, but I wasn't taking any chances.

I tugged the door shut behind me, then finished undressing her and peeling off her small blue panties and red bra.

"I would've made sure they matched if I knew we were gonna fang," she said.

I laughed. "Please don't call it fanging."

"Oh, it's done and decided. Vampire sex will henceforth be known as fanging. All applicable euphemisms of the word 'fang' will be used with extreme prejudice."

I stripped out of my shirt, deciding we could argue about the minor details later. Cara Skies was completely naked, lying on her back, and waiting. Those horrible clothes were removed from myself, and there finally wasn't a single thing standing between us from doing exactly what we'd been wanting to do since our first day together.

I hooked my arms underneath her knees and tugged her toward me, making her lay completely flat on the backseat. There wasn't limitless room to work with, which meant I was bending my neck and positioned on one knee while she had to keep her legs bent. But complaining would've made as much sense as a starving man saying there wasn't enough salt on his steak.

I lifted Cara's leg, kissing from her ankle up to her sensitive inner thighs, which drew blushing giggles from her.

I kissed everywhere, feeling myself slip into what felt like an automatic state of consciousness. I'd deprived myself of her for so long that I no longer felt in control. She was here, and I was going to take every inch of her.

I buried my face between her legs, kissing and teasing moans from her with my tongue. I greedily explored her body with my hands while I worked, eventually sliding fingers inside her tight entrance.

But Cara started tugging me up by the shoulders before long. "I want you inside me," she breathed. "Please."

I'd planned to plant a kiss on every part of her body—to savor these moments like they could be our last. But there was a desperate sort of need in her eyes that was both impossible to ignore and agonizingly sexy.

I pushed one of her legs open wider and positioned myself above her, lowering my mouth to hers to steal a few kisses while I used my hips to slide my length between her legs. I didn't try to press it inside her at first, enjoying the anticipation of feeling her radiating heat and slick skin against mine.

She rocked her hips upward, gasping into my mouth. Cara slid her hands down my back, fingernails digging into skin until she found my ass and squeezed, pulling me in closer.

All I could think about was how long it had been.

How long since I'd felt anything close to contentment. Happiness. Satisfaction.

They had begun to seem like imaginary things I'd created from my imagination—dream-like figments of a life that was as old as ash.

But I felt it all booming through me with enough force to make my breaths shallow and my head feel light.

I was happy.

Centuries ago, Dominic Undergrove had taken the joy of sunlight from my life. Even now, I could experience the sun, but not without the constant, fatiguing reminder that it was no longer for me. None of it was. I was resigned to the shadows and to a second, lesser life.

Except Cara had given me back the light.

She *was* my light.

37

CARA

Lucian was huge in the cramped backseat of the car. My field of view was dominated by chiseled arms planted on either side of me, his broad shoulders flexing with the effort of holding up his large frame, and a rack of abs that disappeared into the shadow between our bodies.

His eyes were locked on me when I gripped his firm ass with both hands. It drew the faintest of smirks from him.

I pulled him toward me and felt his cock—which he'd been teasing me with—find my entrance and slide in.

I gasped. I'd been watching everything, transfixed, but the feeling of him inside me made me press my head back into the seat and squeeze my eyes shut. I could hear his breathing above me, slow, steady, but growing more rapid.

He eased himself into me like he was worried he might break me. I could imagine what he would be thinking right now. *I must not impale the tiny human with my huge, supernatural cock. She will only be able to handle a little at a time.*

I gripped his ass again and jerked him toward me, forcing his cock to bury itself in me until there was nothing left.

My eyes flashed open and my mouth gaped.

Lucian let out a surprised moan in my ear, then lowered his chest over me and started doing his work. He moved so smoothly it didn't seem real, like his hips were perfectly oiled machines made for this purpose.

It was only seconds before I wasn't able to hold in the sounds escaping my mouth.

And then the strangest thing happened.

The bond always felt a little like being half of a pair of magnets. All it wanted was for us to get close enough to click together—to be joined. That feeling within me started to ramp up in intensity until something inside my head *did* click.

In a confusing blur of sensations, I felt myself plunging into something warm, wet, and perfectly tight. But at the same time, I felt his velvety length pressing against my walls, stretching me and filling me to the brim.

I felt the softness of a breast and a hardened nipple against my calloused palm as well as the broad rippled of muscle across his back that my hand was sliding across.

I felt *everything*.

I felt what he was feeling and what I was feeling.

The realization only had about a second to settle in before the most explosive orgasm of my life burst from the depths of my soul, setting my whole body to shaking. I hugged my arms around his back like I had to hang on to keep from being swept away by its force. At the same time, I felt a blissful release and the sense of something pulsing between my legs. I felt each throb of his cock at the same time I felt his ejaculation land warm and wet across my stomach and breasts.

I blinked rapidly, still riding out the last of the mind-numbing orgasm as the dual sensations started to fade. Little by little, I was just me again, and I could more clearly tell what the hell was going on.

Lucian was on his knees and he just came all over me.

I had been holding my head up to look at him, but I let it flop back down. "What the hell was that?" I asked.

"It's semen. If I release it inside your pussy, there's a chance it will create a vampire baby."

I lifted my head again to make sure he could see me rolling my eyes. "I mean the other thing."

He grinned knowingly. "That's the nature of the bond. What we did seals the connection. It's a sort of sharing of sensation, but it won't usually be perceptible unless we're sleeping together."

I shook my head. "That was weird, but amazing."

He found a towel and carefully cleaned me up. I enjoyed the silent minute or two of his care almost as much as I'd just enjoyed my first experience with supernatural sex. He ran the cloth across me carefully, rubbing the spot with his fingers when he was done as if making sure he'd got me completely clean. Although the amount of time he spent on my breasts made me suspect this little ritual wasn't purely for my sake.

I grinned sleepily. "That feels good."

"You're magnificent," he said quietly. "I've lived a very long time, and no woman has ever captivated me like you do."

"You're just saying that because you were inside my pussy." I paused, then felt my smile widen. "In more ways than one."

Lucian chuckled. "I'm saying that because you've given me something I thought I would never have again. I won't lie. I still feel conflict over the choice to put you in danger by staying. But selfishly, I'm glad you've taken away the choice from me. I want this. I don't know how I would've gone on watching you grow apart from me."

"You don't need to know," I said, reaching up and pulling him in for a kiss. "Because I'm not going anywhere. Unless you make me. And I'm a vampire now, right? So that means I won't be as easy to get rid of. I'll bite you or something."

"I suppose you are. Especially now that we've done what we just did."

"Yeah," I said, play biting his chin. "So don't cross me."

"I wouldn't dare."

I think we both knew danger was still out there—still planning to come for us before we could really rest—but neither of us seemed to want to be the first to move.

I dozed off with his naked body on top of mine, relishing the comfort of his weight on top of me and his breath against my neck.

When I woke, he was dressed again and my clothes were laid over me to keep me covered, but my stomach was cramping angrily. "Uh," I said, trying to make sence of my surroundings. It was still dark, but I sensed that some time had passed, and Lucian was sitting up like he was keeping watch. "I think I'm hungry." My stomach let out another low, keening groan. "I'm really hungry."

Lucian nodded. "You may need human food, or…"

"Let's test the human food theory first."

He got out of the car and slid into the driver's seat. "Is there any place you like that's open this late?"

38

LUCIAN

We were in a horrible, mustard colored diner with depressed employees wearing ridiculous uniforms. They had on white, crinkly paper hats and frocks. A sweaty man with as much knuckle hair as Vlad was pushing eggs around on a cooktop and occasionally mopping his forehead with the back of his hand.

"You're sure this is where you want to eat?" I asked Cara as we were led to a table and sat down.

"Where'd you find this absolute *snack*, girl?" Our waitress asked as she sway-walked us to our table. She looked like she was in her mid-forties and was the proud owner of a literal tower of tightly curled red hair. She ran her eyes up and down me as she abused a piece of gum, rolling it between yellowing teeth and cherry-red lips.

"Huh?" Cara said.

The waitress poked me. "He's yummy. Y'all ever swing? 'Cause I got this guy I kind of hook up with named Clint. I'd share if you will. He's got a prosthetic leg, but what he lacks in the leg department he makes up for in the—"

"What?" Cara said. "No." She hesitated, then shook her head more firmly. "*No*. We're just here for food."

The waitress gave me one last lingering look, then sighed. "I gotta grab a smoke. I'll be back in ten." Without waiting for a response, the woman huffed off.

"There aren't many places open this late. It's like three in the morning," Cara said. "Besides, waffles and pancakes sound perfect right now."

She lifted the menu and started scanning it. I'd hardly been away from her, but I was struck by how much I'd missed her. I'd missed those thick eyelashes and the delicately curved nose. I missed the big eyes and her tendency to flash shy half smiles, as if she was never quite sure if it was okay to be amused.

I found myself marveling as I watched her drag her short finger down the menu, chewing her lip in thought. She'd occasionally stop on an item, roll her head from side to side as she debated, and then move on. By the time she was done, she had several fingers splayed out as if holding all the items she was considering for one last final review.

Cara was an injection of color. *Of life.* She was a constant, mostly painful reminder to me of what I'd left behind. Cara was so full of life and energy that I couldn't help being taken back to those days when I was a young man with no idea what the future held for me.

Letting her go had been like getting turned all over again. Now that I had her back, I couldn't quite believe I'd done what I did. I left her. I walked away from the most perfect thing I'd ever been given in my miserable life. All I could do was be glad she was so magnificently stubborn and refused to be walked away from.

"What?" she asked, tucking some of her silky black hair behind her ear. They were slightly big ears, which I found I enjoyed. She was showing that half smile of hers as her eyes self-consciously darted from the menu to me and back again.

"I was just thinking how glad I am that you're obstinate and stubborn."

She squinted. "That doesn't sound like a good thing."

"You're strong. And we'll need that strength to make it through what's coming."

Cara smiled a little. "You really think they'll still keep trying?"

"Yes. And we'll likely have to fight them off again. But I think the time for half-measures is done. This may only end if Bennigan does."

"I mean, if we're being technical here... You haven't really fought at all. It's more like you valiantly run away with me in your arms while Vlad and Alaric do the dirty work. Not that I'm complaining, of course. You still get macho points for charging in by yourself like an idiot tonight."

"Bennigan is still alive because I didn't want to start an all-out war. Killing him might. But I'm not even sure if there's enough of The Order left to wage war against. The truth may be it's only us at risk. Bennigan wants us dead if we run, and he'll want us dead if we fight. So we might as well fight."

"What if we just left the country? I'm not sure I'm actually ready for that, but I mean... Is there some kind of vampire trick he'd use to find us?"

"He'll have connections. Bennigan is old, and he has many friends. The only thing working in our favor is that he is the only one with a personal grudge against us. If we removed him from the equation, his allies might not care enough to pursue the grudge."

Cara let out a long sigh, then looked back at the menu. "Well, all this talk of killing evil vampires is reminding me how hungry I am. Where is that stupid waitress?"

"Do you think you could fix this? Using your knowledge of blood," I added. "Maybe there would be a way you could find a way to stop the transformation, or even reverse it."

"You think you can *fix* making yourself a vampire?"

"I don't know," I said. "But you know so much about blood. Maybe you could find a way."

She looked thoughtful. "There was this one sample of blood that kept reacting strange with the black spikey things in my blood. It was like they didn't go anywhere, but it kind of made them seem to go dormant."

"Meaning?"

She shrugged. "Meaning I want to eat some pancakes, and then I'll think more about it." Cara gave me an adorable wink, then got up from the table with the menu in her hand.

When the waitress finally brought her food out, Cara started to eat. A few bites in, she started chewing more slowly and got a worried look in her eyes. "Lucian," she said, mouth full.

"What is it?"

"This doesn't taste right."

I glanced at the hairy, sweaty man who was cooking everything. "I'm not surprised. This place is a cesspool."

"No, like—" She put her fist over her mouth. "Just a sec." Cara rushed over to the nearest trash can and violently threw up, drawing disgusted looks from nearby tables. "I'm still starving," she said, sinking back into her seat. She looked pale and sweaty.

"I feared this would happen. Then you're already craving blood. You won't be able to keep down human food until you get some fresh blood in your system."

She shook her head, laughing. "Lucian. I am *not* going to go bite somebody. I mean, do you guys have like teeth condoms or something? What if I get a disease?"

"We don't get diseases."

We.

I tried to keep my expression neutral because I didn't want to scare her, but my heart was thudding in my chest. I hadn't had enough time to fully grasp the gravity of what had happened.

Cara was becoming a vampire.

I'd known it as soon as I caught her scent, but that knowing hadn't come all at once. It came as little pieces I wasn't ready to put together—pieces I'd deliberately kept apart until the number grew so overwhelming that it all clicked into a crystal-clear image.

But maybe she *could* fix it. I decided to cling to that instead of facing the other option. I could still have her if she was human. I could watch her grow old and die happy, never having to know what it meant to live an eternity in the dark with me.

"Come on," I said.

We got up just as Vlad and Alaric burst through the door. Unfortunately. Vlad was once again naked. He was also spattered with blood—some of which appeared to be his own. He roared like an ancient king coming to the feast hall after a battle.

"Where's my fookin' apple juice, wench!" he demanded, laughing deeply at himself as he waddled toward the counter and took a cup from a startled looking homeless man. Vlad drained the cup, swished it around his mouth, then spit it violently all over the floor. "Gah! Delicious."

"Sir, you can't be naked in here. You have to at least wear pants." The woman speaking looked like she was only halfway sure she wanted to confront Vlad. She was behind the counter with her head slightly ducked and her shoulders slouched.

"Aye? Well bring me some fookin' britches then!"

Vlad had a tendency to switch his accents depending on his mood. Given how long he'd lived, I suspected he was calling up previous lives he'd lived when he did. Either that, or he'd lost his mind long ago. I supposed both were just as likely, or maybe no different.

I pulled Alaric aside while Vlad caused terror and began talking a homeless man out of his jacket. Vlad stuck his meaty legs through the arm holes and zipped the whole thing on upside down so his belly bulged over the top of it. Thankfully, his hairy ass was now hidden from view. This apparently brought the sight of him down to a level the establishment was equipped to handle, because everybody resumed business as usual once Vlad's cock and ass were put away.

"Did he kill anyone?" I asked Alaric.

"No, but he bit off one of Leah's arms," he said with a wicked smile.

"When he was a bat?" I asked.

"No. Just naked Vlad, apparently."

Cara looked like she wanted to ask several questions, but she stayed quiet. I imagined she had plenty on her mind at the moment without trying to visualize what Alaric was describing better.

"Any sign of the fourth person Cara mentioned?"

"Yes. And you're not going to like who it was."

"Okay?" I said.

"It was Dominic."

I stared. I felt my stomach seize into a tight fist and my mind immediately start racing as it tried to connect the dots to figure out how that was possible. "You're sure?"

Alaric nodded. "Yep."

Cara looked up at me. "Wait. The same Dominic who turned you? What does this mean?"

"It means the stories that he'd been dead for centuries were exaggerated," I said. "Greatly exaggerated."

Alaric leaned in toward Cara. "It also means him showing up and helping somebody who wants to fuck us over is a mighty fine mystery. Also, a mighty big problem, given that this fucker is old as rocks."

Alaric was right. Dominic and I had never been on great terms to start, and at the time he disappeared, they'd been downright hostile. If he was still around, it meant I had bigger problems to worry about than Bennigan. Bigger, much more capable problems.

"Me and Cara need to go. Now."

Alaric shrugged. "Watch your backs. Vlad said he's going to power nap and 'poke some virgins.' That means he won't be around to save your ass if you get captured again."

I sighed. I'd need to check in on Vlad and make sure he wasn't planning to go on a murderous rampage, but that could come once I had helped Cara feed.

39

CARA

I sat with Lucian at a seedy bar that served barbeque pork sandwiches on sugary doughnuts instead of buns. As weirdly delicious as those usually were, I couldn't stomach the idea of eating one. I found myself looking around at everybody's neck like it was a jumbo-sized candy bar.

My gaze would fixate on a vein until I swore I could see it pulsing. Until I could practically feel the warm rush that would fill my mouth if I just...

Ugh.

I rubbed at my eyes and shook my head a little. "What happens if I just don't feed?" I asked.

"You will die. First, you'll go into a sort of hibernation. Then you will waste away."

"Wonderful." I tapped my canine tooth, noting that it felt just as nubby and round as usual. No peculiar sharpness. I briefly considered that maybe Lucian was mistaken. After all, I was going to go out on a limb and assume I would be the first lab grown vampire he'd ever encountered. What if that meant the rules were different for me? Or what if I just needed to wait a little bit until the little black specks in my blood went dormant and died?

My stomach gurgled like the traitor it was.

"So what are we going to do?" I asked.

Lucian looked around the room discreetly.

"We find you someone to feed on. A woman. I don't want your mouth on another man's neck."

I raised an eyebrow. "You fed on *two* women in front of me. Aren't we being a little hypocritical?"

"No," he said. "Maybe. But I get to make the rules, because you need me to wipe their memory, so I am picking the mark."

I rolled my eyes but couldn't help smiling. "How do you know I couldn't use my freshly made vampire powers to wipe their memories?"

He grinned. "That's something I'll need to teach you. For now, you need me."

I gave him a goofy smile, then hugged his arm. "That's not all I need from you."

Lucian chuckled, then lowered his voice, leaning closer. "What else do you need from me?"

"Various things," I said, feeling my embarrassment rise.

"Such as?"

"More of what we did in the back seat of that car. More of you. A *lot* more." I laughed a little to myself. "Maybe I'm supposed to be coy, but I don't want to. I just want to tell you how much you mean to me every chance I get."

Lucian's gaze was deadly serious. He put his hands on my arms, thumbs running idle circles that gave me goosebumps while he stared into my eyes. "You're sure you want this?"

I met his eyes, nodding. "I've never been more sure of anything. I love you. I don't care if that's a death sentence or if you don't think I should. It's how I feel, and I'm not going to—"

"I love you too. Even though I wish I didn't."

I gave his shoulder a little punch. "Well, you better learn to accept it, because you're stuck with me." I poked my canines again, making sure they hadn't gone all pointy on me. "Maybe for eternity if Bennigan doesn't manage to off us."

"I could imagine worse ways to spend eternity." Lucian looked down, then his face grew serious. "It's time I told you exactly what we're really up against."

"You mean I'm in the vampire club now and get to know all the secrets?"

"As much as we have time to discuss before I need to get food in you."

"Okay..."

"Dominic isn't just any vampire. For hundreds of years, he was the reason The Order was able to enforce The Pact. Nobody could oppose him."

"Why?"

"Some believed he was the original vampire. The first and the oldest. The most powerful by far. But just a few years after turning me, he vanished. Before long, there was a list of those who claimed to have been the ones to kill him, including Bennigan. I thought it was ridiculous, but decades and then centuries passed and he never returned. The Order managed to enforce The Pact without him, but just barely."

"Wait," I said. "I thought Alaric and Seraphina were your sort of vampire family, right? If you're older than them and Dominic disappeared right after he turned you—"

"I turned them. But that's a story for another day."

"So if you turned me, does that mean in the vampire world... you're like my dad and we just fanged in the back of a car?"

"No," he said. "It's not that sort of family. It's more like a clan, and vampires within clans date and marry often. Also, I technically wasn't the one who turned you. I bonded you, but you are unique. You turned yourself. *Somehow.*"

"That's a relief. I definitely wasn't going to start calling you daddy."

Lucian grinned. "A shame."

I smiled back, then frowned while I thought over what he'd said so far. "So the original vampire was the one who turned you? Why did he do it?"

"Do you recall when I said there was another way to turn a vampire? A ritual?"

I nodded. "Vaguely."

"I was supposed to be a sacrifice to him. He would feed on my life force and make himself grow stronger. These things were unfortunately commonplace in the past. But the process involves turning the sacrifice briefly before the execution, and he didn't anticipate how strong my ability to heal would be. Imagine his surprise when I walked away from the sacrificial stone the following morning."

Lucian's grin was wicked, but there was a twinge of sadness there, too.

"What did you do after that?"

"What could I do? I wasn't strong enough to day walk for nearly a century after that, and I only discovered I *could* when an enemy of mine tied me and left me in the sun to die. Dominic wanted nothing to do with me. He pointed me in the direction of The Order, and I've been devoted to it ever since."

"What about your family? Did they know what happened?"

"I watched them grow old and die, along with everyone else I ever cared about. Just like you will if you don't find a way to undo this."

I swallowed. My throat had gone suddenly dry. It was one thing to hear an immortal being talk about these sorts of things when I thought I'd never have to personally face them. Now I tried to imagine checking in on Zack, Niles, Mooney, and Parker as they ribbed one another at the old folk's home sixty years from now. I thought about my parents passing and looking around one day to realize nobody who knew the real me was left.

But the catch was I'd still get to have Lucian. Maybe I wouldn't be able to undo what had been done, but at least I'd have him.

"I'll try," I said. "But as much as it feels weird to say this, I think you really need to find me someone to drink from. I feel like I'm about to pass out."

It was only ten minutes before Lucian had lured a woman from the bar outside and down to the historic part of town. The three of us discreetly went into an old hollowed out section of the wall encased in brick. The woman laughed nervously.

She had the sort of long, acrylic nails that made me seriously question her ability to perform basic hygiene tasks like wiping herself. She also jingled with every movement because of the excessive amount of jewelry she wore. "It's dark here," she said.

"Forget," Lucian commanded in a hypnotic voice. "Be still."

The woman slumped against his arms. He gestured for me to come closer, then pushed her hair away from her neck and let her head lull to the side.

"Do what feels natural," he said.

The strangest tingling sensation started to spread in my mouth. It was oddly pleasant, and I felt a swelling beneath my teeth. Then two points were pressing against my lower lip.

In disbelief, I raised my hand and touched my sharp, elongated canines. I was lightheaded with hunger but couldn't stop myself from thinking how completely insane this was. I looked up at Lucian, trying to smile and feeling ridiculous with my protruding teeth. "Do I look hot?" I asked, struggling to talk around the large teeth.

Lucian gave me a suffering, but adoring look, showing his dimple when he smiled. "You look wonderful. Now please stop playing with your teeth and feed."

I gulped, stepping closer to the woman. "It won't hurt her?"

"She won't remember a thing."

I took a deep breath, then lowered my mouth toward her neck. It all felt wrong in so many ways. For starters, crazy nails or no nails, I had no idea if this woman even showered. What if she never washed her neck? Or what if her boyfriend had just slobbered all over it before she got to the bar?

I paused. "Do you carry any wet wipes to clean it off before, or—"

"Cara," Lucian said in a deep rumble. "You are immune to sickness and disease. You will be fine. *Now feed.*"

I closed my eyes and opened my mouth, fighting the natural instinct not to bite a random ass stranger in a darkened corner of the city. I felt my teeth punch through skin and then the blood spurted into my mouth like I'd just bitten into a grape. If grapes were full of blood that tasted nothing like blood was supposed to taste, that was.

I nearly fell back at how good it felt.

Silky, rich waves of her blood filled my mouth and it was better than any meal I'd ever had. Each drop seemed to make me swell with boundless energy and a sort of buzzing, internal electricity.

"That's enough," Lucian said, pulling the woman away from me. I was left hunched forward, mouth open and blood dripping from my chin. I ran my index finger up against one of the drops and sucked it dry, then felt incredibly dirty and gross when I thought about what I'd just done.

"Ugh." I stepped back, wishing I had something to wipe myself clean with.

Lucian searched my eyes. "How do you feel?"

I ran the back of my hand across my chin. "Good. Weird, but good?" I was still not used to talking with elongated teeth poking my lips and made a mental note that I would need to practice that at some point.

"You'll grow used to it. If we can't find a way to undo this," he added quickly.

He took out a cloth and cleaned my chin delicately, then used it to clean up the wound on the woman's neck from my bite. Next, he gave instructions to the dazed woman on how she could find her way back home safely.

When she was gone, Lucian focused on me again, concern clouding his expression. "You will probably crave human food next. Do you feel hungry?"

"A little, yeah."

"We'll go back to my house and call delivery. It will be safer there."

I started walking beside him, mind racing with all the questions I wasn't allowed answers to before now. There were so many more things I probably should've wanted to know about the danger we were in, but I found myself asking the least important question first. "Werewolves," I said. "Are they real?"

Lucian sighed. "Yes. And I've never met one who isn't a complete asshole."

40

LUCIAN

The vague yellow glow of streetlights filtered through the hazy windows of my home in Savannah. Cara sat on the couch with a box of pizza in her lap and a nervous look on her face while she ate ravenously.

"You're sure it's normal to be this hungry?"

I nodded. "Your body is changing. It needs fuel."

Vlad poured himself some bourbon, took a mouthful, then spit it on the floor with a grimace. He was wearing a pink bathrobe today that he mostly had tied around his sizable waist. His bare belly and chest along with glimpses of his legs were still unfortunately included in the outfit. "I still remember when I first got turned." Vlad leaned against the wall, folding his arms. "Feels like it was only a thousand years ago."

"You told me you forgot all about it," I said.

"Yes, well, you're a fucker and I like to lie to you. This one," he said, pointing to Cara. "I like her. She has some spunk. So I'll tell her the story. Anyway, I was a young beautiful prostitute in my city. Royalty from across the world came to have just one night with me. I was gorgeous, elegant, absolutely deadly with my tongue—"

I shook my head. "We stop aging after we're turned. You don't need to describe the way you look as if it was any different."

"Underneath this padded exterior lies the body of a lithe panther," he said. "And that was when I met her. Ana Black. The original vampire. Hundreds of years old even then. Smoking hot. Absolute pair of tits that—"

"Vlad," I said, cutting him off. "That would make her older than Dominic."

"And?"

"And the rumor has always been that he's the oldest of us."

"Rumors are shit. Rumors say I never met a pussy I didn't like. That rumor is absurdly false. There was once a pussy in the canals of—" Vlad interrupted himself, frowning as he used his hands to try to gauge the size of this supposed pussy.

I ignored him, turning to look at Cara, who was watching with interest. "How do you kill a vampire, exactly?" she asked.

Vlad stopped talking, then pursed his lips. "Not so hard, really. A little sunlight. Or you could always cut off their head and bury it in sacred ground. Personally, I never understood the point of going to all that trouble. I say you just tie them up and let the sun come. Much less messy and you don't even need to find a shovel."

Cara set down the pizza she'd been about to bite as if she was having second thoughts. "So that's what we need to do to Bennigan? Expose him to sunlight?"

Vlad rubbed his hands together excitedly, then gave me a wide-eyed look. "See? This is why I like her. The girl is vicious."

"He's not going to stop until we're dead, right?" Cara asked. "It sounds like it's us or him."

"That's probably true," I agreed. "But he has dozens of allies under his spell. We couldn't hope to outnumber him and hold him in place until the sun came. Our best chance would be to find where he rests and surprise him."

"How do you find that out?"

"A vampire's resting place is his most carefully guarded secret," Vlad said, taking another sip of bourbon and spitting it. "Good luck."

Cara frowned. "But I found your coffin really easy. Shouldn't it be better hidden if it's such a big secret?"

"You found what Vlad let you find," he said. "Besides, I sleep with one tooth sharpened. Let my enemies come. They'll be the ones regretting it."

"They will regret the smells you omit while you sleep," I muttered.

"Hey!" Vlad said, throwing his hands up. "That was one time. And I swear, that human had gotten into something foul before I fed on him." He clutched his stomach at the memory. "The world should thank me for what I did to him the next day."

Cara narrowed her eyes. "What did you do to him the next day?"

"Just some light poking," Vlad said easily. "Well, it *started* light. But the little bastard spit on me. And you know my rule about humans who spit on me during torture."

"He's just kidding," I said.

"Oh, no," Vlad insisted. "It's a hard and fast rule. 'You spit, you *get lit*,' as the kids say."

"You get them drunk?" Cara asked.

"Lit doesn't mean engulfed in flames? *Whoops.* Vlad has been using that wrong." He looked deep in thought, then his eyes went a little wide and haunted. For the sake of unknowing humans he'd crossed paths with, I hoped no college kids had ever told Vlad they wanted to get "lit."

Seraphina and Alaric thankfully arrived, saving us from more of Vlad's grisly details. Seraphina was wearing a sleek, black, no frills dress and a pissed off expression. Alaric had on some fluffy sleeved nonsense with a high cream-colored collar and a stupid, confused look on his face.

"I see you survived," I said.

Alaric saluted. "I'll be pissing out a few new holes tonight, but yes. I do appear to still be here."

"We're all thrilled about that," Seraphina said dryly.

"Thanks for your help, Seraph," Alaric said, slapping her back. "Really appreciated you coming to our aid in the life or death situation a few hours ago. That was fantastic."

"I had things to do," she said.

"We can point fingers later, but here's our situation." I spent a few minutes filling them in on Cara's status as a new vampire, what I suspected about Dominic's involvement in the evil organization of vampires formerly and ridiculously known as Shadow Force that were trying to overthrow humanity for their own benefit.

When I was finished, Alaric let out a long whistle of appreciation. "Shadow Force?" he said, laughing. "They really went with that as a name? Was their leader a twelve-year-old boy who spends his days playing video games and threatening to sleep with the mothers of his enemies?"

Vlad clapped his hands and let out a victorious sound. "I know! But I told Jewel to tell them that Vlad said their name was shit stupid." He winked. "They changed it."

I sighed. "This is the least important detail of everything I just said."

"The name *is* stupid," Seraphina agreed. "But what are we going to do about them?"

"This Ana White person," Cara said around a mouthful of pizza, which she'd apparently found her appetite for again. "Do you still have a way to get in touch with her, Vlad?"

He looked suddenly smug. "She still keeps me on deck for the occasional booty call. Yes."

I was skeptical, but then remembered his idea of "smoking hot" was Jewel and her body like an old warship.

"So," Cara said. "What if you call her? Tell her she doesn't actually need to do anything. We just need her to say she supports The Order, or whatever? It sounds like all you guys—*we*—care about is how old and powerful people are, right? It's not really about actually winning the fight? So if they think this ultra-old, ancient lady is backing us, they'll have to hold off on making a move. Right?"

I nodded slowly. "It could work. Assuming she agrees."

"Vlad can be very persuasive." He emphasized his point by planting his fists on his hips and starting to gyrate his round body in circles like some kind of warm up.

"Then get to persuading," Seraphina said.

"It will take some time. You four try not to get yourselves killed while Vlad works."

Cara stuck up a greasy thumb and nodded, polishing off the last of the pizza crust with her free hand. She noticed me looking, then did an exaggerated wink in my direction.

I smiled to myself. Resisting the woman had been foolish. I'd started falling for her from the first moment, and every day had only drawn me deeper into the depths.

41

CARA

It had been two days since Vlad disappeared into God knew where to find this Ana woman. I still hadn't become used to the daily need to bite a stranger's neck and drink their blood. *But,* disturbingly, I'd come to look forward to it for the burst of energy and delicious taste of it. I'd also been troubled to find that I almost couldn't resist crossing my arms over my chest and lying on my back when I went to sleep.

I'd already felt my cravings for human food dwindling as well, which was bittersweet.

Lucian insisted we needed to lay low as much as we possibly could while we waited for Vlad. That meant his usual house was deemed too conspicuous and we had to move to a house in another part of the city for the time being. I was making him watch *Twilight* on a small, ancient box of a TV when I started to get restless. "I have to do something about my old life," I said. It was a conversation we already had the previous day, but I wasn't satisfied with the conclusion. He wanted me to wait until we settled things, and I didn't want to risk dying and never getting a chance to tell my parents or roommates where I was.

I was sitting with my head on his shoulder. Lucian had finally lightened up a little on his dress code, but not much. He at least set the jacket of his suit to the side and had the sleeves of his button down rolled up as we sat on the couch. He hardly ever took off his dress shoes, which was something I decided I would work on with him if we survived long enough.

Lucian still hadn't answered, and I decided I wasn't going to let him off that easy.

"I could just text them. Make up some kind of story so they know I'm not dead in a ditch somewhere."

Lucian shook his head. "You've got to let that life go. For now. Once we are sure it's safe, you can go back to Anya's and see about finding a way to reverse this, if it's possible. But there are rules. Traditions."

"The guys will worry. They probably already sent out search parties."

"What about your parents? You're not going to try to convince me to let you tell them?"

I hesitated. "They chose to remove themselves from my life a long time before any of this happened. Maybe I'll tell them eventually, but my only priority right now is my roommates."

Lucian clenched his jaw. "I suppose the majority of vampires already want us dead. It's not as if they can threaten to make us even more dead."

I sat up straight, clenching my hands together. "Does this mean we can go talk to them and tell them I'm okay?"

He sighed. "Yes. But I'm coming with you to supervise."

"Fine. No problem."

"We'll need to think of a convincing story."

"I'm sure we can come up with something."

42

CARA

It hadn't been that long since all this began, but I already felt strange standing outside my apartment. I guessed it was now "my old apartment", which meant the guys were going to need to find a fifth roommate to cover my portion of the rent. I'd also need to get my things out of the room at some point. But I decided to worry about that later. Right now, I just wanted to leave them with some sort of closure so they didn't worry I was dead.

Parker was the only one in the kitchen when we came in. He came toward me and gave me an awkward, lanky hug while Lucian stood by stiffly.

"Jesus," he said. "We thought something happened." He stepped back, looking me up and down, then let out a relieved sigh. He pulled out his phone and fired off a quick text. "The guys should be here soon. We were going out looking for you in shifts."

"Sorry," I said, rubbing the back of my neck.

Parker got busy making coffee for me like a worried mother while me and Lucian took spots at the breakfast table.

It was only a few minutes before Zack burst through the door, repeated the relieved hug and look-over like Parker had done. Mooney and Niles came next, almost mirroring the exact same procedure.

I realized how much I missed all of them, and how bad I felt for making them worry.

Once I had warm coffee in front of me—coffee I was pretty sure would turn my vampire stomach if I dared to drink it—they all sat around the table.

Zack folded his hands, leaning forward. "We haven't said a thing to Niles and Parker, but I think they deserve to know the truth."

Niles and Parker both looked accusingly at Zack and Mooney.

I sighed, then ditched the far-fetched story I'd planned to tell about a surprise cruise we'd decided to go on at the last minute. I spent the next few minutes explaining everything I could about what had happened so far to the guys, stopping every couple seconds when Parker asked clarifying questions.

When I was done, all four guys were staring at us in disbelief.

Zack was the first to speak. "So you're a vampire now, but other vampires want you dead?"

"Basically."

"How can we help?" Niles asked.

"Yeah," Mooney said. "I was the state champ in wrestling back in high school. I bet I could handle a vampire or two."

Parker nodded. "I could help you find their lair."

Zack got up, then went to the kitchen. "I'm super hungry right now, but yeah. Hell yeah," he said over his shoulder as he rummaged through the fridge. "Just tell us what to do and we'll be your personal ass kickers."

I smiled. I'd expected them to be mad or act weirded out. I should've known better. Just a few hours ago, I'd felt like this whole thing was bittersweet.

I was getting Lucian, but I was losing everything else.

Now it didn't feel that way at all.

43

LUCIAN

Despite my arguments, Cara insisted on letting her roommates become involved in the planning process, which we began in earnest at my temporary and hopefully hidden home in Savannah. It was hardly more than an empty space with a bedroom, and it felt even more cramped with Cara, myself, all four of Cara's roommates, Vlad, Alaric, and Seraphina crowded in the room.

The honest truth was that I wished I could just take Cara and leave it all behind. I suspected we could find some semblance of safety if we were willing to go far enough. But I also didn't want to see a world where The Pact was a memory. I knew there were terribly cruel vampires who would do horrible things if unleashed.

Vlad belched loudly, then covered his mouth. "So, what's the plan?"

"Did you get to Ana Black?" I asked.

Vlad held the fingers on one of his hands in a circle and then crudely inserted his stubby finger in and out of the circle a few times. "Got in 'er. Out 'er. Then back in. Quite enjoyable."

Seraphina let out a disgusted noise. "Do we really need him?"

"Yes. Unfortunately," I said. "Did you get her to agree to help us?"

"She wasn't too keen on the whole thing with the pact. But, lucky for you, old Vlad knows she hates Dominic. Once she learned he was still toolin' around, she agreed on the spot. Except, well, she said she couldn't be bothered to actually show up. We can pretend she's backing us without her removing our heads in our sleep, but it'll just be words."

"Will that be enough?" Cara asked me. She was standing close with her hands wrapped around my arm. She liked to stand like that, hugging some part of me she could reach.

I put my arm around her, pulling her a little closer. "If we make a wave. It might be. But I think we need to take Bennigan out of the picture."

"You mean find where he sleeps, right?" Parker asked.

Vlad sniffed the air. "Who brought the virgin?"

Parker's cheeks went red. "I know a lot about vampires. Okay? I've read all sorts of stuff online. But that's true, right? You find where they sleep and that's where they're vulnerable."

"And all you have to do to kill a tiger with your bare hands is punch through its chest and rip out its still-beating heart," Alaric said. "Knowing is one thing. Doing is another."

"Vampires still have to use money, right? Like you pay someone for your properties, I assume?" Parker asked.

"Yes," I said.

"People sell information on the dark web. If one of you has the money to spare, I could probably buy a list of his expenditures for the last several years. It'd be pretty hard to hide where he's got property, at the very least. If we were lucky, maybe one would be a place he sleeps."

I raised my eyebrows. "I can give you the money you need. How long will this take?"

Parker shrugged. "It depends how careful he is. If he's funneling money through other people, there will be more steps. But it is worth trying, right?"

"Give the virgin his money," Seraphina said.

Parker cleared his throat. "When did we agree I was a virgin?"

Mooney laughed. "Everybody with functioning eyeballs agrees you're a virgin the moment they see you, dork."

We spent the next few hours making plans to find Bennigan's resting place and hopefully put an end to him.

Cara's roommates kept working with Alaric and Seraphina. Vlad had some mysterious place he needed to be, and I took Cara into one of the side rooms once our input wasn't needed.

She slumped against the wall, resting her arms on her knees. "This is crazy. It feels like we're planning some kind of military operation out there."

"More or less," I said. I took a spot beside her with my back against the wall.

Cara rested her head on my shoulder. "What happens to the bond now that I'm a vampire, anyway?"

"It'll come and go. When we slept together, we sealed it. There will always be a faint connection. Extreme emotions or sensations may make it feel more intense at times."

She was quiet for a while. "I'd kill to look at my blood under the microscope right about now. Yours, too. But I'm guessing they would be watching Anya's. It's where they've come for me twice now."

I nodded. "It's unfortunately out of the question, for the moment. I may not be able to promise your old life back to you, but I swear if we make it through this, I'll try to find a way to give you as much of it back as I can."

"It's okay," she said. She planted a soft kiss on my neck. "This new life has at least one major perk."

"I'm going to get us through this." I clenched my jaw, staring ahead at the peeling wallpaper. I wasn't sure what it would take, but I was going to find a way to do what needed to be done. Dispatching Bennigan. Protecting The Pact. Finding Dominic and convincing him he had too much opposition to keep pressing for an uprising. I didn't know how, but I knew I had to do it.

"You know how your specialty is healing and Alaric's is speed? What if mine is resisting suggestion?"

"What do you mean?"

"I don't know. Vlad wasn't able to change my thoughts when he tried and Bennigan only managed once. Just try it on me."

"Cara, I've never heard of someone who has a specialty in resisting suggestion. It's typically just—"

"Try it," she said. She got up and sat across from me. "Make me do something I don't want to do."

I stared at her. "Take off your shirt," I said, smirking.

Cara didn't flinch. She just flicked her eyebrow upward and titled her head. "We can do that in a few minutes. But I'm serious. Try your thing on me."

I frowned. I *had* tried my "thing." I tried to focus more, delving my concentration into her thoughts. "Stand up on one leg," I commanded.

Cara didn't move again.

She clapped her hands, smiling before rushing to hug me.

"See?" she said. "And I have an idea you're not going to like."

"Cara..." I said, not liking where she was going with this in the slightest.

44

CARA

Lucian only agreed to my plan with about fifty precautions put in place. That meant I was being constantly followed on rooftops by Lucian, Alaric, and Seraphina.

The riskiest part of my plan was relying on the information Parker had dug up and hoping Mooney, Zack, and Niles weren't going to put themselves in too much danger.

I walked toward Anya's just after sunset, knowing that the guys were currently on their way to the place Parker found Bennigan spent a sizable amount of money nearly every night. Lucian was fairly confident Bennigan and his harem were no threat to ordinary humans for the time being. That made my roommates the perfect bait to buy me time. They'd hopefully distract Bennigan into feeding on them, which would let Vlad get eyes on him and hopefully give me enough of a warning if he was coming for me.

And if Bennigan did come before I finished, we'd move to my Plan "B," which was what had Lucian practically shaking with anger when I'd proposed it. But he eventually agreed to trust me and admitted it was the best idea we had.

Anya opened the door, looking surprised. She had a cat on her shoulder and her eyes were bleary. "Thought you quit." It wasn't a question, and it was all she offered before turning to head back to the basement.

I felt a brief rush of relief. I'd been afraid she might ask too many questions or try to pin me down for some task she'd been saving. Instead, I closed the door behind us and was able to get straight to the samples I'd been working on. As soon as Anya wasn't looking, I pricked myself and took a look at my own blood under the microscope.

Sure enough, the spikey little Lucios were in my blood. The strange part was that my red blood cells were all engorged to three or four times normal size. There were normal sized blood cells floating around in the mixture, which were getting absorbed into the massive cells when they drifted too close.

I watched the tiny ecosystem with blind fascination for a minute before remembering I didn't have time for curiosity.

I rushed over to my samples, pulling out the handful of diseases, chemicals, and materials I'd noticed had the most dramatic negative impact on the spikey Lucios.

I used the sample of blood I'd drawn from myself to set up several slides, injecting foreign agents into each and making as quick an observation as I dared. Most had almost no effect, except to excite the Lucios into a sort of cleansing frenzy—making them dart around the sample to eradicate the newly introduced material.

I put my head in my palms, trying to think quickly. I was painfully aware of how many people I cared about were currently putting themselves in danger to give me time to do this, and how little time I had.

Think, Cara.

I visualized the large, vampiric red blood cells absorbing the smaller cells. The larger cells seemed to produce enormous amounts of energy, which meant they needed a constant influx of fresh material to fuel the process.

On a hunch, I grabbed a few vials of dehydrating agents and started creating mixtures with binding agents that would make them cling to the red blood cells in my samples.

After I was nearly out of ideas, I put my eyes to the microscope and watched the latest sample. The red blood cells were carrying bits of the dehydrating chemicals, and the large vampiric cells sucked them up hungrily. I was about to look away when I saw small cracks start forming in the cells. Within seconds, they were breaking apart and flaking away.

My heart started to pound with excitement. I rushed over to mix up as much as I could manage and then discreetly flooded a syringe with the mixture, then capped it and shoved it in my jacket.

My phone buzzed with a text. It was from Lucian telling me that my time was up.

I started up the stairs, ignoring Anya's question about where I was going so soon. I sent Lucian another text because he hadn't responded to my last question. When I got outside, I was immediately confronted by Bennigan, Jezebel, and Leah.

I looked up toward the rooftop where Lucian was supposed to be with Alaric and Seraphina.

Bennigan moved closer, his smile triumphant and cocky. He was wearing the same large fur coat that he'd worn the first time I saw him. It made his shoulders look inhumanly broad. With the bald head and scars on his face, he looked like some kind of Russian mafia boss. "You're a difficult one to catch, aren't you? I can see why Lucian prizes you so highly."

"Where are they?"

"You mean the three Undergroves you thought could keep you safe from all of us? You all really have no idea what you're up against, do you?"

"Is Lucian okay? What did you do with my roommates?"

"Your distraction, you mean?" He grinned wickedly. "The plan was cute, but we've been watching you too closely. I grew tired of you slipping through my hands. This time, you won't want to leave."

He stepped closer, eyes blazing as he stared at me. "You are mine now. I am the only thing you care about. The only thing you will ever love. You would lay down your life for me."

I felt the faintest swirl of dizziness as he spoke. There was a vague sense of losing consciousness, but I found if I just focused, I could keep it at bay. He was trying to charm me, and it seemed I'd been right, because I still loved Lucian. I felt nothing for the hulking vampire with the shaved head who was looming over me.

I tried to think of what someone would do if his little trick *had* worked. I let my eyes grow a little heavy, then nodded my head, almost sleepily. "Yes. Everything you just said."

Shit. That probably wasn't the most convincing line.

I discreetly looked at Bennigan and the two women. They were watching me with a twinge of suspicion but seemed to trust in his abilities too much to let their doubt take hold.

"Come," Bennigan said. "We'll get you somewhere Lucian won't find you before I call my allies off."

"Yes," I said in my best zombie impression. "Whatever you say."

He gave me one last odd look, then seemed to decide it was better to just get moving. I followed the three vampires for a long while, letting them lead me through an abandoned subway station. We went down darkened stairs, through a long tunnel, and then stepped through a crumbled section of the wall to a room that had been hollowed out of the dirt.

I tried my best to stay calm. My heart was thudding so hard I worried one of my captors might hear it, but I was otherwise doing a convincing job of keeping my face neutral. I had one hand in the pocket of my jacket, clutching the syringe I'd whipped up. I had no idea how or when I planned to use it, but I had hoped Lucian would be within "save my ass" distance before I revealed Bennigan's little charming technique hadn't worked on me.

Jezabel sat down against the far wall, watching me closely. Leah pulled out a phone and smiled at something as she swiped her thumb, apparently unconcerned with my addition to their strange life as Bennigan's pets.

I felt a pang of sympathy for the women. If he'd just used his power to force them into servitude, then they weren't really to blame for anything they'd done.

"How many others are there?" I asked, hoping I still sounded like a zombie.

"Jealous, already?" Bennigan chuckled. "I have thirty others like you who are bound to me. Jezabel and Leah are my favorites, but I still make time for all of my pets."

Bennigan made my skin crawl when he patted my head and motioned for me to sit.

I clenched my jaw, then took a spot in the corner. *Come on, Lucian.*

"What will you do with Lucian Undergrove?" I asked.

The question drew a lingering look from Bennigan, but he answered after a few seconds. "I had my people detaining him and his friends. Now that I have you, I'll let him go. I want him to live a long, *long* life. Long enough to imagine all the fun we're having together."

I nodded. "Yes," I said dully.

That was good. It meant Lucian was going to know exactly where to find me, and it meant Bennigan probably still hadn't figured we were still bonded.

I'd wait until I knew he was here, then I'd do my best to weaken Bennigan with the syringe—hopefully—and Lucian could do the rest.

45

LUCIAN

The blood in my body pounded until I could feel it pulsing in my forehead.

Dominic himself was standing in front of us with a smug look on his face. Behind us, there were close to twenty of Bennigan's women and several other vampires I didn't recognize. I thought maybe Alaric would've been fast enough to run and slip through, but I couldn't be sure. Dominic was immensely powerful, and I didn't know what he was capable of.

It meant we had no choice but to stand and let the crowd of hostile vampires keep us trapped on the rooftop outside Anya's, even as I could feel hints of what was happening to Cara through the bond. Bennigan had taken her somewhere, but she'd finally stopped moving farther away.

I cursed at myself for letting her convince me this plan was our best choice. I should have never agreed to anything that put so much distance between the two of us. I'd let her put herself in danger, but the alternative had been to show Cara I didn't trust her judgment. To show that I was too bull-headed to let her use her intelligence to get us through this.

So I'd stupidly agreed, thinking I was doing the right thing.

Now I saw the "right thing" would've been to get her out of danger and trust that I could smooth over her anger with enough years of making amends.

I also knew I wouldn't forgive myself if anything had happened to her roommates, who were supposed to have let us know if Bennigan was coming. Their silence meant he'd made it through them, and they somehow hadn't been able to reach out.

The whole plan had fallen apart in an instant, and now all I could do was stand like an idiot on the roof while Dominic watched me.

"What really happened to you?" I asked.

Dominic had ignored my previous questions, but he finally pursed his lips and gave a little shrug. He looked exactly like he had the last time I'd seen him. Severe, slightly aged, and the owner of the two most dead, empty eyes I'd ever seen. He wore a black ankle-length coat with a high collar and a blood-red tie beneath his vest. "You only supported The Pact because I told you to," he said.

"We have the night and they have the day. There's no need to fight for more," I said.

"You're more of a fool than I thought if you can't see it. How long before they find a way to end us? Some machine smaller than a blood cell? Nanomachines that can unmake us—can seek us out and neutralize our kind? What do you think they would do if they knew about us and had the means to destroy us?"

I swallowed. "I think they would try to find out more about us before they made imaginary machines commit genocide."

"Then you're naïve. Humanity's greatest fear is being lesser than. We are better than they are. They will never abide our existence."

"Why are you helping a thug like Bennigan?"

"Bennigan is a tool. A wise man uses the tools he's provided. The dull blades can be used to chip away at the objective until the sharper tools are needed. That's all."

"Ana Black won't let you do what you're wanting."

The mention of her name caused the faintest reaction in Dominic's face—a twitch of his eyebrow and a narrowing of his hooded eyes. "Ana Black doesn't concern herself with mortal or immortal affairs any longer."

"Maybe you should ask her, then."

A female vampire emerged onto the rooftop, then whispered something in Dominic's ear. He gave me one last, lingering look, and snapped his fingers. In an instant, the vampires surrounding us were gone.

I let out a long breath, finally feeling like my lungs weren't compressed by some unseen fist.

Alaric whistled long and low. "That guy is a dick."

Seraphina rolled her neck. "Did you see how he reacted when Lucian mentioned Ana Black?"

Alaric nodded. "He was scared. I'm guessing Vlad was telling the truth. This woman must be even more powerful than him."

I grunted my agreement. "We can talk about that later. Follow me. I can sense where he took Cara."

"What about Vlad and the humans?" Seraphina asked.

"Cara first," I said.

I felt a twinge of guilt at that, but I wasn't going to change my mind. I could deal with guilt and responsibility later. Right now, I needed to get to Cara.

46

CARA

I tried not to sit up straighter when I sensed Lucian coming toward me. It seemed like Bennigan really had called off his people, and that meant Lucian was okay. He was also closing the distance between us fast enough that I could feel it in my chest.

I started breathing heavier in anticipation. I'd need to act fast when the opportunity came.

Bennigan was speaking in quiet tones with Jezabel about something I couldn't quite pick up when I sensed Lucian was close.

He appeared in the doorway without a word, flanked by Seraphina and Alaric.

A rush of emotion overcame me to see him there. He met my eyes, and I silently tried to communicate that Bennigan's power hadn't worked on me—that I was ready to help.

Bennigan, Jezabel, and Leah were all standing in an instant. I saw Bennigan reaching behind his back for a pistol. Before I could think logically and remember it didn't pose the same threat to Lucian that it would to a human, I lunged toward him.

I stuck the syringe in his neck and pushed most of the fluid into him before he swung his arm behind himself and sent me colliding with the wall like I'd just been hit by a bus.

I gasped, watching the close-quarters brawl that ensued through double and triple vision.

I tried to blink through the pain, but it felt like several somethings inside me were broken.

Lucian was grappling with Bennigan, trying to wrestle control of the gun from him while Seraphina and Alaric sparred with the two women.

I lost consciousness for a few moments, and when I was aware again, Bennigan was on his knees, clutching at his face. I saw blood but couldn't make out what was happening before Lucian scooped me up and carried me over his shoulder. Jezabel and Leah were lying on the ground, apparently unconscious.

"What happened?" I mumbled.

"Whatever you put in him made him dry out," Lucian said. "The women will be incapacitated long enough for us to wall them in."

"What will stop them from breaking out?"

"This," Alaric said. He pulled out a small container that looked thick and heavy with metal. He carefully opened it, then rolled out a single, small onion into the room.

"An onion?" I asked.

"The garlic thing is bogus," Alaric explained. "But fucking onions... They weaken us. It's how my love managed to keep us trapped in the wall at the Mercer house for so long."

"Wait. Jezabel and Leah were charmed by him. They shouldn't be punished."

"There's no way to know his power will fade if he's detained here," Lucian said.

"Then let's take his head," Alaric suggested.

I gritted my teeth. I knew he had done terrible things, but it felt so final. So wrong. I realized Lucian was waiting for my approval. I shook my head. "We should at least see if his powers fade before we do anything we can't un-do. And we'll know where he is down here."

Lucian nodded. "It's settled then. Grab the women and let's go."

"You can put me down," I said, patting Lucian's shoulder. "I'm feeling better already."

He set me down while Alaric and Seraphina went into the room, treating the onion like it was a live snake and circling wide around it.

I tested my feet on the ground, somewhat surprised to find they were working like I hadn't just been hurled into a wall hard enough to break concrete.

Bennigan reached toward Alaric's leg, but Alaric kicked him away as he carried Jezabel out of the room. "Fuck off," he muttered.

"Wait," Bennigan croaked.

I could see now that his skin was cracked like a dried-out piece of clay. Some small part of me felt guilty to do that to him, especially since I didn't know what the long-term effects would be. I hadn't had time to study that. I suspected he'd recover in time, but likely not fast enough to stop Lucian from trapping him in the room. *With the onion.*

"You deserve this," I said to him.

He glowered.

Lucian started gathering loose stones, which were all over the abandoned subway. "Go get me some supplies to make this permanent," he said to Alaric.

Alaric nodded, then zipped off with his supernatural speed.

It was only a few minutes before he returned with the things Lucian needed to seal the bricks and create a permanent wall.

"Did you pay for these?" Lucian asked.

"Left my wallet at home," Alaric said, shrugging.

With a sigh, Lucian began working while Alaric helped him. Seraphina kept watch over the unconscious women.

In a surprisingly short time, the men had cobbled together a complete wall to close Bennigan into the small space.

"You're sure that'll hold him?" I asked.

"Unless someone comes along and breaks it by mistake a few hundred years from now." Lucian gave me a little wink, then pulled me in for a hug. "And that is the last time you get to make the plan. I nearly lost you."

"But it worked," I said into his chest, hugging him back.

"I may be immortal, but I will die of a heart attack if you get yourself kidnapped *again*. So, yes. It worked, but a man can only survive having the woman he loves taken so many times."

"Then I guess you'll just have to take me yourself," I said, biting my lip.

"Barf," Seraphina said dryly. She was hoisting both unconscious women on her shoulders. "When you're done playing footsie with each other, can we decide where to take these women and how to make sure they aren't going to try to claw our eyes out when they recover?"

Lucian kissed the bridge of my nose, giving me a lingering look before responding to Seraphina. "Take them to the safe house. Alaric, go make sure Cara's roommates are okay."

"What about Vlad?" he asked.

"I'm sure Vlad is fine. Just find her roommates and make sure they get to the safe house in one piece."

"Thank you," I whispered to Lucian.

47

LUCIAN

I hugged Cara from behind, pulling her into my chest as we overlooked the river. Above us, the headlights of cars shot yellow beams into the darkness, tires crunching on the asphalt.

I knew we weren't finished with Dominic or the events Bennigan had set into motion. But the threat of Ana Black would at least buy us time.

For now, that was enough. *Time.*

It meant I could finally enjoy being with Cara. Yes, I still needed to keep alert for any efforts from my enemies—*our enemies*. But the level of threat had subsided enough that we didn't need to hide. The danger was a low pulse in the background, not a deafening roar that demanded our full attention.

I softly lifted her chin, studying the curves of her face and her full lips.

That mouth of hers held a language I felt I'd quickly become a master of decoding. Subtle twitches spoke volumes from her, and

I thoroughly enjoyed having my own private window to her thoughts.

I kissed her.

Her body relaxed instantly as if she was melting into my arms. There was the familiar rush of warmth that spread through my body like sunlight sinking into my skin.

My phone vibrated. I pulled it out and saw a text from Alaric. It was an image. *Two* images, actually. The first was his penis, which I quickly deleted. The second was him smiling and flashing a peace sign in front of Cara's roommates, who looked tired but otherwise serviceable. I showed her.

"Thank God," she breathed.

I hugged her tighter, watching the way the rippling river distorted the reflection of the stars and moon. "I can't believe you managed to make something so effective against Bennigan in such a short time. You really are brilliant."

"Thank you." She pulled my hand up from her shoulder and gave it a quick kiss. "I am, aren't I?"

I chuckled. "It's one of your many charms." I hesitated, then asked the question that was already beginning to eat at me. "Did you see anything when you examined your blood? Any possible routes to a cure?"

"It's different than I thought," she said. "It's not just an additional element added into my blood like it was during the bond. It's the blood cells themselves that are changed. I'm not sure how you'd even start trying to change that. But... I'm also not sure I'd want to."

"You don't mean that," I said, even though my pulse was quickening because I guiltily hoped she did.

She turned toward me, resting her head on my chest so she could look up at me. "I know you think I'd be leaving too much behind. Maybe this is sad, but you're more than I had. Just you. So when the choice is to give you up or get everything I'd be walking away from back, I choose you."

"What about your aspirations to keep working on some sort of miracle blood? You'd need to leave all that behind as well."

"No. I don't think I would. Because this awesome, immortal weirdo I fell head over heels for is actually a good guy. And I know he wouldn't stop me from discreetly finding ways to help people if I could, even if it did ruffle some vampire feathers."

"You're sure I know this guy?"

Cara swatted softly at me, head still on my chest so I could feel her voice vibrate through me. "So what's it going to be? Can I keep looking at my blood and trying to find a way to help people with it?"

I narrowed my eyes, already sensing the danger in what she was suggesting. "You would need to promise to be discreet. I couldn't give you my blessing to do something that would make you a target."

"I could do it anonymously, but I need to do it. If there's some way to use our blood to create cures for diseases, then I'm going to do it. I don't care if I get money or credit. I can just drop it off at Anya's with instructions on how to use it and what it does. Assuming my generous, kind vampire boyfriend is willing to buy me just a few scientific tools to do my work?"

"Boyfriend?"

She blushed. "I kind of assumed that—"

"I want to be more than that."

Her eyes widened. "You mean—"

"I want you to bite me."

"Lucian. That's pretty kinky. But I don't see what that has to do with our relationship status."

"The effects of our bond will still fade with time. But if we feed on each other, it will be sealed. For as long as we live." I got down on one knee, holding her hands and meeting her eyes. "Cara Skies. Will you bite me?"

She snorted, then covered her mouth, fighting between smiling, laughing, and looking touched. "Um, yes. Just anywhere? Or—"

I rolled my head to the side, showing her my neck. Cara stared at the spot, canines enlarging until they formed points just past her lower lip.

She ran her tongue over them, hesitating. After a few seconds, she lowered her mouth to my neck. I felt her silky hair tickle my skin before she bit, sinking her teeth into me.

I sucked in a breath as the rush of energy flowed from me to her. Cara moaned against my neck, hands clutching my back harder. I let her drink her fill, even as she squeezed her eyes shut and gasped from the pleasure.

When she pulled back, I had to help hold her upright. "Wow," she gasped. "Was that supposed to be kinda hot?"

I grinned. "I've never done it. I guess I'll find out."

"You've never fed on another vampire?"

"No," I said. "This is a permanent act. It's not just a physical sealing of a bond, it's also symbolic. Much like marriage between humans."

Cara gave me a soft slap on the shoulder. "You didn't think that was an important detail to mention before you asked me to *bite you*?"

I grinned. "The ceremony isn't complete unless I bite you, too. If you're opposed, all you need to do is withhold permission. If you want to seal the ceremony, you can ask."

She raised a playful eyebrow. "What if I prefer to make you wait as punishment?"

"Then you would be very cruel."

She rubbed a little of the blood from her chin with the pad of her thumb and licked it clean, never taking her eyes from mine. I felt my teeth—and another part of my anatomy—start to enlarge.

"Bite me, Lucian Undergrove."

"I'm fairly sure you're not supposed to say it like that," I said.

"Fang me, you dirty, sexy vampire."

I laughed. "That's definitely not right."

Cara chewed her lip, a gesture made all the more alluring with her enlarged fangs protruding over her blood-stained lips. "Lucian Undergrove, will you bite me?"

I bent to her neck, pressing my fangs through her soft flesh. Her blood rushed into my mouth like the finest wine. I felt its aphrodisiac qualities pulsing through me instantly and my hands gripped her narrow waist tighter, pushing her body into me.

She let out a low moan, fingers running through my hair.

I had to make myself stop before I took too much. When I pulled back, my body was singing like I was in the middle of the most intense sexual experience of my life.

"Feels good, right?" she asked.

I nodded. "And now you're mine." I cupped her cheeks, kissing her and tasting a hint of my blood on her lips. "Like it or not."

"Like it," she muttered against my lips.

48

EPILOGUE - CARA

Two Weeks Later

∽

I woke up and looked down, realizing my arms were crossed over my chest. I jolted a little, quickly uncrossing them.

It was just after sunset. The windows were open, but the bug screens were up, which was good because I could hear the insects outside buzzing wildly. Lucian had moved us out to a rural farm an hour outside Savannah for the time being. He said if the others wanted to find us, they could, but that it would be safer not to keep showing our faces for a while.

For a few days, we kept Leah and Jezabel under lock and key in a shed outside the property. Eventually, Lucian was convinced they were telling the truth about not being bound to Bennigan any longer. It seemed that without Bennigan renewing his charm on them, they could think clearly for the first time in a long time. We'd let the woman go, even though Vlad had begged to torture them "just a little" for all the trouble they'd caused. We compromised by letting him blindfold them and drive them in circles for a few hours so they wouldn't be able to tell anyone were we were. Alaric had followed along to make sure there was no unapproved "poking" before they were released.

The place Lucian purchased was essentially a mansion with two sprawling wings for guests, several grand rooms for the homeowners, and gorgeous libraries, sitting rooms, and even a ballroom for us all to spread out without stepping on each other's toes. I was glad for all the extra space, because Alaric, Seraphina, and Vlad were all staying with us while we waited for things to cool down.

Lucian apparently preferred to sleep in tight, coffin-like boxes. When I asked him if there was a reason we couldn't sleep in the bed like normal people, he muttered something about vampires not feeling discomfort and dignity.

He had also explained that vampire couples don't typically sleep in the same place because of more mysterious vampire reasons he wouldn't get into. I decided if he wanted me to obey his stupid traditions, he could give me a good explanation. If he couldn't, I wasn't going to follow them.

So I was currently wedged into his tiny little coffin with my ass smooshed against his thigh and my shoulder digging into his neck.

Whoops.

I remembered going to sleep curled up against him in a more lady-like way. But ever since I'd been turned, I kept waking up stiff as a board with my arms crossed over my chest. It was easily the dumbest thing about being a vampire, and the list of dumb things was a quickly growing list.

Another item on the "why is this part of being a vampire" list was that my teeth got longer when I was turned on, not just hungry. Lucian said it wasn't like that for every vampire, but he seemed to thoroughly enjoy how he could tell I was in the mood just by looking at my teeth. Personally, I felt like it took away some of my mysterious feminine charm.

Lucian let out a low sound, then stroked my hair. "What would I do without my lovely Cara jamming her shoulder into my neck all night?"

I shifted a little, trying to take some of my weight off him. "You could always get a bigger coffin. Or, you know, a bed like a normal person."

"There are traditions," he said.

"As far as I can tell, we've kind of made enemies of the whole vampire establishment. I feel like we might as well enjoy the perks of creating our own traditions."

He grinned. "You raise a valid point. Maybe we could give sleeping in the bed tomorrow a try."

"See?" I said, kissing his jaw. "You're not an ancient, stuck-in-the-mud geezer. Not completely, at least."

He rolled me over, putting me on my back as he held himself over me. "You weren't complaining about how old I was last night."

"Who said I was complaining?" I asked, flicking his chin.

Lucian's eyes twinkled. "I love you."

I smiled. "I love you too, but don't change the subject."

"You're still sure you don't want to try to find a way to become human again?"

"I'm sure that I want you. Forever."

"What about your old life?"

I shrugged. "My old life? The one where I already felt like I was running out of time when I was only thirty? Being this way means I get as much time as I need to make my discoveries. And it means I get to have the guy of my dreams I never thought I'd find when I was finally done chasing my career."

"The guy of your dreams was a couple hundred year old vampire?"

I shrugged. "I always thought older guys were kinda hot."

He laughed. "Is that right?"

"Mhm. And you can stop asking me if I'm sure about this. I'm sure. My parents know the truth. My roommates know the truth. Anya knows I'm not dead, even if she doesn't know why I disappeared. The guys found a new roommate to cover my rent. It's all taken care of. All the loose ends of my old life are wrapped up tight, okay? And that microscope and centrifuge you ordered me should be here any day. What else could I ask for?"

"Sunlight," he suggested.

"Overrated."

"You say that now. Let's see how you feel in a hundred years."

The door to our room burst open. Vlad was standing in the doorway with his hairy belly hanging out and a bottle of liquor in his hand. He took a swig, then sprayed it all over our floor. "Slight problem. I need a conference in the kitchen."

Lucian threw something within his arm's reach at Vlad, who ducked it and gave us a thumbs up. "See you in a minute, then."

. . .

I sat at the large dining table next to Lucian. Alaric, Seraphina, and Vlad were also at the table. There was a woman I'd never seen sitting beside Vlad as well. She had cat-like eyes, an aged kind of beauty, and a regal bearing.

Vlad cleared his throat. I wasn't sure, but it looked like he'd actually run a comb through his unruly hair. "This is Ana Black," he said a little shakily. "And she's pregnant. I did it. I fooked her good. Put a baby in—"

"Thank you, Vladimir," Ana said, cutting him off. "As he says, I am with child. And my isolated lifestyle will not suit a new life. I've asked Vladimir if my child could stay here with you all and he has graciously agreed. I've decided I will also move in with you all as well."

Lucian made a choking sound beside me. "Just a moment," he said, leaning forward like something inside of him had just given out. "Vlad got you pregnant?"

Vlad smugly brushed his shoulder. "You think Vlad convinced Ana to back us with words? No. It was his cock! His impressively massive, full-figured—"

Seraphina held up her hand. "Should we get a say in whether we want you to live with us? Or some baby in our lives?"

Ana fixed Seraphina with all of her ancient authority. When she spoke, her voice was quiet. "I could, of course, remove your heads from your bodies one by one until you come to the conclusion that this is in the best interest for all of you."

Alaric spread his palms. "I don't see why we can't make room for two more."

"Will the baby be born a vampire?" I asked.

"Yes," Lucian said. "Births between vampires are extremely rare. The result is typically abnormally powerful for its age. But that makes them targets. Typically, older vampires see them as threats and find a way to exterminate them before they grow too strong."

"And that will not happen with our child," Ana said. "I'll personally see to it."

Vlad clapped his hands. "Then it's settled! Wonderful. And now that my lady is here, I think we can all agree that Vlad could set up a small, modest torture chamber again. Just for the occasional poking, of course."

Alaric glared at him. "No torture chambers."

"You promised you would let me have a torture chamber if I helped you."

He sighed. "If you torture any humans, you will make sure it's not fatal, they are fully healed, and their memories are wiped before you release them."

Vlad held up his palms. "Vlad is a man of the times. Of course. The victims of my torture will never have any idea."

"Alaric," Ana said, snapping her fingers. "You will help me move my things into my room. Come, come."

Alaric raised his eyebrow at Lucian, who shrugged, then gestured for him to go along with her.

I put my chin on Lucian's shoulder, whispering in his ear. "How hard could it *really* be for you to put a baby in me?"

A jolt of excitement and arousal ran through me just to voice the question.

"Statistically, it could be difficult. But that doesn't mean we shouldn't enjoy the challenge."

I wiggled my eyebrows at him. "Is it improper for you to put a baby in your vampire lady when you're not married? Or does the whole mutual biting thing put us in the clear."

Lucian chuckled. "If your human sensibilities would be more at ease with a ring on your finger, I would be happy to make arrangements."

"No," she said. "I was never really one to dream about wedding rings and white weddings. Maybe someday. But I kind of like the whole biting thing."

"Remember," he said. "It's highly unlikely that we'll be able to get you pregnant. Even after decades of trying."

"Then we should probably stop talking and get started," I said.

Lucian needed no further encouragement. He stood, then reached his hand out toward me. "Come."

"Don't mind if I do."

EPILOGUE - LUCIAN

One Year Later

∼

I watched Cara lead an elderly woman into our country home outside Savannah, Georgia. The woman had arrived in a taxi and had given the house a firm, suspicious look before agreeing to follow Cara inside.

Cara was dressed in jeans and a torn t-shirt from some band she'd seen at a show in her youth. She took the woman carefully by the arm and guided her through the house.

I tried to be discreet, since I wasn't needed for any of this. But I knew how much today meant to Cara, and I wasn't going to miss the moment she saw if her prototype treatment worked.

She had explained the process to me several times in the way she always did when she talked about blood and medical things—breathlessly and so excitable that she often interrupted herself and hardly made sense at all. My understanding was that she'd chosen an obscure, relatively minor disease that caused tremors and some occasional issues with fine motor functions as her first test case. She had gradually worked her way up from animal tests until she found a woman who was willing to try the experimental treatment.

Of course, I'd had to make a few phone calls and pull some strings—namely providing bribes—to get the appropriate certifications to allow her to do human testing. When submitting the paperwork about her treatment, she claimed the "Lucios," as she called them, were a lab grown synthetic agent, or something along those lines.

The woman sat down in what had quickly become a fully-fledged laboratory in the room that was once the ballroom. Beakers of colored fluids were neatly arranged and labeled. Microscopes of varying power were arranged on a long workbench with endless racks of sample slides. I hardly knew what half the things in here did, except that my Cara loved to spend her time in here searching for ways to use our blood to make some sort of miracle cure for humans.

I took a seat at the edge of the room, trying to be nothing but a fly on the wall. Cara reassured the woman, who sat down and looked around the room with calm, resigned eyes.

Cara retrieved a small vial from the fridge, explained exactly what was in it to the woman—minus the origin of the Lucios—and had her sign one last release form.

The woman nodded, then let Cara inject the serum into her arm.

I watched the elderly woman's trembling hands for what felt like an eternity. I wanted the shaking to stop for Cara's sake. I wanted to see the delight I knew I'd find on her face when she saw that her hard work had paid off.

But eventually, Cara forced a smile and helped the woman to stand. "It's hard to say if it will work right away. I was hopeful, but it's possible that your system may take some time to circulate the serum. I will check in with you first thing tomorrow to see how you're doing, okay?"

The woman nodded, shuffling her slipper-clad feet as Cara guided her back out of the small lab. She gave me a sad smile as she passed where I sat, but I was glad to see none of the determined fire had left her eyes.

THE FOLLOWING EVENING, I MET CARA AT A BASKETBALL GAME where her roommates were playing. I still wasn't used to being around so many humans, but Cara had helped to get me out of my shell to some extent.

Mooney seemed to be the only one of her roommates having a good game tonight, but it didn't look like it would be enough to earn his team the points they'd need to win. Still, Cara was having fun whooping and clapping her hands every time their team did something good.

I spent most of my time looking around the arena. There must've been nearly ten thousand students crammed into the relatively small space. They all cheered and watched the game like it was the most important thing in the world—completely absorbed in the moment.

I watched them all and was reminded why I cared as much as I did about The Pact. This wasn't just the world I'd left behind anymore. It was the one Cara had left behind. These people were worth saving, and so long as I was able, I planned to keep doing my part. That meant I'd continue to try to rebuild what was left of The Order and recruit more vampires to my cause. It also meant supporting Cara in her research to help humans fight sickness and disease.

Unfortunately, it also meant keeping an eye on Vlad.

He bellowed loudly with a small baby held precariously in one arm. He was decked out in the school's athletic gear, except for a suede robe with black fur he wore over it all. Behind him, Ana wore a wide brimmed black hat with lace covering her face and an incredibly attention-grabbing dress that might've been hand-sewn in biblical times.

Vlad sipped the beer he held in his free hand, spit it on a student wearing the opposing school's colors, and nearly got into a fist fight. Fortunately, the human decided he didn't want to fight someone who was holding a baby like a hand grenade.

"Vlad," I said as he sat down beside us. "At least try to act like your baby isn't almost indestructible. Humans carry their babies like they are made of glass."

"A few drops are good for 'em. Builds character," Vlad complained.

"Whether that is the case or not, it would be best if we didn't try to aggressively demonstrate what we are in crowded places?"

Vlad sighed, then made a show of coddling the baby. "There? How's that?"

"Better. Somewhat."

Ana gave Vlad a solid whack on the back of his head, which drew a yelp from him.

For months, I had viewed their partnership as a sort of strange, loveless but sexual affair. But I'd learned to notice the subtle signs of something more, such as the faintest curl of Ana's lips after she whacked Vlad's head. In their own, very strange way, the two were in some sort of love, I decided.

Good for them.

For the past few months, the house we were all sharing had been emptier with Alaric and Seraphina as busy as they were. Alaric was doing the work I planned to resume when things with Cara were more settled—traveling the country and trying to establish ties with vampires who might be willing to come back to The Order and support the pact.

Seraphina had been mysteriously aloof and unwilling to commit herself to doing much of anything helpful. I suspected she was involved in something she wasn't going to admit to me. I knew her well enough to know that pushing for information would've only made her withdraw more, so I left it alone.

Cara's phone rang. She picked it up, plugging her other ear with her finger and leaning forward to listen closer.

"Yes," she said, hand shaking a little. She smiled, then bit her lip, looking at me with wide, excited eyes. "Oh my God. That's incredible. Would she be able to come in tomorrow so I can get a sample from her blood? Okay. Perfect. Thank you so much."

"Good news?" I asked.

"The woman from last night," Cara said. "My serum didn't just fix what I tried to make it fix. It also cured her tremors."

I kissed her. "You're amazing."

She kissed me back, but I could see in her eyes that her thoughts were elsewhere. She stared off into nothing for a few seconds before speaking. "I mean, we won't know if any of these changes are permanent. But looking at her blood could help give me some idea. And there's still a chance of some unforeseen side effects. So we'll have to monitor for that."

"And I'm sure it's going to be perfect," I said, taking her hands and trying to calm her nerves.

She let out a shuddering breath, then smiled wider and squealed, fists bunched up and shaking as she danced in her seat. "Yes!"

I laughed. "So, what's next if this works? Cancer?"

She kissed me, and this time her thoughts didn't seem to be elsewhere. "Yes," she said, lips brushing mine as she spoke. "But if you don't get a little vampire baby in me soon, I may have to put a brief pause on my research to figure out some fertilization techniques."

"There's nothing I would like more than to continue trying to get you pregnant."

"Aww," Vlad said. "Listen to the little fuck bunnies. He can barely keep his dick in his pants. Remember when we were like that, Ana?"

"I still can't get you to keep it in your pants. So, yes. I remember very clearly."

Vlad let out a low growling noise, then nipped at her ear. "The beast gets hungry. Even Vlad can't contain the beast."

Cara had her back to the two of them, and she gave me a somewhat frightened but amused look. I smiled back at her, then kissed the tip of her nose. "I've been giving some thought to whole human tradition of marriage."

"Have you?"

I nodded. "I've decided the more ways I can say you're mine, the better. And what better way than to mark you as off-limits for all of humanity with a ring?"

She showed a lopsided smile. "I don't care about a ring or whether you've bitten me or anything else." Cara searched my face with her wide eyes. "I'm yours. In every way I can be."

I pulled the ring out of my jacket pocket and held it up for her to see. "So I should just toss this, or—"

She snatched it from me, sliding it on her finger with a wink. "I guess a little tradition wouldn't hurt."

-THE END

SIGN UP FOR MY VIP LIST TO GET A BONUS SCENE WITH LUCIAN AND Cara as well as a free book instantly! Tap here>>

WANT MORE BOOKS LIKE THIS? I HAVEN'T WRITTEN ANY MORE paranormal rom coms (yet!), but all my rom coms have the same type of humor and feel to them. A great place to jump in is with... Well, this is always kind of awkward to type out. But you should read my very first rom com, His Banana!

My new boss likes rules, but there's one nobody dares to break...

No touching his banana.

Seriously. The guy is like a potassium addict.

Of course, I touched it.

If you want to get technical, I actually put it in my mouth.

I chewed it up, too... I even swallowed.

I know. Bad, bad, girl.

Then I saw him, and believe it or not, choking on a guy's banana does not make the best first impression. Tap Here To Read His Banana>>

Printed in Great Britain
by Amazon